W9-BWO-365

SUMMER OF SECRETS

SUMMER OF SECRETS

Cora Harrison

severn
House

This first world edition published 2020
in Great Britain and 2021 in the USA by
SEVERN HOUSE PUBLISHERS LTD of
Eardley House, 4 Uxbridge Street, London W8 7SY.
Trade paperback edition first published
in Great Britain and the USA 2021 by
SEVERN HOUSE PUBLISHERS LTD.

British Library Cataloguing in Publication Data
A CIP catalogue record for this title is available from the British Library.

ISBN-13: 978-0-7278-9039-9 (cased)
ISBN-13: 978-1-78029-751-4 (trade paper)
ISBN-13: 978-1-4483-0489-9 (e-book)

All Severn House titles are printed on acid-free paper.

Severn House Publishers support the Forest Stewardship Council™ [FSC™],
the leading international forest certification organisation. All our titles
that are printed on FSC certified paper carry the FSC logo.

MIX
Paper from
responsible sources
FSC® C013056

Typeset by Palimpsest Book Production Ltd.,
Falkirk, Stirlingshire, Scotland.
Printed and bound in Great Britain by
TJ Books Limited, Padstow, Cornwall.

ONE

In the miserable monotony of the lives led by a large
section of the middle classes of England, anything is
welcome to the women which offers them any sort of
harmless refuge from the established tyranny of the
principle that all human happiness begins and ends at
home . . . The hungry eyes of every woman in the
company overlooked the doctor as if no such person
had existed; and, fixing on the strange lady, devoured
her from head to foot in an instant. 'My First
Inmate,' said the doctor.

Wilkie Collins, *Armadale*

'My dear Collins, take my word for it. As sure as my
name is Charles Dickens, I know that you are about
to have the most wonderful time.'

I took a quick glance around the railway carriage. Not too
full, I was glad to see, but at the mention of '*Charles Dickens*',
enunciated with all the clarity of its owner's public speaking
experience, every head in the seats beyond us turned and eyed
us with curiosity. The rest of the carriage listened in with huge
interest.

I felt my face warm with embarrassment, but Dickens, of
course, took absolutely no notice, no more than if he had been
an actor on the stage. He even raised his voice a tone as though
to make sure that it was easily heard at the back of the carriage.

'You will fall on your knees, my dear Collins, and thank
me for bringing you into Hertfordshire. I'm certain that you
will love the house, a magnificent place, steeped in history,
you will love the company, a fine crowd of fellows, all friends
of mine, and you know that there is always something special
about a friend of mine. I am,' said Dickens, tapping his finger
on the carriage window to lend emphasis to his words and

looking around with a benevolent air, 'I am, without doubt, the world's best judge of a man, not to mention a woman, so you can rest assured that you will enjoy their company. And as for your host, Lord Edward Bulwer-Lytton, well, what a very good fellow he is, famous all over the world for his books, but he sits there at the head of his own table, and, would you believe it, he hardly says a word.'

I didn't think that was much of a recommendation for a host that he would sit at the top of his own table and say hardly a word, but I refrained from further comment and not just because the whole carriage was listening with such interest. Dickens' tone was light, but he was a man who liked his friends to agree with him. I had noted that after weeks of calling me 'Wilkie' he had now slipped back to the more formal 'Collins'. I had ventured to criticize the most recent work from the pen of our host, Lord Edward Bulwer-Lytton, and express the opinion that it was a work of sheer plagiarism. Dickens didn't like it. He had given the book high praise in a review which he had written, and he never liked to be contradicted. Jokingly he used to say, 'I'm always right!' but deep down that was what he believed.

'You will have the time of your life, young Wilkie,' he said with emphasis.

But he was wrong. Now that we had been at Knebworth for a week, I knew that he was wrong.

Knebworth House was a magnificent place with wonderful grounds; its cook produced ravishingly tasty food and the wines were excellent. Nevertheless, I missed London and missed my casual friends, who would dine informally and enjoy the food and the conversation more than the pomp and ceremony.

It had seemed an exciting late-summer expedition. Myself, Wilkie Collins – former law student and now at the beginning of a career as a writer – my friend and employer, Charles Dickens and other relations and friends of his: Mark Lemon, editor of the hugely popular, satirical magazine *Punch*; John Foster, a journalist; and a handful of artists – Clarkson Stanfield, Augustus Egg and the caricaturist John Leech – had all been invited by Lord Edward Bulwer-Lytton to his home at Knebworth in order to put on a play in the magnificent banqueting hall of that Gothic castle.

Dickens, of course, was in his element. He was a born organizer and if he had not, by now, been a successful writer, he could undoubtedly have been an actor or even an actor manager. The noble lord was a generous host – his truly splendid castle had been renovated by the huge sum which he earned from his immensely successful books and plays. And the play, *The Lady of Lyons*, we were about to put on for the gentry of Hertfordshire in order to raise money for the widow and children of an actor who had recently died, certainly was one of the noble lord's most successful works.

Nevertheless, I was bored. Most of the guests were a good ten to twenty years older than me. I was in my twenties – they were in their forties, fifties and even sixties. The play, after the innumerable rehearsals demanded by a perfectionist Dickens, was becoming stale, the company too staid and the heavy, ceremonious meals were beginning to pall when compared with the more bohemian life I led in London.

However, all that changed on the evening of the seventh day when the footman threw open the door to the library, where the male guests were smoking and chatting before the hour of dinner and announced the name of Lady Rosina Bulwer-Lytton.

I had heard about Lady Rosina Bulwer-Lytton, of course. Who hadn't? She was a headstrong, opinionated Irish beauty whom Edward Lytton, as he was then, had married against the wishes of his mother. And lived to rue his decision.

It had been, so I had heard, a stormy marriage, and it had culminated in a separation about twenty years ago. Rosina had then done her best to ruin the reputation of her husband by writing a book about him, *The Man of Honour*, a near-libellous fiction, bitterly satirising her husband's alleged hypocrisy. But when she interrupted the hustings, as he stood as parliamentary candidate for Hertfordshire, with an impassioned speech about her wrongs at his hands, he decided to be finished with her for ever.

My eyes widened with excitement at the implications of

her presence here at Knebworth, the magnificent home from which she had been banished.

Her husband had put her in a lunatic asylum – nothing very unusual about that, according to what I heard. Women were prone to mental disorders; they became depressed and then irrational, caused trouble to their husbands, and that was the husbands' solution. It was expensive, said my friend Gabriel Rossetti, explaining how these private asylums charged extremely high fees with more extras than the most expensive of girls' boarding schools, but it was better than having the peace of the home destroyed. Once a wife was lodged in these places, treated with the greatest of care, given all possible little luxuries, chef-cooked meals, plenty of servants to wait upon her, the unfortunate husband could return to living a peaceful life, so said Rossetti.

As had Lord Edward Bulwer-Lytton, the most prominent author in the whole country of England, far, far more famous than my friend, Charles Dickens. Though, personally, I thought Dickens the better writer of the two, few would agree with me. His lordship was legendary for making a fortune through his many books and plays and volumes of poetry. Friends and admirers, according to Dickens, had applauded his decision to seek a peaceful life away from his tempestuous wife. And that was what Edward Bulwer-Lytton tried to do. But Lady Rosina had not faded into obscurity. She had written letters, so Dickens told me. Letters to her son, now grown-up; letters to Disraeli in Parliament; letters to everyone whom she had known when she lived in the splendid castle in Hertfordshire. Her husband had to give way and make her a small allowance – enough to keep herself in rooms in London. And now she was here in the house from which she had been banished, had probably swept past the footman and was in before he could summon the butler. More than fifty years old, I reckoned, but still a beauty, her lustrous dark hair framing the perfect oval of her face and matching the dark eyes that now stared at us all.

'Lady Bulwer-Lytton,' announced the footman as he flung open the door to the library in Knebworth House and after a moment's stunned silence, we all rose to our feet. I thought about offering her my chair, but Clarkson Stanfield was before me. He and Mark Lemon had been quarrelling in undertones so he may have been glad to move his place, but I had an impression that he was moved at the sight of a woman whom he had probably known for over thirty years.

'My dear Lady Bulwer,' he said, the old name coming instinctively to his lips as he rose to his feet and placed his chair close to the fire. 'Do sit here,' he said, waving her to his seat. 'You look tired and cold,' he added in low tones with a hasty glance towards his host, the lady's husband.

'I'm sick to death, worn to a thread and so would everyone here be if they had been incarcerated by two such scoundrels as Dr Hill and fat old Dr Connolly,' she replied, sinking gratefully into the padded armchair and smiling graciously at all the men seated around the room. Her husband, I noticed, had still made no acknowledgement of his wife's presence. Unlike the other men, Lord Edward Bulwer-Lytton had not moved from a seated position when his wife arrived in the room and now did not glance in her direction as the rest of his guests sat down again and looked with ill-concealed interest at the new arrival. She looked back at them, lips curved into a smile, dark eyes alert with interest as she scanned the room.

'My goodness,' she said to Clarkson Stanfield in a feigned confidential whisper, 'what has he done to this library? Who, on earth, chose that carpet? And the books, the lovely old books that belonged to his grandfather, they are smothered by all of those vulgar new books.' Mockingly she read aloud the titles of her husband's own books: *The Last Days of Pompeii, Paul Clifford, Eugene Aram, Ernest Maltravers.* Her voice made a sneer out of every title and her eyes travelled up and down the serried ranks of shiningly new books gilt-edged and bound in red and dark-blue leather.

'Oh! My!' she added, slightly raising her voice. 'What a lot of rubbish that man has written!'

I found it hard to keep a smile from my lips. I had already noticed that my host's enormous collection of novels and of plays had been augmented by shelving two or three different editions of each book. Almost every inch of the rose-red walls of the library had been covered by floor-to-ceiling bookcases and a large proportion had been filled with books bearing the name of Edward Bulwer-Lytton. She saw me smile and her beautiful lips curved in response. Emboldened, I hitched my chair across the patterned crimson glow of the carpet and placed it a few feet nearer to her and waited for a response.

'Now, who is this young man?' she said to Clarkson Stanfield, with a playful, almost flirtatious smile at me.

'This is Mr Wilkie Collins, the much-talked-about new young novelist,' said Stanfield. A nice old man, always kind and most encouraging to up-and-coming young men like me.

'I am a friend of Mr Charles Dickens,' I said to her with an ingratiating smile, but it was the wrong thing to say. I saw her face darken.

'Don't mention that name to me,' she said vehemently. 'No friend of his can be a friend of mine. He has sided with my husband in his inhumane treatment of me.' But then her face softened. 'Don't take any notice of me,' she said, her dark eyes luminous with tears, 'I have suffered so much that I am prickly as a hedgehog.' She reached a soft white hand across and took mine for a moment. 'Forgive me and say that you will sit beside me at dinner.'

'I shall be honoured,' I said and endeavoured to bow, despite being sunken into soft cushions. There was an intoxicating smell of jasmine perfume from her and I noticed that unlike most women of her age, she was dressed in pure white from head to toe. Not in tulle, or poplin or faille such as young girls would wear, but in a soft, deep-textured white velvet. I found her ravishing.

But at that moment, Bulwer-Lytton's secretary, Tom Maguire, approached us – not a man whom I liked much, though I supposed that his position in the household and the distant, haughty air of his master accounted for his fawning manner.

'Excuse me, my lady,' he said, 'my lord has asked me to conduct you to the housekeeper.'

'Perhaps he'd like to send me straight into the kitchen to scrub the saucepans,' she replied. There was some exotic musical lilt in her voice that made her words resound against the stone busts on top of the bookcases and against the chandeliers.

All conversation ceased instantly, and every eye was turned towards us. The secretary stared at her helplessly. I smiled happily and began to enjoy myself for the first time that evening. I eyed Maguire's embarrassed face and waited for his next move. Between a rock and a hard place, I thought, with my mind on the Greek mythologies which my mother used to read to us. My eyes, slightly maliciously, I'm sure, were attracted to the long-nosed, melancholy face of Bulwer-Lytton. What would he do now with the whole roomful of men staring at him? After a moment he lifted a delicate, white finger and beckoned to Tom Maguire who immediately left us and scurried back to his master's side, bending over the low easy chair and listening attentively for his commands. There was an air of excitement in the room. Dickens looked distressed, his sharp glance going from husband to wife and then across to John Foster whose jowls were heavy with disapproval. Augustus Egg pressed two fingers over his sensitive lips, hiding a smile, but intent with interest. Young Mr Charles Dickens looked embarrassed, but excited. Mark Lemon quickly sketched on the back of an envelope and I wondered whether the scene might end up as an inspiration for a cartoon in *Punch* magazine. Indeed, I thought to myself, this room was full of writers and artists and the dramatic scene might sooner or later find its way into a future work. Augustus Egg could turn it into a melodramatic picture entitled *The Cast-Off Wife*; Clarkson Stanfield could use her as a fore piece in a panoramic view of the romantic exterior of the castle with its turrets, domes and gargoyles silhouetted against the night sky; the estranged husband might well write a novel about it – though I doubted that. Dickens would introduce her as a minor, perhaps slightly comic character and I . . . well, my mind was quite excited, and I thought I knew the sort of novel that I could write where this scene could be shown in its full dramatic splendour. A wronged woman – a woman dressed in pure white – a woman who was incarcerated within the walls of a lunatic asylum in order that a villain could get his hands upon her fortune. My eyes were on Tom Maguire, the secretary. He would be one of the villains, I decided. A two-faced man, a plotter and one who surreptitiously stirred trouble from behind a blankly polite mask. I had observed him during the last few days, whispering in the ears of various guests, causing trouble and anxiety wherever he went.

He was back now. More instructions from his master, leaning over Lady Rosina's chair and whispering in her ear. I caught the words 'ladies', and then 'drawing room'. 'Ladies,' she said aloud, looking from one face to another. 'What ladies?'

Tom Maguire looked embarrassed. I wondered sharply whether his expression was feigned. And I was sure of it when he said in a loud whisper towards her ear. 'Two actresses, from Drury Lane.'

'Actresses!' She pounced upon the word like a tigress. 'So that's what my husband does when he has managed to place me in the custody of a lunatic asylum! I see it all now. He fills the place with actresses. Shame on you, my lord!'

Her voice rang out and the whole room watched her. She was enjoying herself immensely. I could tell that. I couldn't help a smile, though I bit my lips to suppress it. I rose to my feet. 'Let me escort you, my lady. You will find Mrs Lemon, the wife of your old friend, Mr Mark Lemon, in the drawing room. Come along, Mr Young Charles,' I said jokingly to Dickens' young son, using the name that his father had christened him with on the playbills, 'Lady Rosina would like to have a handsome young man like you to escort her as well as myself.' I half thought that Mark Lemon would come too and ease the situation, but he gave an uneasy glance first at the secretary and then at Lord Edward and kept to his seat.

Mr Young Charles, though, came with alacrity, blushing a rosy shade of bright red, and I could see that the unexpected visitor was pleased by that and distracted from her bitterness. He bowed and kissed the hand she held out to him in quite a theatrical manner, though I guessed that it was the prospect of seeing little Nelly which had made him spring to his feet without a glance at his father nor at his host. Between us we got Lady Rosina to the door. Charley had it open in a few seconds and bowed again as she passed through. I found it difficult to keep a smile from my lips. There was no doubt that acting plays, even under the stern supervision of his father, had changed this Mr Young Charles from the shy schoolboy from Eton into a polished young man. I allowed him to offer his arm to the lady and followed the two of them across the hall to the foot of the double flight of oak stairs.

'Goodness, he has been spending money! No wonder he can spare so little to maintain his wife,' said Lady Rosina. 'This is all new since my time. Where on earth did those shield-bearing lions come from? And all that stained glass? I suppose his family coat of arms has to appear everywhere,' she added, looking distastefully from the two long mullion windows to the coats of armour. 'Are you going to be a writer also?' she asked Charley, touched, I thought, by his youthful blushes and his awkward gallantry.

'No, I'd like to be an actor,' he said, blushing even more and then smiling a little to himself. Thinking about Nelly, I thought, and remembered myself in my youth. Not as shy as this Mr Young Charles, I thought, but I, too, found actresses to be mostly alluring when I was his age. 'Though I'll probably end up as a banker,' he continued with such a tragic tone in his voice that the unexpected visitor threw her head back and laughed.

'Dear boy, you do me such good,' she said affectionately. 'How lucky your father and mother are to have you.'

'In a minute, you'll guess why he wants to be an actor,' I said to her in a stage whisper. 'Wait till you see pretty little Nelly.' Poor Charley was the youngest of the players and he suffered for it! Everyone teased him about Nelly. It wasn't fair of me to add my voice, but I was willing to sacrifice him now to bring a smile to the tragic face of the beautiful Lady Rosina.

'So, who is this Nelly, then?' she replied in the same exaggerated stage whisper.

'Wait and see,' I said. Charley blushed even more, and Lady Rosina laughed again. I led the way across the landing and threw open the drawing-room door.

'Now ladies, I've brought you a surprise visitor,' I said, still in a theatrical manner. I had, indeed, the feeling that I was taking part in some melodramatic play. The young hero and the wronged wife, I thought with a slight smile at the absurdity. 'Lady Rosina,' I said with great formality, 'I'm sure that you remember Mrs Mark Lemon, and this is Mrs Frances Jarman and this is Nelly.' I had a feeling that Nelly had a different surname, though her mother was always addressed by her stage name as Frances Jarman or Mrs Jarman, but Nelly was young enough to be just known as Nelly. Important, I thought, to get the visitor settled down by the fire and on friendly terms, so I did not worry too much about the formalities, but instantly sacrificed poor young Charley.

'I couldn't keep him away, Nelly,' I said in a stage whisper as Lady Rosina shook hands with Mark Lemon's enormously fat wife. 'We tried to tie him by the leg to that enormous marble bird in the fireplace, but it was no good. He escaped. Lady Rosina and I went flying after him, but it was no good. He was up the stairs and across the landing before we caught up with him.'

They all laughed, even Lady Rosina. I breathed a sigh of relief. This was going to work out. She had shaken hands, not very cordially, but certainly politely, with Mrs Lemon and now I introduced Frances Jarman more formally. A pale, refined face, blonde hair and delicate features – she looked too young to be the mother of three girls in their teens, but nevertheless, Frances Jarman held herself like a discreet matron. She did not attempt to shake hands – I had already noticed how quickly she summed up social situations. Now she merely dropped a slight curtsey, smiled politely and bowed her head. An eminently respectable woman, a great Shakespearean actress and at the forefront of her profession. I did hope that Lady Rosina, despite her many grievances against her own husband, would say nothing offensive to this dignified woman and after a moment's tense silence my wish was granted. Lady Rosina gravely bowed her head and uttered a few confidential words in the ear of Mrs Lemon.

'And here is the beautiful Nelly,' I said enthusiastically. Nelly, of course, was in no way as beautiful as her mother, in fact she was singularly unlike her, but she was a sweet-looking girl with a mass of yellow curls and a pair of large innocent eyes, bearing the slightly puzzled expression of a shy kitten.

She nervously dropped a most professional and very deep curtsey and Lady Rosina's face softened. 'How lucky you are to have such a pretty daughter,' she said graciously, and Frances Jarman dropped another curtsey in acknowledgement.

'Brrr,' I said, rubbing my hands and feigning extreme cold. 'A lovely house, or castle, I should say, but my goodness, the bigger the place, the colder it is. What a cold, wet, foggy August this is turning out to be! Let's go and sit by the fire.' I ushered the three ladies to seats by the fire, making sure to turn the backs of all four chairs to the windows. I would give Mr Young Charles his reward for patiently enduring my jokes, I thought, and now he had the opportunity to withdraw into the window recess with pretty little Nelly. Dickens, I knew, was not pleased by his son's interest in the girl, muttering savagely, 'What business has he with girls when he can't earn a living sufficient to keep himself!' But that, I thought, was just hard luck on Dickens. He, himself, had married early. Charley had been born when his father was barely twenty-four.

Oddly, though, there was also a look of anxiety and displeasure on Frances' face as her eyes followed her daughter and Dickens' son. Nelly was not misbehaving in anyway; in fact, she was blushing shyly as Charley took her arm. After all, they had been in the same house for days now and they were acting in the same play, and actors under Dickens' supervision were always very friendly and at ease with one another. There was no doubt, though, that Frances was worried about the friendship between Charley and her daughter. I had noticed this before now and how Nelly, when having a whispered conversation with the boy, would be called away by her mother. I decided to turn the attention of all away from the young couple.

'What an absolutely beautiful mirror,' I said enthusiastically, going towards the fireplace and touching the intricately woven gilt frame. And then I pretended to give a violent start. 'Oh, my goodness me, just look at the image of that ugly man wearing glasses. Oh dear, how it ruins the beautiful looking glass! Do come, Lady Rosina, come and stand here and let me stand back and admire the mirror and its mirrored reflection.'

She did come and I knew then that all would go well. Mark

Lemon's comfortable wife was chuckling heartily, Frances
Jarman had stopped looking at Nelly in a worried fashion and
was now smiling quietly and Lady Rosina's face relaxed at
the sight of her own beauty.

'Oh, Wilkie,' she said, and there was a note of sadness in
her voice, 'if only you had seen me thirty years ago when I
was still young.'

There was a moment's silence while I wondered what to
say and then Frances Jarman broke it. She had, I thought, a
most mellifluous voice with such perfect enunciation that every
word gained distinction. 'I always think, Lady Bulwer-Lytton,'
she said, 'that it is a mistake to look back. I acted Lady
Macbeth with dear Mr Macready a few weeks ago. It was our
second time, as we had played the same roles before Nelly
was born, or even thought of, and Mr Macready told me that
I had surpassed myself. I think that he was right. I am very
sure that now, with much of my life behind me, I had the
maturity, and the wisdom and the experience of life which
enabled me to give a far superior performance. And maturity,
wisdom and experience of life adds master touches to a
woman's face. Lady Macbeth is, I reckon, not young, and yet
she is adored by her husband and her beauty enraptures the
king. There was one thing lacking to her, of course,' went on
Frances, speaking to herself now. 'Just one thing to secure her
happiness.'

'One thing . . . of course! He wanted a child, didn't he?'
Suddenly Lady Rosina became animated. 'He envies Banquo,
doesn't he? Banquo has a son – that's right, isn't it? What's
that line? "Your children shall be kings". And he should say
it with a note of jealousy in his voice, shouldn't he? That's
how it should be played, isn't it?'

'And yet Lady Macbeth says, "I have given suck . . ."'
Frances Jarman's voice was plaintive and underscored with
deep emotion. I looked at her with interest. I had observed
the respect with which my friend Dickens treated her and now
resolved to see her in a Shakespearean part as soon as possible.
'She has had a child, hasn't she? A child who died, perhaps,
or more likely, a child that is now grownup.'

'A second marriage, this one with Macbeth, don't you

think?' Lady Rosina's dark eyes were glowing with interest. 'She would have been a widow, wouldn't she? Older than he, perhaps. Is that how you would play her?'

'A very beautiful woman, still.' Frances' voice had a plaintive note.

'Yes, of course. After all, he was high in the land, high in the favour of the king. Knew his own worth, of course, like all men. She would have been very beautiful.'

'And she so loved him that she wanted him to have all that he desired.' Frances had the air of one who was looking back into the past. I wondered whether she was remembering playing the part of Lady Macbeth, or whether she had recollected some more personal memory.

'And she feared that the delay in conception was making her place insecure, that he might cast her off.' Now Lady Rosina spoke with bitterness.

'And so, the bloody plot was hatched. She planned it and almost executed it, not just for love, but for fear of being cast off. Remember she is alone in the world. There is that hint about her father having recently died.' And Frances Jarman lifted her voice slightly as though to make its timbre reverberate to the back of a theatre, '"Had he not resembled my father as he slept, I would have done it." That's what she said, was it not?' Frances was so immersed in the conversation that she forgot to look in that worried fashion at her daughter. 'She was willing to do anything in order to keep his love, wasn't she?'

'She paid for it – bitterly in the end. She paid with her reason! But I,' said Lady Rosina with a lift of her beautiful head, 'will not allow that to happen to me. He won't lock me up in a madhouse, not ever again. I carry a gun and I will defend my reason against such treatment.'

I felt embarrassed and uncomfortable. Unlike Dickens, I was no admirer of Lord Edward, but I was, after all, a guest in his house. Mrs Mark Lemon, I saw, was also taken aback by the bitterness of the words, though I was sure that the story was as well-known to her as it was to me. All London had talked about it when dark rumours had been resurrected about the solitary and terrible death of the couple's daughter after her mother had been driven from her home and the custody of the boy and girl had been handed over to the father. '*In the bosom of her father*' had said the obituary, but everyone knew that the girl had died of an overdose of laudanum in a solitary room in a squalid part of London. I looked appealingly across at Mark Lemon's wife and hoped that she could say something tactful.

But once again, Frances Jarman came to our rescue. 'Ah, but we have resources that Lady Macbeth did not have. She was dependent on him, dependent on his love enduring. I, now, well . . . I earn my living on the stage and am reliant on no man. You have the resources of your mind. You write books. Dear Lady Rosina, do tell me,' she said with such earnestness that no offence could be taken at the use of the first name. 'Do tell me, how many books have you written? I so loved your *Miriam Sedley*.'

'Oh, just ten or eleven.' Lady Rosina was immensely cheered. Her eyes sparkled and her lips curved in a smile. 'Think of all that Shakespeare has written!'

'Ah, but only about ten that I would reckon as excellent,' said I quickly, putting this in before Lady Rosina became abusive or melancholy or both.

She ignored me. 'Which is your favourite play?' she asked the actress. I thought I could hear a note of desperation in her voice. Was it, I wondered, an effort to keep the conversation going and distracting her from her troubles or, had she some other motive at the back of her mind?

'It has to be *Macbeth* or *Cleopatra*. I'm too old now to play the young girls: Juliet, Rosalind and Desdemona or Portia. I think, though, if you gave me a chance, I'd play Cleopatra well, even now. I love that play so much. It has such a happy ending.'

I started slightly. 'A happy ending! What! Cleopatra! But didn't she commit suicide, at the end of the play?' I said, incredulously, but neither woman even looked at me.

Lady Rosina did not hesitate. 'Yes, of course,' she said with a nod of approval. And then quoted dreamily, '"It was well done. And fitting for a princess. Descended of so many royal kings".' She thought about this for a moment and then said decisively, 'But a love like the love Cleopatra has for Anthony, well, that is unknown to me, but Lady Macbeth, now, I can see myself in her place and if I were she, I would use a knife, again, and this time, use it on my husband when he condemned me to the care of that sinister doctor. Or not a knife, no, nowadays a pistol. Look at mine.' And she took from a small handbag a neat and lethal-looking pistol and then replaced it with loving care. To my slight astonishment, Frances Jarman showed no sign of surprise or even of disapproval.

'I'll just pop downstairs and have a word with the house-keeper about Lady Bulwer's arrival,' I said to Mark Lemon's wife. Helen, she had told me to call her, but I thought I'd wait a little longer before I accepted the informality. As I left the room, I noticed that neither the ladies quoting Shakespeare, nor the young couple by the window, even turned to look in my direction. I closed the door quietly behind me and went off on a diplomatic mission. The house was not mine and the owner of the house was not a friend. I peeped into the library, but the men had all dispersed.

And so, I went looking for my friend, Charles Dickens. He was the one who knew Lord Edward-Bulwer intimately and he was the right man to persuade him that there could be no justification to put the woman out of the house, unfed and unrested at this late hour in the evening. In all decency, she had to be offered dinner and a bed for the night. Hopefully, after breakfast she might take herself off and we could all get on with staging the play that was to be held in these splendid surroundings in order to raise money for the widow and children of the actor who had recently died.

I ran Dickens to earth in a shed in the garden where he was superintending Clarkson Stanfield as he painted finishing touches upon a magnificent panorama of the French city of Lyons which was to be used as a backdrop for our play *Lady of Lyons*. Bulwer-Lytton had had huge success with this play of his, in New York as well as in London, but this time the new thing about the play was that it was to be acted by a group of well-known, even famous, writers and artists. The only professionals were Frances Jarman and her youngest daughter, Nelly, and they had just been drafted in a couple of days ago after Dickens' wife had fallen and broken her ankle and his seventeen-year-old daughter, Katey, had developed measles.

I was glad to see Clarkson. He would back me up, I thought, and I burst into speech the moment I opened the door. 'I say, Dickens, that poor woman has to be invited to stay to dinner and has to have a bed for this night at least. Do be a good chap and have a word with Bulwer-Lytton. I'm sure that he shouldn't turn her out of doors at this late hour.'

'No, indeed, that can't be allowed to happen. I'll go and have a word with Edward.' It was Clarkson Stanfield who spoke and he put down his paintbrush before Dickens had opened his mouth. Despite his age he bustled out of the door and had crossed the lawn before Dickens spoke.

'Let him go; he'll do it better than I. He and Lord Edward have been friends since long before I ever arrived on the scene. Anyway, a word from me might be presumed to be a liberty, particularly.' Here Dickens lowered his voice and glanced over his shoulder before finishing his sentence. 'You must understand, Wilkie, that I may be deemed to be presumptuous. Although he is very kind to me also, Lord Edward may view me as a young interloper, a man who, perhaps dares to challenge him for the crown of novelist. I mind my Ps and Qs when I am with him.'

I could not help myself there and I didn't even bother to look around. 'Dick,' I said earnestly, 'you are by far the better writer of the two. Bulwer-Lytton is old-fashioned, long-winded, melodramatic and quite honestly, can be boring. There will come a time when your books and your characters, Little Nell, Mr Micawber, Pickwick, Oliver Twist, Mr Tulkinghorn, will have their names written in the stars and people will wonder who Bulwer-Lytton was, or question whether anyone really ploughed through *The Last Days of Pompeii.*'

'Hush; don't let anyone hear you say such nonsense,' he said, but he said it with a smile. 'Now I'm off to see the village of Knebworth. How would you like to come too?'

'No, thank you,' I said. 'Dinner is in an hour's time and someone has told me that it takes a good forty minutes to walk to the village.'

'Come on,' he said. 'The walk will do you good. I bet that

I will be there and back long before forty minutes are up. Come on, Wilkie, you need exercise. Look at that stomach of yours!'

I shook my head with a laugh. I knew his rate of walking and I knew that I had no hope of keeping up with him if he were determined to set that pace.

'See you at dinner,' I said, and I strolled back through the gardens towards the house, admiring the contrast of the statues placed against the dark green of the yew hedges, and pausing in front of an ornate piece of sculpture in the centre of a pond and waterfall. When I saw the lord of the castle approach, I diverted my steps and decided to have a walk through the maze instead.

I felt very out of sympathy with Lord Edward Bulwer-Lytton and doubted whether I could bring myself to be polite to him. His treatment of his wife and his daughter, his haughty manner and his literary pretensions made him anathema to me and so I decided to seek better company. Bruno and I would enjoy each other's company and we would have a nice stroll for half an hour or so and I would have plenty of time to spruce up before dinner. I was looking forward to sitting beside Lady Rosina.

TWO

There are periods in a man's life when he finds the
society that walks on four feet a welcome relief from
the society that walks on two.

Wilkie Collins, *The Fallen Leaves*, 1879

Bruno was a Great Dane – the biggest dog I had ever
seen. I had first met him on my second day at Knebworth.
I had been passing the stable yard and saw him stretched
out, chained to the wall behind his kennel. An enormous and
most magnificent dog with an amber coat and a smoke-dark
muzzle, he lay patiently and quietly, chained like a convict. I
had always been fond of dogs, but all the dogs that I had
owned had been small dogs and I was taken aback by the size
of this one. I stopped, looked at him and he looked back at
me. My father had always told me that I should never approach
a chained dog, especially, he had emphasized, a dog on a short
chain. And this dog was on a very short chain indeed.

Nevertheless, he had not barked at the sight of me.

I took a step nearer and then another step. The dog watched
me, but there was no alarm shown. I examined him carefully,
but no hackles were raised. The dark eyes touched my heart.
They had, I thought, a lonely look about them. I took from
my pocket a small red apple which I had picked up earlier as
I had passed the orchard and took another few steps forward
with the apple held out towards the dog.

'Go on, Bruno, good dog.' A stable lad, pushing a wheelbarrow, had come into the yard. The dog's tail wagged now.

'He knows you, doesn't he?' I said with a certain amount
of relief. 'Is he safe?' I added, more for the sake of keeping
the conversation going, than from any remaining nervousness.
Bruno delicately picked the apple from my outstretched hand
and scrunched it noisily.

'He's a lovely boy, aren't you, Bruno?' The lad put down the wheelbarrow and selected a large shovel.

'Why does he have to be chained up like that?' In my mother's house, my dog sat on the sofa before transferring to my knee when I was at home.

'Dunno, sir. Master's orders. Looks best like that, I s'ppose.'

'And he isn't dangerous in any way.' I knew, once I had said the words that I meant them as a statement, not as a question. Gently I pulled the soft ears.

I didn't press the questions any further. Not for this lad to question orders. And I didn't want to get him into any trouble. I waited until he went into a stable before I reached over and stroked the dog's head. He looked grateful – in a dignified way, I thought. I took the staple from the end of the chain and freed the dog, holding the end of the chain loosely in my hand. He got to his feet, but he didn't run away.

'I'll just take him for a walk through the maze.' I wouldn't wait for an answer. The stable boy could always say that he didn't know what I was up to. I gave the dog another pat. He strolled beside me like a best friend and we made our way rapidly towards the shelter of the eight-foot-high hawthorn hedges that marked out the complicated design of the maze. It took us a good half hour to find our way out that first time, but on an impulse I took him through for a second time and somehow the sagacious animal sensed the purpose – to get from the entrance to the exit – and cleverly took me straight through at a speed which we both enjoyed. I praised him so much that his air of gentle melancholy left him, and he pranced about like a puppy with his tail wagging and his eyes full of fun.

And from that day onwards, I slipped into the stable yard whenever I got a chance and went to the kennel to release the dog and to enjoy a walk with Bruno. On my third day of this routine, a beautiful leather lead, supple with a copious dressing of saddle soap, appeared on the top of the kennel and I borrowed it with thankfulness. By now the energetic members of the house party had all sampled the maze and no one seemed keen to repeat the experience, Bruno and I had the place to ourselves.

So on this day, with Lady Rosina in the care of Frances Jarman and of Mrs Mark Lemon; Lord Edward talking to his estate agent; Dickens striding out towards Knebworth village, Bruno and I went out together in order to play our usual game where I led him to some obscure part of the maze and gave him the command of 'seek'.

But we didn't have the place to ourselves today. Two fresh young voices and then just the pleasant baritone of Young Charles Dickens enumerating, in a slow, rhythmic fashion, the numbers from one to a hundred. I heard also a light-hearted feminine giggle and smiled to myself. The pair were engaged in the favourite childhood game of 'hide and go seek' and Nelly had gone to hide in the maze while young Charley gave her a hundred-second start.

We wouldn't alarm them, I was sure. By now I had full confidence in Bruno. He would not frighten young Nelly; I was sure of that. These young actresses were not cosseted young ladies, but tough, steady-nerved, young ladies who had been earning their living since even before they were chris-tened. A hard life for these girls! Nelly had told me once how her young brother, only an infant, had died and she had been left to watch his body while her mother and two older sisters had performed in a theatre in order to earn the money for the baby's funeral. The story had brought tears to my eyes and I thought about it as Bruno and I wandered through the maze. We had a habit now of exploring all its paths and its dead ends and its little secret squares, and then when time demanded I would tell him to go 'home' and Bruno would instantly lead me in the right direction.

I was pondering over the idea of buying Bruno from Lord Edward; would it be fair to keep him in London, or should I perhaps present him to Dickens who loved dogs and whose family all loved dogs? Dickens had enough acres in Gad's Hill to satisfy the largest and most energetic of dogs and I could visit Bruno there, though I wanted him for myself, wanted to present him with an armchair all for himself instead of a draughty kennel, wanted him to sit by me in the evening and walk with me in Hampstead Park on fine mornings. I was amusing myself with these little dreams when suddenly a scream came from some part of the maze – a scream and then a tearful, agitated voice – 'Don't! Oh, please, don't! Let me go!' Another scream and then indistinguishable sounds from a girl's stifled voice. The villain was choking her, holding his hand over her mouth. I could hear the thud of feet on the grass paths. Young Charles was pounding along, shouting at the top of his voice, but I knew this maze and knew that once the girl was silenced the villain could escape. Humans relied on their eyes and ears, but here with me today, there was another being with superior abilities. I bent down and unclicked the lead from Bruno's collar.

'Seek, boy, seek!' I said softly. I would have to rely on his sagacity. 'Seek' so far had meant to find the way out, but I have always believed that dogs can read the mind of those that they love and I trusted that this immensely superior dog would know what I wanted him to do. I wished that Young Charles would stop shouting, but at that moment Nelly uttered a stifled cry. It was immediately cut off, but it was enough for Bruno. I had never seen him run before, normally he strolled politely by my side, but now I could hardly believe his speed – as fast as any horse, I just had time to think, before he had disappeared from view. I had never seen him run, nor had I ever heard him bark, but now, like cracks of thunder, the air was filled with his deep-throated anger.

Nelly screamed again and though it was instantly stifled I recognized it was not the helpless sound of a girl caught in a trap, but a shout for help and I blessed her quick-wittedness. She must know that the villain who attacked her was more dangerous to her than a barking dog. I was no runner, but I could follow in the direction of those thunderous barks.

'Oh my God, what a scoundrel! Nelly, I'm coming, I'm coming.' I took no notice of Young Charles's cries and tried to stretch my too-short legs into moving more quickly in the direction of the dog. Luckily, I was by now familiar with the dead-end passages, had noted a cluster of red haws at the entrance to one and a clump of meadowsweet at another. I knew where I was going. This path led to the innermost and most central part of the maze: a tiny grassy square with a statue of a weeping boy in the centre of it and a few benches

where the baffled explorers could recline before resuming their
search for the way out.

Another bark from Bruno and then – very deep, very
menacing – an angry growl. But then the girl's voice saying
something – something I could not hear, but the tone was
enough for me. I slowed down, gasping and clutching my side.
All was over. I had not heard the words, but Nelly's voice had
been light and caressing. The dog had arrived. There was, I
remembered, just one entrance to that centre of the maze and
I could trust, I thought, to Bruno's intelligence, to stand in
the way of the girl's assailant. I turned into another alley. Yes,
this was the right way. I recognized that disused song thrush's
nest with its cork-like, smooth lining of pale clay.

Bruno had heard me, or, with the wonderful gifts of dogs,
had scented me on the breeze. He gave one joyous bark, very
different from the harsh aggressive thunderous growl, but he
did not run to greet me. His breeding was as a protector of
his master's property and now he had scented wrongdoing and
the mastiff strain which had gone into that breeding made him
stay on guard. I still said nothing, though; nothing that would
distract him from his duty to protect the girl and to imprison
the villain who had tried to assault her.

Another light welcoming bark. I turned again to the left and
this time I was certain of my way. The head of the statue rose
just inches above the hawthorn hedges, but the sun gleamed
on its marble and made it like a beacon. I entered the little
enclosure. Yes, it was Nelly, pale, but smiling; Bruno acknowledging my presence with an enthusiastic swing of his tail,
but still keeping a stern eye upon a man: Tom Maguire, secretary to our host, Lord Edward.

He recovered himself quickly. 'Thank goodness, you have
come, Mr Collins,' he said in his oily way. 'I'm afraid that
this dog has frightened Miss Nelly badly. He will have to be
shot. I've always thought that he was a dangerous dog.' His
eye went to the lead in my hand, and a little of the confidence
evaporated from his unpleasant face.

'No, no!' Nelly's nerves were shaken, and she began to sob
broken-heartedly and buried her face in her hands. The dog
looked at her and I could swear I saw worry in his eyes and

a desire to comfort her. But he was a dog bred to guard property and to run beside carriages; a dog bred to catch thieves and assassins and so he did not move from his position beside Tom Maguire. He gave a low growl and Maguire stopped abruptly, foiled in his attempt to go over towards the weeping girl.

'Charley,' I called out as loudly as I could. 'Charley, we're here in the centre of the maze. Nelly is safe. Keep turning in the direction of my voice. Come on, Charley.' I would not, I thought, question the girl until he arrived. He would be the one to comfort her and so I allowed her to weep silently, with her back turned towards us and her hand resting on the plinth of the statue while I encouraged the boy with shouts. This fellow, Tom Maguire, was an unpleasant man, but he seemed to have a great hold over his master and now that little Nelly was safe, I was mainly concerned about my friend Bruno. It was obvious that his master had no interest in the dog and no affection for him. Another dog could easily be bought by a man as rich as Edward Bulwer-Lytton. 'Come on, Charley,' I shouted impatiently. 'Come on, man, Miss Nelly has had a terrible shock. She has been assaulted by a villain. That's right. I can hear you now. Keep coming, keep turning to your left. You'll soon be with us. Look out for the head of the statue above the hedges.' I kept on shouting encouragements and I could hear, below the sound of my own bellowing, that Nelly's sobs were growing less. She had her handkerchief out now and was drying her eyes and patting her face. She looked across at me with a pathetic effort at a smile and I smiled back. 'Good girl,' I said. 'Play the part of a heroine, Nelly,' I advised, before shouting once again at Charley.

She had managed to choke back her sobs and to pat some colour into her cheeks before he came blundering through.

'Quiet, Bruno,' I said, but Bruno saw the meeting of the two lovers and relaxed, only rousing himself to give a low growl when Maguire made a slight move. It was intended as a warning to the villain, but the man was quicker-witted with more evil cunning than the dog.

'Miss Nelly has been attacked by this dangerous dog, Mr

Young Charles,' he said with all the smooth oiliness at his
command. 'No harm has been done, fortunately, as I was
quickly on the scene and managed to take her in my arms and
save her from the dog.'

'No, no,' gasped Nelly, bursting into fresh tears. 'It was
him; him, not the dog,' she said to Charley, but her sobs
prevented her from saying more.

'Yes, indeed, it was,' I assured Charley, who now had Nelly
in his arms. He was a sweet-natured, easy-going boy, but at
this moment he was a man in love. I felt that I could rely on
him to back me up. 'I am certain that it was this villain who
attacked her. The dog was with me, was on the lead when we
heard her scream. He's a very good dog. See how friendly he
is to her.'

I waited for Nelly to respond, but she said nothing, just
sobbed slightly and didn't raise her head from Mr Young
Charles's chest. I looked towards Maguire and saw a nasty
smile spread over his ugly face.

'You have made a very, very serious accusation towards me,
Mr Collins. I'm sure that Miss Nelly, once she has gathered
her wits to her and *remembers* her position in the house . . .?'
He stopped after his last words and waited. Nelly raised a
tear-stained face from Mr Young Charles's waistcoat and
looked towards him. I could see how her face changed at his
words and how she bit her lips and raised her chin – the
automatic small gestures of a woman regaining control over
her emotions.

Maguire gave a satisfied nod and went on smoothly, 'Yes,
I'm sure that Miss Nelly will be happy to confirm my master's
good opinion of me and will tell the truth – that the dog
attacked her and I came to the rescue. I suggest that we all
come out of this absurd place, and as I believe that my master
is sitting on a chair on the front lawn, let us make our way
there. He will be glad to hear that I have been of service to
this young actress and will, I'm sure, order that the dog, which
has frightened her, almost out of her wits, to be shot by one
of the men.'

I said no more, just took a firm hold of Bruno's lead, whispered to him and allowed him to lead the party out from the

depths of the maze and to its entrance. I half-wondered whether to put him back into his kennel but then decided that his calm, affable presence might be of use in what could turn out to be a trial for his life.

Lord Edward was reading a book when we arrived on the terrace. He placed a leather bookmark on the page and laid the book aside on a small table beside him. He did not get to his feet, I noticed. Obviously none of us was of importance. Charley and I were the youngest of his male guests and Nelly, as an actress and the daughter of an actress, was not considered worthy of his usual politeness.

'Yes,' he said, addressing the monosyllable to his secretary.

'I'm sorry to interrupt you, sir,' said Maguire smoothly. 'But Miss Nelly, conscious of how much she and her mother owe to you, did not want to complain, but I persuaded her that you would want to know the truth.'

'Complain!' Lord Edward looked from one to the other of us. I said nothing. It was, I decided, for Nelly to tell her story and then I would back her up. In the meantime, we stood, all of us, in front of his chair, as though summoned to the headmaster's study for a misdemeanour.

'Tell Lord Edward about the dog attacking you, Miss Nelly,' prompted the secretary.

'Attacked,' said the owner of the dog.

Again, I said nothing. Lord Edward looked from one of us to the other with an air of growing irritation. The dog, also, got a cursory glance, but no appearance of affection. Nelly looked from one to another and then she fainted.

It was, I recognized, a theatrical faint. Dickens and I haunted every playhouse in London, and I had seen dozens of actresses who could faint just like that, I could even, by heart, enumerate the steps which were taken. The slight sigh, the tentative step forward, the slow dropping of both shoulders, the head flopping forward on to the chest, arms falling limply and then the collapse. Very efficiently done, I thought.

'Oh, my God, oh my darling,' said Charley and Lord Edward gave him a cold look.

'Fetch the young lady's mother if you would be so kind,

Mr Young Charles,' he said. Calling Charley by this rather absurd name which Dickens had allocated to his eldest son on the playbill, was, I recognized, a way of putting the young man in his place. 'No, do leave her, please. Mr Maguire, fetch a cushion for the young lady's head. She will come to her senses within minutes. Go now, if you please, young sir.' His voice had a frigid politeness which silenced the young man and sent him stumbling across the terrace towards the front door of the castle.

'Perhaps, Mr Collins, you will return the dog to the stables,' he said, and I left instantly. Nelly, I was sure, would tell the truth to her mother and in the meantime, the dog was safer out of sight. I took him back, made sure that cool, fresh water was available and with a heavy heart refastened his chain.

And then I went in search of Dickens. The clock in the stable yard tower had showed that only twenty minutes were left before the first bell for dinner so I hurried down the avenue as quickly as I could force my legs to move. I had gone the whole way to North Lodge before I caught sight of him.

North Lodge was a brick gateway, flanked by two lodges recently re-built by Lord Edward in the Tudor style and Dickens was at the door of one, leisurely drinking a mug of water and patting a small, extremely ugly terrier who had perched on a low wall beside his leg.

My heart lifted at the sight. Dickens was erratic, sometimes he liked the world, sometimes almost everyone came under criticism, sometimes I was right, in his estimation, and sometimes I was wrong. But he never varied in his liking for dogs.

I said nothing of what was on my mind, though. I had to be careful. Dickens was defensive about his relationship with Bulwer-Lytton. He knew that many of his friends, including one of his best friends, the actor, Macready, were critical of the noble lord, finding him irritable, defensive and immensely snobbish. Dickens, however, persisted in finding nuggets of gold beneath the scornfully contemptuous façade and insisted that he was the only person who knew the real man.

Dinner, I thought, could wait. 'Call that a dog,' I scoffed, taking care to keep my voice low so that I didn't offend the lodge keeper. 'Come on, Dick! Let me show you the biggest dog you have ever seen, bigger than that St Bernard or that Newfoundland dog of yours.'

I didn't wait for an answer but set off down the avenue at top speed. He followed; I knew that he would. I had not mentioned Bruno to him previously; I was not sure why, but it may have been because Bruno was my friend, and Dickens, much as I liked him and valued his friendship, had a habit of taking over one's friends and making them his own. But now Bruno's life was in danger and so, breathlessly, I poured out the whole story as soon as he caught up with me and managed to finish before we arrived at the stable yard and Bruno rose to his feet to observe us.

Dickens coveted him, instantly. I heard his breath draw in and, turning around, saw his eyes widen as they passed over that magnificently noble dog. He did not offer to approach, though, and so I swaggered across the yard and laid my hand on Bruno's broad forehead as he rose to a sitting position.

'Hallo, old boy,' I said affectionately, and stroked him with a hand which was now steady, though for minutes I had dreaded the thought of seeing an empty kennel and knowing that I was too late. Deliberately I reached back and removed the staple from the chain and held it loosely in one hand.

'Come and meet another friend of mine, Bruno, old boy,' I said and escorted him towards where Dickens stood. In the distance I heard the chime of the dinner bell, but I ignored it. Who cared if I turned up at dinner in muddy boots and crumpled trousers? This was more important. I looked at Dickens and saw a smile edge his lips. He held out one hand, quite steadily but I knew that he was very alert.

Bruno watched him for a moment. He had none of the overflowing friendliness of a spaniel or the excitable nature of a terrier. He looked straight into the eyes of the man and made his own judgement. His tail wagged – not exuberantly, but it swung in a dignified fashion. He sniffed the palm politely but did not lick it. Dickens looked at him and nodded.

'An aristocratic gentleman,' he said, while I tried to suppress a feeling of pride that Bruno liked me better than my very famous friend.

But then, quite deliberately, Dickens put his hand into the dog's mouth, and just like any dentist, examined his teeth. He nodded once again after a moment, and took his hand out, wiping it on the dog's glossy fur.

'A very good, steady dog,' he said, and once the words were spoken the tension seemed to break. Bruno wagged more enthusiastically and then licked the hand that had touched his teeth.

'One hundred per cent safe. I'm as sure of that as you are standing there; and you know me, Collins; I'm a man who never makes a mistake about dogs,' pronounced Dickens in his usual dogmatic way. It was at that moment that Tom Maguire arrived on the scene. Bruno immediately reacted with a low growl. He took a step nearer to me and faced the man with bristles elevated on the length of his neck and all down his spine. Maguire took a hasty step backwards.

Dickens looked at him with ill-favour. He had, I thought, taken note of an episode that had taken place earlier that afternoon where Maguire had egged on Mark Lemon in his teasing remarks from *Punch* magazine about Roman Catholics and Irish priests, in the presence of Clarkson Stanfield, a fervent and devout man for whom his Catholic religion was of the greatest importance.

Mark Lemon, of course, was a friend of Dickens; they enjoyed teasing and joking with each other, but dear old Clarkson Stanfield was, I knew, of more importance than Mark Lemon. If Lemon was a literary comrade, Clarkson, almost twenty years older than Dickens, played more the role of a gently admiring father. Lemon might be forgiven an ill-timed jest, but if an underling like the secretary had ruffled the nice old man, well, in Dickens' eyes, he had committed *lèse-majesté*.

'Yes,' he said abruptly, assuming the manner of the master of the house. 'You have a message, Maguire, do you?'

Tom Maguire was assured and belligerent with me, but he crumpled before Dickens. 'I beg your pardon, sir,' he said. 'I do have a message from my master for the stable manager.'

'And, this, I presume, is he,' said Dickens, bestowing a cordial smile upon the stable master who had appeared. 'I must congratulate you upon the excellent condition of this beautiful dog. Deliver your message, Maguire, and then leave us, would you? I wish to speak to this man.'

Maguire looked doubtfully from Dickens to me. I could see how his mind was working. If he delivered the message to the stable master to shoot the dog, Dickens would immediately intervene, I would give my side of the story and the chances were that Dickens might insist on dragging Lord Edward to the scene.

'Come on, man,' said Dickens impatiently. 'Out with it. I haven't got all day, you know. The first bell has gone for dinner. Don't delay me any longer. Smarten yourself up, my good man.'

I suppressed a smile. Dickens never spoke to his own secretary, or indeed to anyone of his own servants, in that tone of voice, but it had the desired effect. Maguire crumpled before him.

'It's of no consequence, Mr Dickens,' he said striving for dignity. 'I'll come back later.' He gave me an angry glance as though blaming me for his reception. He then retreated.

The stable manager watched him with satisfaction. I had little doubt that he had heard the whole story. Voices from the terrace had been loud enough to have been heard by the sharp ears of the boy emptying barrow loads of muck into the purpose-dug hole in the nearby rose garden. He would have told his master who would have been awaiting a summons. Now the man stood respectfully to attention, waiting for instructions from his master's guest.

Dickens immediately turned on his charm. 'And your name. You remind me of my man, Topping, so I'd better get your name into my head before I call you Topping.'

Since Topping was a very small cockney, with bright red hair and this was an elderly grey-haired country man, well-built and with a dignified manner, I didn't think that was likely, but it established a friendly atmosphere. The stable manager said that people mostly called him Dick. He admitted reluctantly to the surname of Baldock but reiterated that his name was Dick and that was what he was always called.

'Well, there you are! And my friends call me Dick, so we're

a pair!' Dickens shook hands instantly with the man and so did I. And then he came straight to the point.

'I understand that my friend here has been borrowing your dog to walk through the maze with him,' he began. 'Have you heard that there was a spot of unpleasantness over there in the maze this afternoon?'

The rural Dick admitted he had heard that a young lady got a fright. And then he tightened his lips.

'Mr Collins was just beginning to tell me the whole story as he was there and he's a lawyer so you can trust him to tell the whole truth, so perhaps you could start again, Wilkie.'

I didn't exactly call myself a lawyer since I had never practised law for a single day and had idled my time at the Temple Inn, scribbling ideas for stories, but I nodded gravely. With my mind on the expectation of hearing the second dinner bell, I went through the whole story as quickly as I could, and the man looked relieved.

'Wouldn't think he would touch the young lady myself, not even in play. A very good, steady dog that, sir.' He looked at Dickens with an air of hope.

'Yes, indeed.' Dickens nodded, and then in his impetuous fashion, he said, 'I have a fancy to buy that dog and I value your good opinion of him. Do you think that your master would sell him to me?'

'I couldn't say, sir.'

'He'd like to go with the other gentleman better. Very fond of the other gentleman, sir,' protested the stable boy, and got a look that sent him scrambling into the nearest stable with pitchfork in hand. Dick, the stable manager, turned to the author.

'Nice boy that,' he said. 'You have to keep boys in order, but he's a good boy.'

'Good with animals; I could see that at a glance.' Dickens always prided himself at seeing things at a glance. It was the right thing to say, though. The stable manager looked pleased.

'You're right, sir,' he said. 'I'll have to tell my wife what you said. Very against taking him in the first place, you know. But she got fond of him after a while. Still throws it up at me

from time to time. You know what women are like, Mr
Dickens.'

'Why was she against him in the beginning?' asked Dickens.
He liked finding out about people. When I knew him first I
thought it was that he was searching for people to put in his
books, but later, when I knew him better, I knew that his mind
was teeming with characters and very few of them were based
on a real person. Now I regarded this curiosity of his to be
based on an irrepressible fascination with his fellow men and
women. He had turned an interested face on the man now,
and I knew that he wouldn't stir until he had heard all about
the wife and why she hadn't wanted to take in the boy. I didn't
mind waiting. Dickens' hand was busy, stroking Bruno's noble
head and the longer we stayed, the more I was convinced that
he would not allow the dog to be shot because of a lie told
by Tom Maguire.

The stable manager gave a quick glance around and then
lowered his voice. 'Well, you see, sir, that boy had a bad
history,' he said and then lowering his voice even more, he
whispered, 'his father shot his mother.'

'God bless my soul,' said Dickens. 'What a terrible thing
to happen.'

'So it was, sir. Jealousy, of course. She was carrying on
with a young lad from the town. Now, the cook, up at the
house, would have it that there was nothing much to it. Said
the young woman was just lonely. Had been a kitchen maid,
you see, sir, and the cook thought she missed the company,
always glad to do a few hours' work when the young lad
started school – they had but the one child, you see.' And
the stable manager jerked his head in the direction of where
vigorous clanging of a shovel on stone flags showed that
the stable boy was hard at work. 'Well, be that as it
may, the husband thought otherwise, and he had the rights
of it. He came home early one day with his gun – he was
the gamekeeper, sir – in he walks, unexpected-like, gun
under his arm, finds the two of them in the kitchen and he
shot the two of them, killed them stone dead. And the boy,
young Jim, came in the door at that very moment, just behind
his father, home early from school that day as they had the

inspector in, and, of course, went straight to find his father. He used always to help him to clean the gun when he came home from school, so I've heard. Happened about a year ago, sir.'

'God bless my soul,' repeated Dickens.

'And the father, the boy's father?' I asked, feeling rather sick.

'Well, the father dashed out of the house, threw the gun into the well, according to young Jim, and was off in two seconds.'

'Was the man caught?' I asked, thinking what a terrible thing it would be for a boy like that to witness the death of his mother and the hanging of his father.

The man shook his head. 'No, he wasn't. You see there was no hue and cry after him, not for hours. He had plenty of time to get away, get himself lost in London for a while, and then go south to Kent or somewhere like that.'

'No hue and cry, not for hours!' I exclaimed and Dickens smiled in a knowing fashion.

'The boy gave him time to get away,' he said with conviction.

'That's right, sir. Nobody knew a thing until six o'clock in the evening. The boy had a queer story about that. He said that he went up to his mother and felt her and knew she was dead and then he felt the young fellow and knew he was dead, too. And then, according to him, he fainted for a couple of hours and then he went up to the house, to the cook who had always been kind to him, and he told her the whole story.'

'Wanted to give his father time to get away,' repeated Dickens with a satisfied nod.

'That was the story in the village, sir; you, being a writer of books, you guessed what happened straight away.' The man's voice was admiring and Dickens, I knew, liked admiration. He had a pleased look on his face.

'But what about his mother? Wouldn't he have wanted to get a doctor, to get help, to make sure that she was really dead?' I was rather repulsed by the story.

'Well, sir,' said the man, turning from Dickens to me, 'that

was what everyone said. But the boy had an answer for
everything. Whenever he wasn't in school, he went to the
school here on the estate – they took good care of him, his
mother and his father – well, whenever he wasn't in school,
he was out with his father and his father taught him how to
make sure that an animal was properly dead, taught him how
to take a pulse, trained him by feeling his own wrist and his
father's wrist – so he said. Well, his story was that he felt
his mother's pulse and his mother was definitely dead and
then he felt the young fellow's pulse and he was dead, too.
So, he said. And, then he fainted. Well, that was his story.
And when he came to and checked the bodies, they were
already stiffening in the heat of the fire. Then cool as you
like, he went up to the house and went into the kitchen and
told the cook – she'd been kind to him, you know, for his
mother's sake, of course; so the boy went straight to her. And,
I must say that the doctor backed him up, looked at the bullet
holes and said that both of them would have died the minute
they were shot. A great man with a gun, of course, the boy's
father. He had been trained up as a gamekeeper by his father
and grandfather, so I've heard.'

'And the gun?' asked Dickens. 'The lad said that his father
threw the gun into the well.'

'Never found, sir. His lordship gave orders for the well to
be drained. There was a thought that the gamekeeper might
have thrown himself in there after the gun, so the well had
to be completely emptied. Going up and down they were for
hours on end. No gun ever found. My own feeling was that
the boy made it up, very fond of his father, he was, poor
lad.'

'And you took him on, despite your wife's hesitations.'

'Like all women, going on about bad blood, but someone
had to do something about the lad. No relations. They were
both strangers in the place. No one knew where that gamekeeper came from, though some said it was Cumbria – and
the wife was an orphan, came from the orphanage at St Albans,
left at the door of the church, usual thing. So, I upped and
said that I would take him. I knew that he was good lad with
animals, even managed the dogs as good as any adult during

the hunts that we used to have up to six or seven years ago, and myself and the wife, we never had no children, and a nice snug house, so I took him on, and I've never regretted it. He's a good worker is young Jim and no more mischief in him than any boy. Costs us nothing but his food. As for pocket money, spending money, well, we don't need to give him anything. Got a small job up in the house. Has to keep clean some rooms in the roof and he gets a bit of money for that. The housekeeper told my wife that Sir Edward suggested it when one of the maids slipped and sprained an ankle. You know what women are like, sir, went to Sir Edward herself, complaining. He was the one that said they'd get an active young boy to do the cleaning up there and he was the one that suggested young Jim. Not long after the inquest, sir, so the boy's name would have been in his mind. No, he don't cost us much and I'm glad to have him.'

'Nevertheless, you're a charitable man and I hope you get your reward,' said Dickens, taking half a crown from his pocket and passing it over. The story, I could see, had moved him and excited his mind. He said nothing for a moment and then seemed to come back to the present with a slight jerk.

'And now about this dog,' he said. 'This is a good dog; I'm sure of that, and I'm very good at picking out a dog. I pride myself on that. I wouldn't like to see him shot for something that he was not responsible for. Mr Collins, my friend here, tells me that he released the dog after he heard the girl scream, not before, and that he is convinced that the dog protected the girl from assault. What do you say to that?'

'Mr Collins is right, sir. This is a very calm, good-tempered dog, sir.' The man hesitated a little for a moment and then finished with the air of one who is picking his words with care. 'I would want to check on any order that came telling me to destroy any animal, not to mention this particular dog, sir, if you know what I mean. You can rely on me for that, sir.'

'So, you understand me, I know,' said Dickens with a satisfied nod. 'I'll speak to your master immediately about this matter. That's a smart lad that you have there – well-trained by you, I can see. Send him for me if you have any worries in the meantime.'

And with that broad hint, Dickens and I made our way quickly back to the Gothic splendours of Knebworth House.

THREE

No man under heaven deserves these sacrifices from us
women. Men! They are the enemies of our innocence
and our peace – they drag us away from our parents'
love and our sisters' friendship – they take us body
and soul to themselves and fasten our helpless lives
to theirs as they chain up a dog to his kennel. And
what does the best of them give us in return?

Wilkie Collins, *The Woman in White*

I guess that before our arrival all meals at Knebworth were
carried out with the greatest solemnity, but Dickens had
put a stop to that, declaring that no crowd of strolling
players could be expected to dress for dinner and that
everyone should choose a place at table that suited him. We
were the last to arrive, but Dickens took, as if by right, his
place beside Lord Edward while I happily ousted a few
people from their positions, insisted that it had been arranged
that I had to sit beside Lady Rosina and in the ensuing
confusion managed to reserve a place for Young Charles
beside little Nelly across the table from us. She was, poor
girl, still rather pale and red-eyed, but she responded with
a brave smile when I told Lady Rosina all about the beautiful
Great Dane dog and how he had protected the young heroine
from attack.

'"The Assyrian came down like a wolf on the fold!"' I
declaimed dramatically, and others chimed in with the lines
of Tennyson's well-known poem, while the well-trained servants refilled glasses as soon as they were emptied of their
choice claret or Chablis.

'Speech! Speech!' shouted the caricaturist Leech and I could
see that he had taken a pencil from his pocket and was busy
drawing on one of the fine linen napkins. 'Go on, Wilkie, let's

hear about the dastardly villain, the beautiful maiden and the noble dog.'

'Stand on the chair, Wilkie, so that we can all see you,' shouted Lemon and I shook my head at him. I had no desire to interrupt the conversation between Dickens and Lord Edward and so on the contrary I sank my voice to a whisper and forced all to lean across the table in order to hear my words.

'Once upon a time, there was a beautiful princess with blue eyes and golden hair,' I said, looking straight across the table at Nelly who blushed attractively and began to smile for the first time that evening. 'And one sunny afternoon in August, when the princess wandered through the secret gardens of the palace, there came upon her an evil wolf.' I let my eyes wander down the table until I met the furious face of Tom Maguire. I smiled innocently and nodded in his direction, noticing that Leech held his pencil poised above the napkin and that his eyes had followed mine.

'And this wolf in man's clothing,' I said, slowly and dramatically, with my eyes still fixed on the secretary's face, 'this wolf in human form, having a wicked and evil nature, frightened the golden-haired princess by trying to assault her. He frightened her so much that she screamed and screamed,' I went on, still with my eyes fixed on Tom Maguire. Young Charles was not even making a pretence to eat or to drink, but sat with both hands clenched and his eyes, also, on Tom Maguire. Leech, I saw, with inner satisfaction, was now adding a prominent pair of dark-rimmed spectacles to perch on the long nose of the wolf. Lady Rosina clasped her hands together with theatrical intensity, uttering a dramatic, 'Oh, *mon Dieu! Quel horreur!* What wickedness!'

John Foster, fanatically religious, frowned disapprovingly at this taking the name of the Lord in vain, scanning the faces on either side of the table and then he also fixed Tom Maguire with a penetrating stare and an air of disgust. I cast a rapid glance towards the top of the table, but Dickens and Lord Edward were deep in conversation and did not appear to be looking in our direction.

'And now,' I said lightly, but still in a very low voice, 'we

come to the happy ending of the story. Unlike the victims in
the poem, my golden-haired princess did not perish, neither
did she come to harm. Because the golden-haired princess had
a young prince nearby who heard her cries and unleased a
noble dog who came to her rescue.' I would, I thought, hand
over the part of rescuer to be shared between Young Mr Charles,
and the gallant, fast-moving Bruno.

'And the wolf,' queried John Foster with a frown on his
face. 'Has the wolf met his just deserts?'

'Not yet,' I said, not looking at Foster, but staring sternly
down at Tom Maguire, sitting at the bottom of the table. He
was looking straight ahead, patches of red on his face and an
untouched plate before him. He took off his spectacles, wiped
them on his handkerchief and then replaced them and had
tried to fix his attention on his knife and fork.

'Should be hanged! Any man who mistreats a woman
should be hanged. It's the worst of all crimes!' said Lady
Rosina with a loud emphasis which, at last, drew her
husband's attention. He frowned slightly, looked down
towards her and scowled angrily. I looked back up at him
with concealed amusement. Why did he have to bother
showing his anger so plainly, so openly? My sympathies
were all for Lady Rosina. Perhaps he was annoyed that she
was still beautiful, and he had lost all the looks he had had
as a young man. He minded that. This much was obvious
by his efforts to disguise his age. A man in his sixties should,
I thought, allow his hair to grow naturally grey and refrain
from dying it that strange and unnatural shade of black.
Moreover, a man in his sixties who looks in the mirror and
sees wrinkles may be allowed to heave a sigh at the signs
of departing youth, but he should, by no means, be tempted
to clog the pores of his skin with flesh-coloured powder and
paint his cheekbones as Lord Edward Bulwer-Lytton so obviously did. I found myself disliking the man even more as I
listened to his authoritative voice pronouncing sentence upon
his unfortunate wife.

'Lady Rosina, could I have your attention please,' he
said, making no effort to leave his seat in order to speak
privately to her. In fact, he sat back in his chair and raised

his voice to the pitch of one delivering an after-dinner speech.

'Lady Rosina,' he continued with a heavy emphasis on the word 'lady', 'you are an uninvited guest here and I would ask you to restrain the language of the gutter while you sit at my table. I would remind you that you still bear my name and so I would ask you not to disgrace it any further.'

A dead silence fell upon the company and all looked from husband to wife. For my part, I felt overwhelmed with anger against a man who could treat his own wife like this, treat any woman, in fact, not to mind a wife whom he must have loved at one stage and who had borne two children to him.

She, however, turned a brave face towards him. 'Go ahead, sir,' she said, her lovely voice filling the whole of that large dining room. 'Tell our whole story. I'm sure that your guests would like to hear from your own lips such a gripping narrative of persecution of the most base and unmanly kind, practised by a wicked man of great talent and resources, upon a noble lady, who had hardly anything to defend her but a high spirit, a consciousness of innocence, and a resolve not to be crushed.'

I bit my lips to conceal a smile. I had a feeling that this 'gripping narrative of persecution of the most base and unmanly kind, practised by a wicked man of great talent and resources, upon a noble lady who had hardly anything to defend her but a high spirit, a consciousness of innocence, and a resolve not to be crushed' had been lifted from the publisher's blurb for one of Lady Rosina's novels. Nevertheless, her impassioned voice rang with truth. I looked around the table. Most faces were filled with embarrassment, Clarkson looked distressed – poor, old man, he would have known both in the days when they lived together as man and wife – there was, I seemed to remember, some talk of him being godfather to the daughter who died before her twentieth year. Dickens, however, smoothed a hand over his mouth and moustache and I suspected that he was hiding a smile, or perhaps saving up the dramatic scene for a future book. As for myself, I felt indignant and was on the lady's side. Lord Edward had brought this upon himself. She had said nothing amiss, just shown a womanly sympathy towards a young girl who had been molested on his property. I looked down at Maguire and saw him rise to his feet. His master had beckoned to his secretary.

Lady Rosina observed the gesture. 'Yes,' she said with an air of high scorn. 'Yes, send your minion to summon your tame medical men. Have me locked up in an asylum again.' She looked from one embarrassed face to another and then spoke in a confidential manner, across the table, to Frances Jarman. 'Never,' she said dramatically, 'was a more criminal or despotic law passed than that which now enables a husband to lock up his wife in a madhouse on the certificate of two medical men, who often in haste, frequently for a bribe, certify to madness where none exists.'

Frances Jarman, I noticed, winced slightly at that, and I remembered that her own history was a sad one where her husband went out of his mind due to a venereal disease and died in a lunatic asylum. I saw Dickens look down the table towards her. They were old friends, of course. Had known each other for about twenty years, had met, I seemed to remember, when he was a stage-struck young man and she a highly successful actress and mother of two little girls. Doubtless, they had kept in touch. He was the one who had recommended her to Lord Edward; I had overheard him negotiating a wage for the services of herself and her youngest daughter with Lord Edward. She glanced at him now but said nothing; merely bowed her head in grave acknowledgement of his look of concern and addressed herself to the plate of rapidly cooling, brown Windsor soup while her daughter crumbled a piece of bread nervously and allowed her own soup to remain untouched.

The secretary, having listened to his master's instructions, did not, as Lady Rosina obviously expected, leave the room to send a messenger to the doctor, but came down the room and gently touched her on the arm. I abandoned my soup, which was over-flavoured for my taste, and watched with amusement. For a moment Lady Rosina stared at Maguire and then at her arm with dignified amazement. She jerked it away from his grasp, reached across the table and helped herself to another piece of bread, ignoring the man as she turned to me.

'The service in this house is very poor, isn't it?' she said in clear, distinct tones. 'You can always tell, can't you, when there isn't a woman supervising the household?'

'So my mother tells me,' I said, trying to inject a note of conversational ease into my voice and wishing that the secretary would have the sense to take himself off. He didn't though. He was made of sterner stuff. This time he reached down and removed the side plate still bearing its slice of bread and placed it in the centre of the table. Now she did turn to look at him and so did the rest of the table. The clank of spoons against china ceased immediately and all eyes were turned in our direction.

'Now, look here, Maguire,' called out Leech angrily.

The secretary turned his attention from Lady Rosina, walked over to Leech, bent down and whispered in his ear. Just one word. A sibilant sound. And Leech, normally an outspoken man, visibly paled and turned his eyes back to his soup plate. I heard John Foster protest from the top of the table and then fall silent as Maguire turned a malevolent gaze in his direction. Then Dickens rose to his feet and walked towards us in a leisurely fashion.

'Collins, my dear fellow, look what I've just found in my pocket,' he said with a novelist's ease in making up stories. He removed his clenched fist from his pocket and held it under my nose and the attention of the table was turned in our direction.

With a man less determined, less malign than the secretary that would have caused a diversion, but Tom Maguire seemed to have a personal grudge against the unfortunate Lady Rosina. He seized her by the arm, attempting to drag her from her chair. She was made of sterner stuff, though, and she took immediate revenge by emptying the remains of her soup over his head.

Dickens dropped his arm, took a step forward towards the secretary. I had to bite back a smile at the sight of the man's face streaked with the glutinous brown liquid as the round bowl crowned his head like the cap worn by farm labourers.

'You'd better go and wash, man,' said Dickens, reaching his side and taking him by the arm. 'Go now. You look quite ridiculous! Come, Collins, let's get this poor fellow washed and presentable.'

I found it hard to resist a laugh. Dickens was so calm and so unemotional. One could have imagined that he was talking to one of his young sons who had got into mischief. Willingly, I jumped to my feet and took Maguire's other arm in a firm grip and, while Dickens solicitously took out his handkerchief and mopped his face, Leech, wearing a broad grin, came and removed the soup plate. I heard a muffled giggle from the two young people on the other side of the table and was glad that Nelly was feeling recovered enough to indulge in a laugh against her attacker.

He didn't struggle as we marched him towards the door. It was hard to withstand Dickens when he was in a determined mood, and all might have been passed off as a joke if the whole table had laughed and then sympathized with the victim, perhaps handed him a glass of wine, but Lord Edward Bulwer-Lytton was not a man possessed of a sense of humour and he dominated his guests, glaring around him with malevolence which wiped smiles from the faces of his guests. I had already begun to think that he was a downright unpleasant character who liked to domineer and now he proved it. We had just reached the tall Tudor cabinet when we were arrested by his voice.

'I thank you, madam. I am grateful to you. You have now proved my point. You are completely insane, completely unfit for ordinary society.'

There was a short silence after those words. All eyes now, including ours, turned towards Lady Rosina. Dickens paused and waited. I expected a passionate outbreak, and was looking forward to her spirited rejoinder, but she said nothing. She sat there, very straight, very upright, her eyes upon her former husband and then quite deliberately she picked up a plate and fired it in the direction of his head. And then another and another. The whole dinner party was immobilized and speechless as the plates, with their delicately painted wreaths of pink

and green, crashed, one after another, against the wall behind
Lord Edward's head.

He bowed mockingly. 'I'm glad to see you reveal yet more
of your insanity, even at the price of the destruction of some
pieces of rare Berlin porcelain. Beautiful china, but, well, so
be it!' he said. 'Anyone watching this exhibition, my dear
wife, must be happy to testify that you are not fit to dwell
outside a sheltered and strictly supervised asylum suited to
your needs. Maguire, go and telephone for Dr Hill and let's
be finished with this unpleasant business.'

There was a moment's pause. The eyes of the guests shut-
tled rapidly from the face of the husband at the top of the
table and the wife towards its end. Both looked the calmest
in the room, but the lady was the one who moved first. Picking
up her handbag from its position on the floor beside her chair,
she extracted from it a small but workmanlike pistol and aimed
it straight at the secretary's heart.

'I bought this pistol with the very first money I earned
from the publication of my first book,' she said dramatically.
'I had sworn,' she continued, 'that never again would I expose
myself to an attack from my dastardly husband who had
kicked me savagely and bit me on the cheek with his great
horse-teeth.' She said the words in a casual manner, the hand
holding the weapon remaining quite steady. 'And now,' she
continued, moving the pistol from man to master and then
back again, 'I will take myself off to my bedroom and direct
the servants to bring me a tray of sandwiches. But remember,
my lord, this pistol stays close to my hand. I'm no longer the
meek, young girl that you married and abused and tormented.
Now I am a woman of experience who knows how to protect
herself.'

And with these magnificent lines which needed, I felt, a
round of applause, Lady Rosina got to her feet and still holding
her pistol in her hand, she bent to pick up her handbag and
then made her way towards the door.

'I'll see you to your room, Lady Rosina,' said Dickens in
his nonchalant manner. He didn't even glance at his host but
relinquished his hold upon Maguire and was at the door before

her. Ceremoniously he held it wide open as Lady Rosina,
pistol in one hand and alligator skin handbag in the other,
passed through, casting a look of disdain over her shoulder at
her former husband.

There was a long silence after they left. I saw Maguire look
at his master a few times, waiting no doubt to see whether
the command to phone for Dr Hill would be repeated, but he
waited in vain. Lord Edward picked up a small bell and rang
it vigorously. A wide-eyed maid entered so quickly that I
guessed she must have been behind the door when Dickens
left the room.

'We are waiting for the next course! Kindly clear away as
quickly as possible and serve us some edible food,' he said
in abrupt tones and I thought, not for the first time, what a
very unpleasant man he was. He made no effort to cover up
the awkwardness of the situation with small talk, but stared
balefully down the table, fixing his eyes on poor Nelly, while
servants scurried around, picking up pieces of broken china
and clearing the undamaged soup plates from the table. He
was, of course, very deaf; Dickens had told me that, but I felt
that he could have made some effort by talking or even asking
a question of someone like John Foster who seldom turned
down any invitation to hold forth on any subject under the
sun. He didn't though, but after a minute got to his feet and
left the room without any attempt at an apology, leaving his
guests looking awkward and ill-at-ease.

I scoured my mind to hit on a subject of interest to all.
However, it wasn't my light, indecisive, rather tentative voice
that broke the uneasy silence, but the rougher, harder notes of
Clarkson Stanfield who, though he had left the sea all those
years ago, when he was quite a young man, still kept in his
voice some of a sailor's bellow.

'I can remember when I met Rosina first,' he said meditatively, addressing his words to John Foster across the table
from him. He looked up to the top of the table, paused for a
second and then, seeing that our host had left the room,
resumed. 'She was over from Ireland and was a pupil at a
school in Kensington run by the poetess, Frances Arabella
Rowden. They say that Frances was not only a poet herself,

but that she had the knack of turning her pupils into writers themselves and that was certainly true. I'm an old man now, but I remember at least three of them, Caroline – what was her name then? Of course, we know her now as the poetess, Caroline Lamb, and there was Laetitia Emma Roberts and Anna Maria Field – all of them writers of prose and poetry, even at that age they were, all three, producing work worthy of being published, but somehow Rosina stood out from them all. I was just there to give the young ladies lessons in painting seascapes, but my goodness, I was enraptured by her. I've never known anyone with such intensity. She burned like a candle in the darkness. Nothing that she did was ordinary. She was fifteen years old, and so beautiful,' said Clarkson, his eyes full of visions of the past. 'She had big dark eyes . . .' He paused for a moment and then resumed. By now the whole table was listening. 'I can see her now,' he said. 'She wore a linen smock for painting – covered with smears of paint – she had no thought of how she looked – would run her fingers through her hair, smudge paint on her cheeks while she was thinking, would hum a tune, dance a few steps, those lovely dark eyes glowing, and then she would stop for a moment, stand very still and then put more paint on to the canvas – a few strokes of a paintbrush and she brought the whole picture miraculously to life!' Clarkson stopped and mused for a moment. 'I loved her then, and I would have killed anyone who injured her,' he said simply.

No one said anything, but glances went from him to the face of our host who had just reappeared. Had Lord Edward heard that last sentence, or was his deafness more profound than we realized? Whatever was the reason, his face showed no glimmer of feeling. He took his seat, drummed with his fingers upon the polished wood of the table and stared stonily ahead. His impassive features displayed no indication that he may have heard his death knell. I didn't like the man, but there was a sharp intelligence in his face and, of course, his prodigious output and the large income which he earned from his literary works had to earn my respect. I wondered what might have happened if they had never met. If Lady Rosina had married someone like Clarkson Stanfield who adored, and worshipped, her. And if Lord Edward had married a meek little woman who admired him immensely and thought that everything that he did was wonderful.

'"Oh God, that one might read the book of fate!",' I said aloud and Frances Jarman, recognizing the quotation, gave me a very sad look.

FOUR

But in these modern times it may be decidedly
asserted as a fact, that vice, in accomplishing the vast
majority of its seductions, uses no disguise at all;
appears impudently in its naked deformity; and, instead
of horrifying all beholders, in accordance with the
prediction of the classical satirist, absolutely attracts a
much more numerous congregation of worshippers
than has ever yet been brought together by the divinest
beauties that virtue can display for the allurement of
mankind.

Wilkie Collins, *Hide and Seek*

Only John Leech, the caricaturist, was at the breakfast table when I came down next morning. He greeted me with relief. No one likes to be the last down for breakfast and no one likes to pass the first meal of the day in solitary confinement.

'Ah, Collins,' said Leech. 'What did you think of our little tableau, yesterday evening?'

'I don't know what you are talking about,' I said grumpily. Leech was not a man I liked much. Too much inclined to worm into people's affairs, to spread gossip and curry favour by that means.

'Come, come,' he said in a lofty fashion. 'Surely you could see the drama. After all, our host was threatened by his wife, and a wife carrying a pistol! I would have thought that a young man like you would be sitting up until three o'clock in the morning, writing out the scene while it was fresh in your mind.'

I grunted, said nothing but helped myself to some ham. The breakfasts at Knebworth were superb, with enough food to feed an army and the service was equally good with a young

maid at my elbow ready to pour my coffee. I took a long drink
and began to feel better. I looked across at my companion.
There was something about Leech which I disliked, I decided.
Something about the tight mouth, the way his hair bulged out
like an additional pair of ears, trying to disguise the two bald
spots on his temples. Dickens was fond of him as he had done
some striking illustrations that added immensely to the success
of one of his most famous books, *A Christmas Carol*.
Nevertheless, Dickens had told me, in a confidential moment,
that he had some difficulty in persuading Lord Edward to have
John Leech as a house guest. I wondered why. After all, he
was, like all the players, a professional and a very well-known
artist. Dickens was adamant about this. The cast had all to be
part of the brotherhood of writers and artists, or their wives or
daughters, of course. If Mrs Dickens hadn't sprained her ankle
and Katey developed measles, we would not have had the two
actresses, Frances and her daughter Nelly. But why should
Lord Edward have objected to Leech? He was as well-known
– better known, indeed, as Clarkson Stanfield, or Augustus
Egg. I decided to pass the time at breakfast, not in discussing
poor Lady Rosina, but in delving into Leech's background.

'You don't care for our host, much,' I said, drawing a long
bow of invention as I had never really talked much to the man
before and certainly had not heard him say anything about
Lord Edward.

'Don't like the way that he treated his family,' he said briefly,
swallowing the last piece of his crumpet and helping himself
to a few more from the plate. At the rate with which he was
swallowing them, there would be none left for me by the time
that I had finished my ham. 'Calls himself a Christian, well,
I know what I would call a man like that.'

'Lady Rosina?' I queried, though with some surprise as he
had sounded cynical and dismissive of her troubles.

'Not Lady Rosina,' he said impatiently. 'That woman can
look after herself. She's like a wild cat. Her claws are out all
the time. No, I'm talking about their daughter.' He stared
meditatively at the wall opposite, looking at the set of pictures
which were lined up in the oak parlour where we breakfasted.
They were all of ancestors and present members of the Lytton

family, but I had a feeling that he was not looking at them, but at a picture within his mind.

'It's not there, I see, but I sketched her, the daughter, once; almost twenty years ago,' he said dreamily. 'For her seventeenth birthday.' And after a moment's pause, he said, still in the same tone, 'Her name was Emily. I always think it is a very pretty name, but she wasn't just pretty, she was very beautiful. I've never seen a face that was such a perfect oval. Lovely eyes, cornflower blue; fine, baby-fine, hair. I had trouble drawing that hair, making the pencil lines show how soft it was. She was very sweet, I thought, but not like the usual seventeen-year-old girl, no giggles, no effort to appear knowledgeable. She sat there in the glory of her youth . . .' Leech paused for a second or two and then finished up, 'And, do you know, Collins, she was like an old, tired woman, sick of life and waiting for the end.'

I was startled into dropping a slice of ham by those last words. I stared across at him. 'Why?' I asked. 'What was wrong with the girl?'

'Her father,' he said bitterly. 'That was what was wrong with her. Her father.'

I was taken aback by that. It was not like Leech, I thought. In fact, I had always thought of him as rather a toadeater, as my mother used to say. I raised my eyes from my plate and looked across at him. He wasn't looking at me but was still eyeing the row of family portraits stretched across the chimney breast.

'Was he unkind to her?' I asked. 'Blamed her for the mother's desertion.'

'She was only eight years old at the time,' he said impatiently. 'How on earth could she be responsible for her mother leaving her father?'

I shrugged. This was typical of Leech. Set you guessing and then scolded if your guess was incorrect.

'I don't know anything much about the daughter,' I said. 'Tell me,' I added invitingly, though I knew that he was going to tell me anyway.

'There were two children, you know,' he said. 'Everyone knows about his son, Robert, who was mainly brought up by

Lord Edward's brother. His father acknowledges him, of
course. He would, wouldn't he? After all, Robert was a success.
But it would have been a different story if he had not been a
success. No thanks to his father that he has become a success.
He threw the two young children, Robert and Emily, out of
the house when their mother left. Sent them to be brought up
like peasants on a farm nearby, never saw them, never commu-
nicated with them, did nothing but pay a monthly stipend to
the farmer's wife.'

'Goodness!' I said, cutting some more ham. It was a deli-
cious joint, moist and tasty, delicately flavoured with salt and
some herb which I could not identify. 'He's an ambassador,
though, isn't he? Robert, the son, I mean,' I added. It didn't
sound like a peasant upbringing to me, I thought, but Leech
was not a man that I particularly wanted to contradict, especially before my breakfast in the morning hours.

'Oh, he shipped Robert off to his uncle, when the boy was
about ten or twelve,' he said impatiently. 'But the daughter, well,
he didn't want the daughter. She had something wrong with her,
a curvature of the spine, some childhood disease, polio, I think.
He didn't want her anyway. Eventually when she was getting
too old for the farm, when the whole business was causing some
scandal in the neighbourhood, he thought he'd better do something with her. Sent her to Switzerland for treatment of her
spine, put her through terrible operations. All to no avail. But
she grew up, pretty as a picture so when she was about sixteen,
he took her into his own house eventually. Should have left her
where she was,' said Leech moodily. 'You ask Foster about
Emily Bulwer-Lytton. She lived there in that house and goodness
knows what he did to her when she was there. He broke her
spirit, anyway. The place was full of his mistresses, of course.'

'Full!' I said. I thought that I would have to tell Dickens
about that. I crafted the way he would tell the story to selected
friends, while Leech swallowed some more tea and demolished
the rest of the crumpets. 'Three mistresses in the attics,' he
would say. 'One in the parlour, two in the banqueting hall and
half a dozen in the cellars . . .' My imagination was preparing
to go off on its own when Leech came to the more dramatic
part of his story.

'She left him,' he said. 'She stole some money from his desk. What could she do? She had nothing of her own, lived there as if she were dog, fed and housed but nothing else. Nothing to do with her life except to write letters.'

'Where did she go?' I asked the question but thought that there was something odd about the account. If the girl was writing letters, then she must have been taught to read and to write. Nevertheless, it was a tragic story that he was unfolding.

'She went to London. I saw her there one day. It was not long after I had sketched her, and I recognized her instantly.' He refreshed himself with some more tea before continuing. 'It was on Westminster Bridge. She was there with a young man. Might have been a student or something, that age, certainly, though he had a rather rough look about him.'

'Did you speak to her?'

Leech shook his head silently. But after a minute and another gulp of tea, he answered my question. 'I was embarrassed,' he said. 'She was behaving strangely, not like the daughter of Lord Edward Bulwer-Lytton, but like a shop girl or a parlour maid on her day out. She was standing on the bridge and she was kissing this young man, out there in the open, under the eyes of all, behaving almost as though she were drunk. I was desperately sorry for her.'

I didn't share his sorrow. I found myself feeling glad that the tragic girl, deserted, in reality, by father, as well as by mother, had found some love, even if it were not from a young man of whom her father would have approved.

'So, you let her go!' I commented, more because he annoyed me, than because I truly thought that it would have been any of his business to interfere. 'Did you ever see her again?' I asked when he did not reply.

A look of pain had come over his sour features. 'Yes, I did,' he said. 'Almost in the same place which made me think that she lived near to Westminster Bridge.'

'Not too nice an area around there,' I said, when he hesitated and seemed reluctant to continue. 'Devil's Acre,' I added with a vague notion of seeing something in the evening papers about that evocatively named slum.

He said nothing in reply to this. Appeared to be thinking

hard, his brow furrowed and his finger and thumb rubbing up and down upon the starched cloth. He had the look of someone who wanted to turn his thoughts into a pencil sketch, and I could see that he was deeply moved.

'She was across the road from me, with a different man this time,' he said after the silence had lengthened to the degree that I felt I would have to ask another question to hear more about the tragic history of the noble lord's only daughter. 'He was a much rougher-looking fellow this time, had a nasty face and dressed badly, almost looking like a dock worker or something like that.' A look of pain came over his face and with an effort, he finished off the story. 'I saw him hit her, slapped her across the face. I couldn't bear that. I went to cross over, I don't know what I was going to do, hit the fellow, take her away, take her back to her father, tell him to look after her. I didn't know. I plunged on to the road and was hit by the hind leg of a jarvey's horse. When I came to, I was lying on the pavement and someone was pouring water into my mouth and a policeman was fanning me with his helmet. There was no sign of Lady Emily, or of the man who had been mistreating her.' Leech was silent for a minute and then said sadly, 'I never saw her again. The next thing I heard of her was the notice of her death in the papers. Died of typhus, so they said, but I heard otherwise. Effie Grey told me that the girl had committed suicide, had died of an overdose of laudanum.'

'And you blame the father, you think that Lord Edward bears some responsibility.' I thought about that lonely death in one of the slum dwellings of Devil's Acre and felt intensely sorry for the young woman. Leech's words had made me see her as a tragic figure and I felt a disgust for any father who could have abandoned his only daughter and allowed her to live alone and unsupervised among thieves, murderers and molesters of the innocent.

'What happened to your picture of the girl?' I asked and Leech shook his head.

'I have no idea,' he said. 'I was paid for it, I know that. No thanks, no praise, just a note from the secretary enclosing a cheque drawn on Coutts Bank and that was that. I wonder whether he put it on the fire when he heard of her death.'

'The secretary,' I said. 'Did he have the same man, then? Mr Tom Maguire.'

A shadow came over his face. 'That's right,' he said. 'An unpleasant man. Came in once or twice when I was sketching the girl. I had a feeling that she was afraid of him.'

I looked at him with interest. 'You don't like Maguire, do you, Leech? I thought there was some sort of trouble between you. I saw him whisper something to you and you looked very annoyed.' Leech had looked not so much annoyed as frightened, I had thought at the time, but I didn't like to say that. It didn't seem to fit with the story that Leech had told me. He made no comment now. Just allowed my words to settle like dust upon the well-polished furniture.

'Where is she buried, Lady Emily?' I asked as I got to my feet. I had, I thought, no more appetite for breakfast after hearing that sad and sordid story. It was fairly near to the time when Dickens wanted to rehearse the scene between me and my stage mother, Mrs Mark Lemon. I would be glad to take my mind off the unfortunate girl once that last question was answered.

'Oh, here, at Knebworth, in the mausoleum, in the bosom of her family,' he said sarcastically. 'The Bulwer-Lyttons think highly of their dead. They even have a cemetery for their pets. Surprised that she wasn't placed there,' he said, as I made my way to the banqueting hall and its improvised stage and did my best with my part as the gardener's son.

Once released from Dickens, with a list of meticulously careful notes about my performance, I walked rapidly down the corridor, past the suits of armour and the framed square of brick walling and stone mullions which marked the original outside wall of the medieval manor house. Lady Rosina was standing there, looking meditatively at the early remains of her husband's sumptuous property. I wondered whether she regretted anything, regretted leaving this magnificent house, but, above all, I told myself, she must regret leaving her children. Her son, yes, although he seemed to have embarked upon a successful career, I knew how important my mother was to myself and the interest that she took in my efforts to become a writer, and how ecstatic she was every time that my brother sold a picture. I felt sure that, despite the universal good opinion earned by Robert and his apparent success in life, he must have missed having a mother to enthuse over his triumphs over the years.

But all that was of small importance compared with abandoning her small daughter, a delicate child who had suffered from polio. How much of her daughter's terrible end did she know about? Enough, I guessed, to fill any normal mother with intense regret. Did she blame herself, I wondered, as I greeted her, or did she, perhaps, blame her husband for everything and feel that if only he were dead, she would have been allowed to care beautifully for their tragic child herself.

FIVE

Darker and darker, he said; farther and farther yet.
Death takes the good, the beautiful, and the young –
and spares me. The Pestilence that wastes, the Arrow
that strikes, the Sea that drowns, the Grave that closes
over Love and Hope, are steps of my journey, and take
me nearer and nearer to the End.

Wilkie Collins, *The Woman in White*

I blame my new-found profession for my next move. I was
a writer. I was firmly convinced of that. The law bored
me. Commerce bored me. I could make a run-of-the-mill
painter, I supposed. Seize on a lucrative line as my father
did when he began to turn out his seascapes and then sell
them as expensive wallpaper for those who had money enough
to pay for them. But no, writing was what I liked and I was
determined to make a success of it and was by now aware
that the difference between a mediocre novel, and one to be
cherished, lay in the strength of the portrayal of the characters. On the advice of Dickens, I studied people carefully
and Lady Rosina was one of the most interesting women
that I had met.

And so, I probed.

'I'm going for a walk in the park, Lady Rosina,' I said
cheerfully. 'Dickens was telling me about a magnificent mausoleum in the grounds, down Old Knebworth Lane, he said.
Could you direct me to Old Knebworth Lane? I must see it
this morning. Dickens likes me to improve myself and he's
bound to ask me about it over lunch.'

She smiled, but there was a slight strain behind that ready
smile, and I saw how her eyes clouded over. I felt guilty but
told myself that she would be bound to visit her daughter's
last resting place and that my company might make it easier

for her. I would encourage her to talk about the girl, to weep
if necessary. Indeed, when I thought of the story that Leech
had told me, I almost felt like weeping, myself. That, or
shooting her selfish, cold father.

'Perhaps you could point me in the right direction.' I waited,
looking at her in a friendly way. She will be better with me,
I repeated internally and that gave me the assurance to wait
with a look of expectancy on my face.

'I'll come with you,' she said with that sudden decisive-
ness which was one of the attractive features of her unusual
personality. Few women, in my experience, tended to make
up their minds quite so suddenly; my mother said it was
because most women saw every side of the matter and only
a few women had the single vision of a man. That may have
been true, but if so, Lady Rosina was certainly one of that
small number. I wondered what more details of her marital
life she would unfold as we strolled together through the
grounds of Knebworth.

'Let's go, then,' I said, opening the hall door. The night-time
fogs with which we had been plagued over the last week had
now dissipated and the day was a fine one with a gentle breeze
ruffling the dark green of the yew hedge that formed the
backdrop for the statuary on the lawn.

'Let's go,' she repeated. She took a shawl from the elaborately carved hall stand and slung it around her shoulders. It
belonged, I knew, to Helen Lemon, but Lady Rosina did
not accord its unfamiliarity a single glance. She had, I
thought admiringly, the assurance of a queen. No worries
about her shoes, either. Unlike most women she did not cast
a worried look down on them when we emerged into the
sunlight.

'You are unmarried, I understand,' she said in her direct
way.

'Yes.' I smiled at her to show that I had taken no offence,
but wondered that she would make no apology for her
inquisitiveness.

'Good,' she said. 'Keep it that way. Have a mistress; every
man needs a mistress. Have lots of mistresses, one in each
street if you wish, but treat them well, and when you fall out

of love, why, just give them a handsome present and part company on amiable terms. Don't make them suffer for your change of feelings.'

I couldn't forbear to laugh. 'I'm going to have to get to work in real earnest if I have to support a mistress in every street and have enough money in the bank to pay them off when I want to get rid of them,' I said.

'That's right,' she said, returning my smile. 'What a good ambition for a young man. Start straight away and work as hard as you possibly can.' The smile had abruptly left her lips and her eyes were stony as they stared straight ahead at the well-groomed fields that surrounded the lane. 'Marriage,' she said, speaking with an intensity which made me feel extremely uncomfortable, 'is a terrible institution. Men talk with horror about the slavery of the black people in America, but they keep very quiet about the slavery of women in that holy institution of marriage. A woman marries because she thinks a man loves her and perhaps, he does, but love, my friend, does not last for ever, and then the cruelty begins. The man sees that he can shout at his wife, that he can make her unhappy by sneering at her, then that he can make her even more unhappy by physical cruelty, that he can slap her, or punch her with impunity as though she were, indeed, a black slave out in America. All the terrible injustices done to these slaves, here in Britain we outlawed the practice over twenty years ago and in Parliament many men speak out against it and try to bring the Americans to their point of view. But do any of them talk of the women in the homes who are treated like slaves by their husbands?'

I was beginning to feel most uncomfortable and hoped that she was not going to tell the stories of what her husband had done to her. And then I felt ashamed of myself. Why should she not tell? Why should it be worse for me to hear than for her to endure?

'It must have been very hard for you to leave your children in order to escape from your husband,' I said bravely.

She thought about that for a few minutes, striding along the gravelled path at my side, and it was only when we reached the gate that she spoke again.

'It's a terrible confession to make, but I didn't really think about them,' she said, and I noticed her voice trembled slightly. 'Yes,' she went on, 'a terrible confession. But, you see, I was desperate. I was in fear of my life. I did really think that one day, when he was in a bad humour, and when I had done something to annoy him, that he might kill me. My son was five years old, very well cared for in the nursery, best of care. His father adored him. He would do anything for that boy.'

She had stopped and now she began to walk quite quickly, to stride along the lane, going ahead of me. I closed the gate with care and then went after her. I thought that she would pause when she heard my footsteps, but she did not, and I was forced almost to run in order to catch up with her.

'What a lovely morning for a walk,' she said, and I understood that the confidences were over. Emily, according to Leech, was about eight years old when her mother left. Just about coming to an age when a mother's love would have been important to her. And, quite possibly, was of little importance to her father. Lord Edward, with his intense pride in his family, and in the five-hundred-year-old seat of his ancestors at Knebworth, was just the kind of man to regard a girl of little importance. In fact, her birth might well have marked the onset of his dislike of Lady Rosina. Some men, I knew, were like that; some men blamed their wives for the lack of an heir. By the time that the boy was born, three or four years later, love had probably completely died, and its place had been taken by hate, on both sides. Lady Rosina had neither the disposition nor the upbringing that would permit her to give into the husband meekly, to remain silent when he was unjust and to hide her shame at his cruelty. The world, I thought, would hear her troubles. I suppressed a slight grin as I remembered the story of the hustings where she made a speech about Lord Edward's brutality to the fascinated villagers.

'I'm more of a Londoner, myself,' I said casually. 'Can never enthuse about fields and cows. Give me people! That's what interests me.'

She smiled at me. 'I could give you people,' she said with a note of slight mockery of my phrase. 'They wouldn't just interest you but would raise the hairs on the back of your neck.'

'That's a bargain, then,' I said merrily. 'You give me the people, I'll write about them and make as much money as possible and then I'll set up a mistress in every one of the streets around my principal residence and I will invite you to come and visit them all.'

To my relief, she laughed at this and said no more about her private life. She was interested in people. I could see that as she cross-questioned me about the guests. Clarkson Stanfield, she knew and loved, Dickens she disliked, and Foster also, I thought from the way that she pronounced his name, but the others were new to her and I passed the time by giving her thumbnail sketches of them all. Away from her obsession with her husband, she was an intelligent woman and made very many sensible observations. But when we came to Leech, her face darkened. 'I've seen a sketch that he did of my daughter and I've heard about his behaviour also,' she said, and instantly changed the conversation to talking about Frances Jarman and asking eager questions about the actress's history and about her daughters. I supplied as many answers as I could but was left wondering about her remark. I didn't much like Leech, myself, and now I began to wonder whether there had been some sort of relationship between himself and the tragic Lady Emily Bulwer-Lytton who died before her twentieth birthday.

It was only when we reached the mausoleum that Lady Rosina mentioned her daughter. 'He buried her here,' she said. 'He told me nothing. Did not even write me a letter. Took her dead body down from London and thrust her in here beside his abominable mother. She built this place, you know. Built it for her own mother and for herself when her time would come. Left all the instructions for her funeral. Even down to the flowers to be placed in that vase there.' She pointed to a beautifully carved stone vase placed within one of the sloping sides of the small stone building. It was almost like a miniature chapel. It had doors on all four sides, but I could see that those on the east and on the west sides were just blank, though the framework and the pediments were delicately carved from stone. I peered in through the southern door – a wooden one, kept in good order, with its frame carved, once again from stone. The roof rose to a central platform of stone and carried, balanced upon it, a sarcophagus, elaborately decorated with sculpted shells, done with marvellous attention to the tiniest details. I looked upon it with delight, wondering what my artistic brother would make of it, but Lady Rosina gave an exclamation of disgust.

'I hate to think of her bones lying there, side by side with that horrible woman and her mother who was probably just as horrible,' she said impetuously. It was the first time that she had spoken of her daughter and even now she did not call her by her name.

'Have you seen the sarcophagus before?' I asked in a low voice.

She had turned away as if she could not bear the sight, but now she stopped, turned back, looked at the mausoleum for a long moment.

'No,' she said and added theatrically, 'and I will never see it again. You go now, Wilkie, I will see myself back to the house.'

I did not argue with her. She needed to be alone. She needed to make her peace with her daughter. Perhaps to send apologies that she had deserted a vulnerable child. The inscription showed that the girl had been nineteen years old at the time of her death, born in 1828, four years younger than I. Tears stung my eyes and I blinked them away hastily. Her mother did not weep. She placed her hand for a moment on the carved stone and I saw her lips move.

It was, I told myself, just a fancy, but I felt, in that moment, that I was witnessing the taking of a solemn vow.

I did not look back when I left her. I took her at her word and walked briskly away in the opposite direction. I would go and see my friend, Bruno, I decided. Somehow the simplicity of a dog's love and of a dog's loyalty was highly attractive at this moment when the complications of human relationships were filling my mind.

As I approached the stable yard, however, I frowned with annoyance. That voice! That Newcastle upon Tyne accent! I knew who was there. It was Foster. Playing his usual role. Hectoring the stable manager, and his unfortunate young assistant. I was glad that Lady Rosina had not come with me. Foster, as Commissioner of Lunacy, a post for which he received a fat salary, would undoubtedly have aroused her ire and there would have been hot words between them both.

Foster was not the only visitor to the stable yard, though. Augustus Egg was also there. An artist and a great friend of my brother, but I did not like him. Dickens described him as 'dear gentle little fellow, always sweet-tempered, humorous, conscientious, thoroughly good, and thoroughly beloved', but I did not care for the man too much, though I didn't dislike him in the way that I disliked Foster.

'Funny fellow,' I said to Dickens once when we were discussing Foster. 'Why on earth did he not marry that woman Laetitia – what was her name? There he was! Engaged to be married year after year! Ten or fifteen years, wasn't it? But not married! Just as though one reserved a prime turkey for some future Christmas celebration. Kept her dangling for years until she finally gave up in despair and went off and married somebody else and then committed suicide. So, I suppose that she must have loved Foster after all and was devastated that he *could not* return her love.'

I remember that I used the words 'could not' with a slight emphasis and searched Dickens' face but got no response. I had heard some odd stories about Foster, but did not know whether they were true, or just idle gossip. But Dickens was always intensely loyal to his friends and Foster, born in the same year and his closest friend for over twenty years, was for Dickens beyond criticism. He was frowning now, and I knew that he was displeased with me.

'There was a reason why that marriage didn't take place,' he said after a few moments. 'The lady had a bit of a

reputation, whether deserved or not I could not say.' He
stopped and wrinkled his upper lip distastefully. 'I hate
that sort of talk,' he said vehemently, and so I guessed that
the rumours told that Laetitia had been having affairs, or
perhaps had borne a child out of wedlock – the one almost
inevitably led to the other, in my experience – were probably
true.

'Went on writing poetry, did she?' I prompted.

'Yes, and a novel, *Romance and Reality* – you can imagine
what that was about.'

I could. And I could see why Dickens didn't like her. He
was fond of women, fond of his wife, but he disliked stories
about marital troubles.

'Anyway, Foster, in a reasonable way, asked her about these
rumours. She had only to deny everything to satisfy him, but
of course, she didn't. Typical poetess! Turned very haughty
and told him to investigate until he was satisfied. And, of
course, being a good, solid north-country man, he did as she
told him and then went to her and told her that he was
satisfied.'

'With a forgiving smile on his face, no doubt.' I couldn't
resist the comment and Dickens gave me a displeased look.

'And then, believe it or not, when he had gone to all that
trouble, she wrote to him breaking off the marriage, wrote a
silly letter saying that the more she thought about it, the more
she thought that he should not unite himself with one accused
of such crimes – and then,' said Dickens, 'the stupid woman
got all dramatic saying that the suspicion was as dreadful as
death. Unhinged, of course. He was better off without her.
Married a man that she hardly knew and then committed
suicide.'

'Women shouldn't be allowed to write poetry or novels. It
just unhinges them.' I couldn't resist the sarcastic remark, but
I was sorry when I saw the hurt look on his face.

'I did not say that, nor do I believe it. You know how much
I esteem Mrs Gaskell, how impressed I was by *Mary Barton*.
Other women writers also. I found *Adam Bede* excellent; I
praised it very much. *Jane Eyre*.' Dickens shrugged his shoulders and left the room. He always claimed never to have read

Jane Eyre, but sometimes I wondered whether the book had hit him hard and had shown him how bland and uninteresting was the profile of his narrator, Esther Summerson, in *Bleak House*.

I gave him a moment to get clear and then decided upon a walk and so made for the stables.

The dog, after my story at table yesterday, had been the subject of much conversation. He had been taken from his kennel and displayed to the two gentlemen, but he was not being patted by Foster. The pats seemed to be reserved for the stable boy who was looking thoroughly embarrassed as the man absent-mindedly stroked his neck and pinched the skin beneath his chin. I greeted Bruno enthusiastically, released him from his chain and authoritatively called upon the lad to find the dog's lead. I could see the lead perfectly well myself, but young Jim seemed relieved to be freed from the embarrassing attentions of a middle-aged man so I allowed him to attach the lead to the collar and to hold the dog at a slight distance from the group of visitors.

'Thanks, Jim. You get back to your work now. I'll take the dog for a walk.' It wasn't my place to order the boy around, but there was no sign of the stable manager. 'Want to come with me?' I extended the invitation to both men, but Foster abruptly declined and made his way back to the house.

'Not the maze,' said Augustus Egg. 'Gives me the shivers that place. I imagine myself being a lost soul and wandering for days, weeks and months around and around and unable to get free.'

'Could be a good symbol for hell, couldn't it?' I said carelessly. 'You could make a great picture out of it, Egg. Why should hell be always painted with fire? Why not a terrible mist, a fog like we had last night. You could paint it with these paths leading to nowhere and the faces of the damned hovering through the mist.'

'Hell, to me, is people thinking up bright ideas for subjects to paint,' he said in a bad-tempered way.

'That's not like you, Egg, old fellow,' I said. 'You're always such an easy-going fellow.' I didn't much care that my idea had been rejected, but I was surprised to see Egg in such a bad mood.

'Sorry,' he apologized, and then he suddenly stopped, stooped down and stroked the dog, minutely parting his fur as though looking for fleas. I wondered what he was doing, but then when he spoke again, I realized that the activity gave him an opportunity of saying something without looking in my face.

'Someone should have a word with that boy's father,' he said. 'Foster is a strange fellow. Hard to know what to make of him.'

I grasped his meaning instantly. There had been a notorious scandal recently and I had often wondered a little about Foster.

'I'll do that,' I said briefly. No need, I thought, to pass on the story of Jim's father and the tragedy. The stable manager was father to him, now. I wondered whether Egg, himself, had had trouble with Foster. He was a good eight years older than I, but he had a girlish face and the adjective 'pretty', rather than the more masculine 'handsome', sprung to the mind. He was looking very embarrassed though, so I did not pursue the subject. I bent down and released Bruno's lead, and walked briskly with him by my side until we reached the maze. Once we entered upon the hawthorn-edged passage-ways, I called upon Egg to witness how cleverly the dog led us through the paths, dodging all the blind alleys until we reached the centre. When we got there, Bruno sat upon his haunches and looked at me expectedly with almost a grin on his face. I was pleased to see how Egg shook off his moody state of embarrassment and we both had fun with the dog before returning him to the stable yard. There was no sign of Foster there, and the boy, Jim, seemed to be his usual cheerful self.

It was only when we were on our way back that I ventured to explore an idea which had come into my mind. We were walking through the orchard and we made several futile attempts to secure a couple of rosy apples from the top branch of a tree. The activity with both of us springing up with sticks in our hands, made my question more casual than it would have been if I had been eyeball to eyeball. And so, it could be responded to without embarrassment.

'I wonder whether that secretary has anything on Foster?'

'Could do,' said Egg. He glanced at me and then looked away and we neither of us pursued the subject further.

SIX

I have always held the old-fashioned opinion
that the primary object of work of fiction should
be to tell a story.

Wilkie Collins, *The Woman in White*

Rehearsals began at ten in the morning. Ten sharp! Everything to do with Dickens was sharp. Parts had to be memorized, had to be delivered without hesitation. Actors had to position themselves on the exact spot of the stage which he had designated. He had provided himself with a packet of coloured chalks and neat crosses decorated the stone floor of this most ancient part of the original medieval building.

To my shame, I was late. I had stayed up until midnight working on my book, musing over and adapting the character of one of the women. By the time I went to bed I was pleased with myself, but very, very tired.

Nevertheless, there was no excuse for me. I knew that this was the all-important dress rehearsal. I knew that we were going to have an audience, that the workers on the estate and the servants in the house had been invited to watch and the last words that Dickens had spoken to us at bedtime on the night before had been to impress upon us all to be on time and word perfect by ten o'clock on the following morning.

And so when I dozed off after my early-morning tea, and woke not long before the magic hour of ten, my better nature urged me to forgo breakfast and hasten to join my fellow actors. But that banqueting hall with its stone floor and its forty-foot-high ceiling was so intensely cold and this play, *The Lady of Lyons* with its snobbish undertones and its dreary dialogue, had begun to bore me so intensely that I told myself that I needed my breakfast. And by the time I had consumed my liver and bacon, had swallowed my third cup of coffee and exchanged a few words of banter with a jolly little maidservant, it was already fifteen minutes past ten.

The play was well into the first scene when I slid behind the curtained entrance to the backstage. All of the women in the first scene were on stage: Nelly, as Pauline Deschappelles, was lying on the sofa; her maid was fanning her while Madame Deschappelles, played by Frances, was, from the depth of her stage experience, giving a superb performance of an ambitious mother. The men were huddled in small groups backstage. The place was very dark: Dickens refused to allow anything other than the bare minimum of light. Nothing must distract from the brightly lit stage. Lord Edward, his face completely overshadowed by his magnificent hat, was anxiously conning his words as near to the prompter's lantern as he could squeeze himself, but the others were whispering to each other in small groups. I tried to relax. Some genuine bursts of laughter from the audience made the tension melt. I crossed my fingers and held them up to Lady Rosina who had appeared out of the gloom and she smiled and then, to my great surprise, she walked over to stand near to her husband. No word was exchanged between them as far as I could see, and I wondered whether she was trying to put him off his big scene. He was still frantically conning his lines, holding the script almost to his nose and I saw Dickens look across at him in a worried way and then take one of the other lanterns from near where I sat and put it beside another on the shelf behind the master of the house. Now the whole backstage was in complete darkness except for one well-lit corner.

But we had not long to wait. A thunder of applause! Real genuine applause and the welcome sound of laughter and chattering voices. The first scene, between mother and daughter, had been a great success. The curtain eventually lowered. And then the activity was all behind stage. The women, one by one, came tripping off the stage, swirling their elaborate eighteenth-century costumes and tossing their powdered curls, pleased and excited. Frances Jarman sat down on a stool and buried her face in her hands for a moment. Nelly went across to stand beside the backstage curtain, ready to hold it back so that the marquis could make a grand entrance. Clarkson Stanfield, his two helpers from the woodyard and my young friend, the boy from the stable yard, climbed up to uncoil the second backdrop showing the exterior of a small village inn, The Golden Lion, with a hazy sketch of the city of Lyons in the distance. They would, I thought fleetingly, all have an excellent view of the stage and hoped that the boy would not be tempted to play any tricks such as flicking horse chestnuts or pieces of gravel on top of the noble lord's huge hat, as I would have done as a boy of his age. I half-smiled to myself at the memory of the tricks that I used to play when dragged to see some boring play by my mother who was stage mad and who used to compel my attendance when my father rebelled. I felt a little ashamed of myself now when I was aware of the huge amount of effort that went into the staging of a play.

And then when all was ready, Lord Edward stood up and adjusted his eighteenth-century costume of a marquis. Despite the lanterns beside him, I could not see his face as it was hidden by the enormous brim of his hat, but I could tell by the convulsive clasping of his hands that he was nervous about carrying out his soliloquy alone on the stage even in front of an audience of his own servants and workmen. Not like him, I thought and wondered whether he was well.

The men who had lowered the backdrop climbed down the ladder and returned backstage, though Clarkson Stanfield and a couple of the workers still perched on high, ready to unfurl the next backdrop once this short scene changed to the interior of the gardener's cottage. One of the workers held a covered lantern and I recognized that it was the boy who cared for the dog, Bruno. I gave him a nod and thought that we both probably wished that we were with the noble Great Dane in the peaceful surroundings of the stable yard.

'Now!' hissed Dickens from above and Lord Edward strode past Nelly and out on to the stage to begin his interminably lengthy soliloquy as a nobleman deeply in love with a flirtatious young girl and wishing that the French Revolution had not robbed him of his title of Marquis. I yawned. I was bored with this play. Everything so predictable, so over-rehearsed. I knew the exact spot of the stage where he would stand to deliver his lines, knew every gesture that he would make, could predict the exact second when he would declare his love, fling himself to lie prone on the stage floor, convince himself that he had no chance of winning the young lady and then he would jump up, plunge into the cottage, come back with pistol in hand – handed to him by Nelly backstage – pretend to kill himself and then aim it at the ceiling before pulling the trigger. The resulting bang would, doubtless, cause the audience to scream, and would make a break in the scene. His friends would pour on stage, attracted by the noise of the shot. And then the plot would be woven. They would humiliate Pauline, make her think that the gardener's son was a noble and monied gentleman. The discussion about Claude, the gardener's son, would give me time to have a final glance through my lines and to get ready for my entrance. I waited in almost total darkness, hearing the breathing of those around me, smelling the perfume of Lady Rosina – a rich, exotic jasmine scent, which wafted back to my nostrils from where she stood peering through the far end of the screen – and the fresh lavender fragrance from young Nelly as she moved closer to the exit on the other side of the stage. In a few minutes now she would pick up the pistol from the table in order to be ready to hand it to Lord Edward – in fact, she had already done so. I could see it gleam in her hand as she stood by the stage entrance.

There was very little light, backstage, now. Dickens had taken over the prompt duties from Mark Lemon and was perched on high, his lantern on the floor beside him. The women were now invisible, and the only glimmer of light came from the lantern beneath the table, left there so that the revolver could be snatched up quickly.

When thinking about it afterwards, I remembered experiencing a feeling of great tension as all waited quietly in the backstage darkness. At the time I suppose that I put it down to stage nerves – though why I should be nervous, I could not have told, as I had no interest in this play, regarded the whole business as a waste of time, could not wait to get back to

London and to make time to write down all the ideas that
were teaming in my head for books that would astonish the
world. Nevertheless, I felt the palms of my hands were damp
and that every nerve in my body was alert, awake, almost
waiting for a catastrophe.

Then there was a bang. Too early! He hadn't come backstage to find the pistol. I had barely time for those words to
flash across my mind when there was a scream and then
another scream from the audience and then a torrent of sounds,
exclamations, chairs scraped back, shouts. I dashed to the
stage entrance and reached it just as Dickens had swung
himself down from the prompter box and landed with a thud
beside me.

The stage was brightly lit with six gas lamps illuminating
every corner of it. Lord Edward's body lay in the centre of it
with blood staining his white shirt front. His head had fallen
to one side and the monstrous hat almost covered his face.
Dickens was on his knees in seconds, his hand on the man's
pulse. I bent down and removed the hat. My legs trembled
and my glasses misted over, but I was conscious of a pair of
staring eyes which could not have belonged to any living
creature.

'My God, Dickens, Lord Edward must have shot himself,'
I said.

He ignored me. He had gone to the edge of the stage.

'I would ask that everyone remain seated for the moment,'
he said. 'There has been an accident. I want one man with a
fast horse to fetch the doctor. Yes, you.' His eye had picked
up the stable manager and he gave him a nod and then beckoned to his white-faced son.

'Charley, you go with him. Tell him about the shooting,' he
said and then turned to me. 'Wilkie, like a good chap run
upstairs and fetch Lord Edward. Break the news to him.'

'Lord Edward!' I could hear my voice crack with disbelief
on the second word and then I saw what I had not observed
at first.

The man with the sightless eyes and the bloody chest wound
was not Lord Edward. Same height, perhaps, same size, but
the face was different. A much younger man. This was Tom

Maguire, Lord Edward's secretary. 'Oh, my God, Dickens!' I said. 'Where's Lord Edward, then?'

'In his bedroom. He's unwell. One of his bad ear inflammations. Go on, Charley, go with the man and fetch a doctor.' By some miracle, Dickens sounded calm, though impatient.

There was a thud from behind me as I got to my feet in a bewildered fashion. Little Nelly had fainted and Charley, summoned by his father's impatient voice, hesitated for a moment, looking back as her mother bent over the girl.

'Take my smelling salts, Mrs Jarman,' said a cool voice, as with trembling limbs I began to climb down from the stage. Lady Rosina sounded in no need for smelling salts, herself, and yet, for a moment or two, she like everyone else, behind and before the stage, must have thought that Lord Edward Bulwer-Lytton had been shot on the stage in his own banqueting hall.

'I'll come with you, Mr Collins,' she said in that same cool and unemotional voice. 'It will be interesting to see how the monster receives the news of his secretary's death. Do you think that Maguire was the intended victim or was it a case of the man taking the shot for the master?'

'I-I don't know.' I could hear my voice coming out in a sort of gasp and my heart was thumping. I took off my spectacles and wiped them before setting foot on the double flight of oak stairs. She went ahead of me, her footstep light and vigorous. When she reached the first landing she stopped and waited for me before turning to scale the second staircase.

'Did you really think that it was our lord and master? From the moment when I saw him first, I knew straight away that it was the secretary, didn't you?' she enquired with an air of calm self-possession which I found hard to comprehend. 'Surely you could see the difference?' she continued. 'They are not particularly alike, except perhaps in sharing a certain unpleasantness in character. Well, getting rid of that secretary will be a relief to Frances Jarman, anyway. She made her daughter sleep in her room last night – they were both afraid of rape. Like master, like man!' she said with an undertone of anger coming into the light, indifferent voice. Then she added, 'Who shot him, do you think? Such an unpleasant man. Like master, like man,' she repeated. 'Look at the way he behaved towards that very sweet little girl, little Nelly.'

I found her insistence on the offence against Nelly a little odd. Was she trying to hint that the girl had shot a man because he attempted to make love to her? Lady Rosina's grievances against her husband were real and very deep. Lord Edward had turned her out of his house, had attempted to have her locked up in a lunatic asylum. She had no reason to shoot the secretary, but plenty of reasons to shoot his master. And had she really recognized who was playing the part of the marquis? I began to feel a little suspicious of her motives in insisting on her recognition of Tom Maguire. After all, the man dressed in the marquis's costume had not moved or spoken in her presence, had just sat there hunched in his chair, that huge hat covering his face. The two men were virtually the same in height and in bulk and Dickens had trained us all in a stage voice which bore little resemblance to our natural speech patterns and which moreover included speaking with an Englishman's idea of a French accent. I had been in the presence of the secretary and the master for over a week now and I had suspected nothing.

'You can't believe that either Nelly or her mother had anything to do with it, can you, Lady Rosina?' I said, and then, when she did not reply, I ventured to say lightly, 'Perhaps it was an accident. Perhaps someone idly picked up the gun and it went off.'

She treated that inane remark with the scorn which it deserved. Gave me an amused glance and prepared to mount the next set of stairs.

'Why on earth does this wretched man choose, from all the rooms in the house, to sleep in that obscure little room at the top of the house? It's as if he wants to hide away from his guests, or perhaps to lose in obscurity all memories of our marriage when we slept on the first floor. You know he keeps his mother's room like a shrine. No one can ever sleep there, and he has placed an inscription over the mantlepiece ordering that the room is never to be changed. Such a strange man,' she added once again as with undefeated energy she prepared to scale the next set of stairs.

'Do you think that anyone in the hall could have shot Maguire?' I asked, doing my best to suppress a breathless note in my voice.

She thought about that for a moment and delivered her answer in slightly regretful tones when we reached the next landing.

'I would have thought that there was too much light in the hall for anyone to go unnoticed if they took out a gun and aimed it. It's a summer morning. There are no curtains drawn over those windows. No, it will have been one of us backstage, not you, not me, so who? *Quis?* as my old Latin master used to say when one of us played a trick upon him, back in those lovely days when I was in school in London.'

'What about Mark Lemon?' I enquired, more to shift her from the subject of Nelly than from any serious suspicion of the editor of the satirical magazine *Punch*.

'The very man,' she said with enormous enthusiasm. 'How clever of you to hit on someone who I dislike so much. How dare he satirise the Irish in the way that he does? I've lived in Ireland for all my girlhood and the Irish are my dearest friends. How dare he call them dirty and ignorant! How dare he imply that the Irish peasantry are below the English peasantry! How dare he make jokes about their religion! Anyone who has seen, as I have done, a church full of the Irish peasants, on their knees, listening with such reverence to the sound of the Latin prayers, would recognize that these are an immensely spiritual people. How dare he sneer at them in that despicable *Punch* magazine! Yes, let's have him as the assassin. I'll swear I saw him move to the table and pick up the gun and you'll have to back me. Two solemn oaths. That should be enough to convict any man.'

I was too out of breath to reply but I looked after her with alarm. I was experiencing the same feeling of panic as when I, from sheer idleness, had unblocked the dam to a land drain in a farmer's field and then was unable to stem the flow as his spring crop of delicate lettuces had become flooded. I hoped she would say no more about that wild idea.

Fortunately, we had eventually reached Lord Edward's room and with a perfunctory knock, Lady Rosina burst in.

There was no doubt of the man's illness. The bedside table
was littered with medicines. He was alone and half sat up with
alarm when we entered. His wife wasted no time on enquiries
after his health but broke the news instantly.

'That man of yours, Edward, that wretched Maguire, well,
he's been shot. Shot on stage, right in the middle of the
rehearsal!

'Oh, bother! The man is as deaf as a doorpost!' she
exclaimed as he looked from one to the other of us with an
expression of alarm and incomprehension. 'Dead! He's dead,
your secretary, he's dead! Been shot!' And with her fist
clenched and one finger outstretched, pointing at her estranged
husband, she feigned a pistol and said as loudly as she could
shout, 'Bang, bang! He's dead, Edward, your secretary is dead.'

He looked alarmed and affronted, shrinking back on his
pillows. He seized a bell from his bedside table and rang it
vigorously. I couldn't tell from his expression whether he had
understood her, but it was obvious that he wanted to get rid
of her. He looked at me with a frown and then rang the bell
again.

With a feeling of deep embarrassment, I went to the door
and opened it, looking down the corridor. Doubtless a valet
was being summoned, but the door of the small dressing room
next to Lord Edward's bedroom was wide open and no one
was there. I hesitated for a moment. Another bell sounded
from overhead and the wire that ran along the wall, above the
picture rail, was jangling raucously. A door at the bottom
of the corridor opened and a man shot out, carrying a pile of
snowy white linen, starched sheets and pillowcases. Bedlinen
for Lord Edward, or else an excuse for his tardy response.

'Lord Edward needs you,' I said curtly, and then thought
to save us all a lot more embarrassment. I walked quickly
beside the man. 'There's been an accident,' I said. 'Someone
has been shot. Mr Maguire, Lord Edward's secretary has been
shot. Lady Rosina and I have come to break the news to Lord
Edward.'

'I didn't know about the accident. I've been downstairs,
down to the laundry to get fresh sheets for the bed. I know
nothing about all of this,' he said rapidly and defensively. He

quickened his step until he was almost running, and I did my best to keep up with him.

Nevertheless, he was well ahead of me and was first into the room. He was through the door and fell to his knees by the head of the overstuffed bed.

'Where the hell have you been?' snarled Lord Edward. 'Leaving a sick man alone and the door unbarred against dangerous lunatics.' He cast a malevolent look at his wife and ignored me.

I looked at him helplessly. It was, after all, a great breach of good manners to enter a sick man's bedroom without any invitation. Somehow, I thought, deafness was more of a barrier to the ordinary forms of social intercourse than is blindness. Words came easily to me; I could explain myself out of trouble on most occasions, but nuance is difficult when shouting your words.

The valet had taken something from the bottom of a small cupboard, had now risen to his feet and in his hand was Lord Edward's hearing trumpet. He delicately placed it in his master's ear, held it in position and looked from Lady Rosina to me. I reproached myself for my stupidity. Why had I not looked for the trumpet? I had seen it often enough during the last few days. It normally lay on a convenient table or cupboard beside the master of the house and whenever he wanted to hear what was going on, he snatched it up and inserted it into his ear, holding it carefully tilted in the direction of the speaker. The bedside cupboard was the ideal spot to hold the cumbersome object.

'You tell him,' I said to the valet. I didn't feel up to any more explanations and if Lord Edward was suffering from an ear infection, especially if the infection or abscess were to be located in his better ear, then he would be deafer than normal.

'I'll tell him,' said Lady Rosina, and her tone bore such a note of authority that the valet relinquished the trumpet into her hand. She wiped it clean with her handkerchief, dropping the delicate piece of lace on the floor with a grimace of dislike, inserted the trumpet into her husband's ear and then shouted into it.

'Your secretary is dead, Edward. He's been shot. Shot dead!'

He heard the words. There was no doubt about that. In fact, I would not have been surprised if the guests, waiting downstairs, for the police and doctor, also heard it. It seemed, I realized with a moment's compunction, almost to cause him physical pain. He jerked his head back from the trumpet, clapped his right hand to his ear, angrily gestured to her to stand back with his other hand and beckoned to his valet. On the table at his bedside was an array of small bottles and syringes and some sachets of laudanum and his eye went to those as if seeking a remedy for his pain.

'I think, my lady,' said the valet respectfully, 'that Lord Edward would like to be alone. He is far too ill to rise from his bed just now. He has a high temperature.'

Lady Rosina ignored him. She snatched the trumpet from her husband's hand. Once again, she inserted it into his ear and then bent her head and bellowed into it. 'The police are on their way, Edward. You had better get up and dress. They will want to question you.'

He winced. I saw him do so. Deaf or not the sound hurt him. I knew that; I could see how his head jerked back and how his hand went to his ear in an effort to block the sound that was causing him so much pain, and, for the first time, I felt slightly sorry for him. The hectic flush on his cheeks and the glitter from his dark eyes seemed to show that he was running a fever, or else he had more face paint than usual. If he had an abscess in the ear, then the amplified sound of Lady Rosina's bellow would probably, indeed, cause him severe pain. There was a leather-bound notebook on the table beside him and I was sorry not to have noticed it earlier; we could have spared him by writing the news on it. I remembered a quote from one of his numerous writings: 'Refuse to be ill. Never tell people you are ill; never own it to yourself. Illness is one of those things which a man should resist on principle at the onset.' A certain sympathy came to me for this stoical man who though approaching his sixties, old and ill, believed it incumbent upon him to appear as neither. There was a certain dignity about him at this moment and I felt that we should spare him and leave him to his valet.

'Let's go downstairs,' I said to her. 'Perhaps the police have come.'

'And who knows but we are missing another murder,' she said in a light-hearted way which though it amused me, also slightly shocked me. I had not liked the secretary, had not liked his supercilious manner, had been angry at his attack on an innocent young girl, but death had a terrible awfulness about it. I could not bring myself to turn it into a joke.

SEVEN

Any woman who is sure of her own wits, is a
match, at any time, for a man who is not
sure of his own temper.

Wilkie Collins, *The Moonstone*

'I wonder whether I could make a book out of this?' said
Lady Rosina. 'Wonderfully dramatic, isn't it? That darkness, the eerie atmosphere backstage, all those people
huddled together, only a gleam of light; the fatal revolver, the
instrument of death, lying there on the table, visible to all,
accessible to all. What a wonderful opening to a book! Yes, I
think that I could write that book.'

'I was thinking about doing it myself,' I confessed. 'It would
be something quite unique, wouldn't it? Not just telling a story,
but engaging with the reader, going hand in hand with him.
Coaxing him to guess who did the deed. And, as I would write
it, the author doesn't know the ending to the book but follows
the pathway with apprehension in his heart, waiting for inspiration to strike.'

'Or *her* heart,' put in Lady Rosina.

'Or her heart,' I amended, but in my mind the book might
be too violent, too terrible for a female sleuth.

'We'll do it together,' said Lady Rosina with an air of great
generosity. 'I'll introduce you to my publisher. I'll say that
you are the most talented young man that I have ever met. I'll
foster your career for you. You'll have to get away from
working for Dickens, writing little stories for that magazine
of his, your work going out under his name.'

I said nothing to that. Dickens had been very generous to
me. He paid me a salary, saved me from being completely
dependent upon my mother; he gave me invaluable advice on
my own writing and I learnt much from seeing him at work

on other people's stories, how he would cut some tedious passages, demand more details on interesting characters. Yes, I had definitely picked up some tricks of the trade from Dickens. He was, in my view, the greatest living writer and I was privileged to be so close to him. Nevertheless, I was enjoying my acquaintance with Lady Rosina, so I gave her a grateful smile and a modest shake of the head.

'Who do you think did it?' I asked in a stage whisper when we reached the next landing.

'John Leech,' she said instantly, and I could swear that the name had just popped into her head. Nevertheless, I nodded wisely.

'Of course,' I said with conviction.

She beamed upon me. 'You noticed, I'm sure, didn't you?'

'Ah, you saw me looking,' I said, thinking this was like a new parlour game. 'What did you think was the motive?'

'Well, it was obvious, wasn't it?' she returned. 'Maguire is a blackmailer. Just because I live on the fringes of polite society doesn't mean that I don't know what is going on in the drawing rooms of the rich, my friend.'

A blackmailer. Well, I thought, she might be right. There was something very unpleasant about that secretary and certainly he had alarmed the cartoonist when he had whispered in his ear. But why Leech?

'These drawings of his,' I ventured. 'These caricatures – he copies them, does he?'

She dismissed that feeble idea with the scorn which it deserved.

'Money,' she hissed, embarking on to the stairs leading down to the banqueting hall.

'Of course,' I said with the air of one who has had a flood of light cast upon his dull brain. What money, I asked myself? Leech was a youngish man, unmarried, lived in lodgings and dressed in an inconspicuous style – quite shabby on occasion. I didn't care greatly for him, disliked his caricatures of Jews and of the unfortunate Irish peasants, not to mention his relentless mocking of those who were poor and homeless. He was a man, I had always thought, who would do anything for money, and I would not have been surprised to hear that he was a blackmailer. Nevertheless, I couldn't quite see how he could have been the victim of blackmail.

'That scurrilous magazine, *Punch*,' she hissed. 'Sells hugely. About 20,000 copies of each number. Think of it, Mr Collins. Three pence a copy. Twenty thousand times three pence. How many shillings and pounds would you get from that?'

My mental arithmetic wasn't up to that piece of gymnastics, so I contented myself with a long, low whistle of astonishment. 'Goodness,' I said feebly, and wondered what she meant to imply. I had never liked John Leech very much, had despised the role he had played in the suppression of the Chartist movement. But, as far as I knew, John Leech's connection with *Punch* magazine was just as a cartoonist, as they had taken to calling the brotherhood who drew caricatures for the magazine. He would get paid, but what had he to do with the takings? I would have to ask Dickens. He always knew the ins and the outs of everyone's business. We were now approaching the door to the hall, so I put my finger to my lips.

'Mum's the word,' I said. And with an expression of delight, she beamed at me and echoed my gesture. I threw open the door for her and waved her into the hall like a well-trained herald.

Everything was very muted in there. The audience still sat on their uncomfortable chairs, probably steadily growing colder as the stoves appeared to have died down and the enormous fireplace now housed only the remnants of a smouldering tree trunk. The rain had fallen upon every day of August and that hall, the core of the original medieval house, was always bitterly chilly and smelled of mould. Four members of the cast, John Leech, Mark Lemon, John Foster and Augustus Egg stood in one corner and in the other young Mr Charles stood protectively beside Nelly and her mother Frances. Clarkson Stanfield and Dickens were displaying the wonders of the opening door and window in the backdrop to the sergeant and the body of Tom Maguire still lay stretched out in the middle of the stage. Beside it was one policeman – a constable, I thought, waiting stolidly until his superior should have finished his conversation with Dickens.

Our arrival caused a welcome break in the boredom of the audience still waiting patiently in the body of the hall. Everyone seated upon the chairs turned to stare. Many, I thought, recognized Lady Rosina and chairs were scraped on the floor as several rose to make clumsy bows in her direction. She seized the opportunity to stamp her authority on the proceedings.

'Oh, you poor, dear people,' she said. 'Is nobody looking after you? How cold it is! What an uncomfortable place this is, even in summertime.' Vigorously she rang a bell at the side of the room. 'You shall all have a hot drink and something to eat,' she promised recklessly.

I saw Dickens whisper an explanation into the ear of the harassed-looking sergeant who nodded and then came to the edge of the stage.

'No need for that, Lady Rosina,' he said. 'I don't think that we need to detain any member of the audience. My constable will go to the door and take everyone's name and anyone who feels that they may have important information may stay behind and wait in their place.'

There may have been a slight struggle between the desire to get away from that cold stone-floored hall and the desire to appear important, but they had already waited for a good twenty minutes and the first desire won. I guessed that the local inn would benefit as all went to have a drink and a discussion of the exciting event. Every member of the audience rose to their feet and made their way towards the door.

'What a good idea,' said Lady Rosina graciously. She advanced down the middle of the hall, climbed the set of stairs to the improvised stage and nodded to the policeman.

'This is Lady Rosina, Sergeant,' said Dickens and I could see a flash of amusement in his eyes. He was in his element, I guessed, controlling all and explaining all. 'The mistress of the house,' he added with a polite bow in her direction and I saw a look of pleasure come to her face.

'Lord Edward will be down shortly,' said Lady Rosina in a patronizing fashion to the embarrassed policeman. He had obviously, I thought, heard all about the notorious Lady Rosina. That time when she had appeared at the nearby hustings of Hertfordshire and publicly denounced her husband would have been a staple item of fireside stories for the last winter in the local inn and cottages around the estate. 'Why don't we all go into the library and have some hot toddies and sit cosily over the fire,' she proposed in her impulsive fashion. I could see a look of indecision come across the sergeant's business-like exterior. It had been a wet summer and Knebworth House was a place that soaked up the damp and exhaled it with a damp cold that put spots of grey mould on the furniture and filled the rooms with an icy chill.

'Perhaps wait for Lord Edward,' proposed Dickens. He spoke quietly, but he was a famous man with a very assured manner and the sergeant had heard many a story about Lady Rosina. In any case, he ignored the suggestion of hot toddies sipped in the comfort of the fireplace by the simple method of pretending not to hear and fixed his attention on the motley mixture of estate worker and maidservants who were filing out of the banqueting hall, some of them spelling their names, others chattering cheerfully to each other. The arrival of Lady Rosina seemed to have lightened the atmosphere, caused the actors to cluster in groups and whisper to each other and so I made my way over to the drooping figure of little Nelly who was as white as the marbled fireplace.

'What a dreadful thing to happen,' I said to her mother and Frances smiled upon me with her professional ease.

'"In the midst of life . . ."' she quoted, though I noticed that her eyes slid back to her daughter's tearstained face.

'Yes, indeed,' I said and sought to find something conventional to say about the deceased man. 'His master will miss his efficient presence,' was the best that I could come up with and Frances gave me a nod of approval.

'Indeed,' she said with dignity. 'Quite a shock, though, for us all.'

'Of course,' I murmured, noting that Frances was using her stage voice, not raised, but perfectly pitched so that every calm observation reached the ear of the sergeant. Here is a rational woman who has witnessed an unfortunate event but who knows nothing about it and is sensible enough to be positive that it would have nothing whatsoever to do with either herself or her daughter. That, I thought, was the message that those calm words from Frances was intended to convey to the sergeant and she had done it very well. I looked at Nelly's white and tear-stained face and her shaking hands, one of which young Charley was stroking and thought that she would never be the woman that her mother was.

I wasn't the only one to notice Mr Charles's actions. His father, also, had an eye to his son and his voice came across with an unaccustomed note of sharpness.

'Charley,' he said. 'Lord Edward may need a little help on the stairs. He has been quite ill last night, I believe. I think it would be kind of you to go and see whether you can do anything for him. That would be in order, Sergeant, wouldn't it?'

'Yes, certainly, Mr Dickens,' said the sergeant obediently while I heard distinctly from the background Lady Rosina's voice saying to Clarkson Stanfield, 'He's got a valet, hasn't he? What else does the man need to get him downstairs? A wet nurse?'

I suppressed a grin. 'I'll go with you, Mr Young Charles,' I said jokingly, taking pity on the boy's alarmed and very pale face. 'If he's weak, why then a strong man on either side will assist him in coming down all those flights of stairs.'

I didn't wait for an answer but took him by the arm and led him out. Why was the lad looking so upset, I asked myself and put the question to him as soon as I had shut the door to the banqueting hall.

'What's the matter, Charley?' I asked, looking curiously into his eyes. I could have sworn that there was a frightened look in them. He wasn't, I remembered, much more than three years younger than myself, but I thought of him as a boy. It was his father's fault, I thought. Dickens was very fond of his son, but he had a poor idea of his ability and the boy was sensitive enough to absorb that. And, of course, he always referred to him as a boy and even the jocose nickname of Mr Young Charles made his eldest son sound faintly ridiculous.

'You're not upset about Maguire, are you?' I asked. 'Between ourselves, he's no loss, is he? A fairly unpleasant fellow, to put it mildly,' I added as the image of poor little Nelly struggling in the arms of the brute came to me.

'No, of course not,' he said, but there was still an uneasy look about him and a tremor in his voice.

'You seem upset,' I said, looking back at him as we mounted the stairs. Our feet made quite a noise on the oaken steps and I purposefully spoke in a low voice which would not carry. 'Is it Nelly?' I asked.

'No, no, no, not at all!' There was almost a note of panic in his voice. I wondered whether he suspected that Nelly, standing so near to the gun, had picked it up and aimed it at her tormentor. But who had inserted the bullet into the gun and was it that gun which had killed the man?

'I'm worried about my future,' he blurted out. 'I wanted to be a writer, like my father, but he won't hear of it. He doesn't feel that I am any good. He won't even look at anything that I write, or if he does, he just seizes on some small detail and gives me a lesson in grammar or in syntax.'

'What does your father want you to do?' I asked curiously.

'He wants me to be an accountant.' Mr Young Charles sounded acutely miserable. 'I have no head for figures. I hate that bank. And now he's got John Leech to pester me about what a good career it is.'

That interested me. 'John Leech,' I said, stopping on the top step and looking around at him. 'Why John Leech? He's a cartoonist, draws caricatures for *Punch* magazine.'

'Well, apparently he said to my father that he wished he had stuck to the accountancy. He says that a regular salary is better than being paid for pieces of work that you might or might not be able to finish or be able even to start. My father thinks that is very sensible and that I should follow that advice. He says that I shouldn't think of being a writer, that I have not the tenacity of purpose to stick at finishing a whole book. He didn't exactly say that I have no talent, but I knew that was in his mind.' Young Charles sounded acutely miserable.

'And that you might not be able to find a publisher even if you have finished and liked the result,' I said. Dickens had shown me something of Charley's and I had to agree with his father that he should probably find some other profession.

'But you did it, didn't you? Became a writer. You've had three books published and lots of short stories,' said Mr Young Charles, embarking on the next flight with renewed energy.

'Well, yes,' I said absentmindedly. 'But I can't say that I've been making a living at it. I live in my mother's house. My mother pays all of my expenses.' And of my brother's, I thought, and remembered that Dickens had eight sons, all of them to be established in the world of money-making independence. 'My hair stands on end at the cost of these boys,' he was wont to say from time to time. He meant it as a joke; I was sure of that, but a sensitive fellow like young Charley must have winced at the delivery of the oft repeated phrase.

'Your father wants the best for you,' I said, but I don't think that I put much conviction into the phrase. I was busy thinking about John Leech and his startling reaction when the secretary had whispered something in his ear. I had the picture very clearly in my mind. Malevolence and a threat on one face, and surprised horror on that of the cartoonist. So, Lady Rosina was right. Leech had been an accountant. Perhaps he had come on the staff of *Punch* in order to work on their accounts and only later was accepted as a brilliant caricaturist. Or perhaps he still did the important, if less glamorous, job of banking the money and totting up the accounts. No need for anyone except the directors of *Punch* to know who did the books and Leech might just sketch out these drawings in an idle moment, or else in the evening at home. Shouldn't take long, I thought. Not like writing a novel and penning 150,000 words or even 200,000 allowing for different drafts and revisions.

'Your father has a high opinion of John Leech, does he?' I asked idly as we turned to ascend another flight of stairs. If Lady Rosina had heard a rumour that Leech may have helped himself to some funds from the overflowing bank account of the popular magazine, then I would expect Dickens to know all about it. After all, not only was Leech one of his group of friends, but Dickens had contacts all over London and was usually the first to hear scraps of gossip.

'He has a high opinion of everyone except of his sons,' said Young Charles glumly. 'Nothing I do pleases him. He even interferes in my private life and tells me who should be my friends.'

I could guess which friend was objected to. After all, an

actress and the daughter of an actress would not be suitable
for the son of a famous man like Dickens. I clapped him on
the back in cheerful fashion. 'Don't worry,' I said. 'My own
father wanted me to be a lawyer, but he got to be resigned to
the fact that I was spending most of my time scribbling stories.'
Guiltily I remembered that it was only after the death of my
father and the substantial sum of money which he left behind
– that and the generosity of my mother – which allowed me
the time and means to devote myself to literature. Before that
I had been immured in a tea company and had almost gone
out of my mind with boredom.

'Anyway,' I said, 'tell me about John Leech. Why don't you
like him – don't deny it? I can hear it from the sound of
your voice. Do you think that he, too, is after your pretty little
Nelly, standing beside her, backstage, was he this morning?'

A fairly clumsy effort, but it worked. Mr Young Charles
turned a puzzled face back to me as I toiled behind him on
the last few steps of stairs.

'Well, he was, but that was because he wanted to be first
on stage. Oh, Nelly doesn't like him. She doesn't say anything
about him, but I could see that she moves away when he comes
near to her. All these men think that because she is an actress
. . . I wish that she didn't have to lead this sort of life. I wish
that I could get married. My father was married when he was
only a few years older than I and his father was very poor
and mine is very rich.'

But Charles Dickens, before his early marriage, had
published *The Pickwick Papers* and was earning large sums
– I knew for a fact that he was paid twenty pounds for each
of the nineteen instalments of *The Pickwick Papers*. A huge
sum for a man of twenty-one. Most people were only earning
about five shillings a week and so would take almost a year
to earn that amount. And then there was *Oliver Twist* – a brilliant success. And published a year later.

Young Charles's father was a rich man when he embarked
on matrimony, but he himself would just have to be dependent
upon his father. No wonder Dickens looked so unfavourably
on this flirtation with Nelly.

* * *

Lord Edward was already dressed when we were admitted to his room by his valet. He looked at us sourly and declined our help. He was, I noticed, very deaf, more so than usual, and his valet was packing his ear tube into a leather box padded with glossy satin. I volunteered to take charge of the ear tube box and allowed Mr Young Charles to walk falteringly beside the valet and the sick man. Lord Edward was, I decided, acting like a man who was quite unwell. He hung on to the banister rail like one whose legs were most unsteady, and the valet was visibly holding him up on the other side.

'Has a doctor seen him?' I said in the valet's ear, feeling quite confident that there was little or no chance of Lord Edward even realizing that I had spoken. I had never seen him so deaf before and wondered whether the good ear had become quite inflamed. Oddly, though, I saw his head move and his eyes scanned my face in an unfriendly manner. Perhaps all deaf people were like this, suspicious that they were being talked about.

'He has not had the doctor, but he should have had. Lord Edward is not at all well and should not have got up,' replied the man rather reproachfully. 'He had just wanted to sleep peacefully for the morning. In fact, he had forbidden me to disturb him after he had his breakfast and told me only to come if he rang the bell. He had just summoned me, probably because you and Lady Rosina arrived.' He added the last words with an air of reproof, and I bowed my head and slackened my steps as Lord Edward shot me one of his angry looks.

I abandoned Lord Edward once he was inside the banqueting hall and had been ensconced in an easy chair in a corner of the stage by a solicitous Dickens, who sent servants flying to fetch rugs, cushions, a hot bottle for the man's feet and a draught screen to put around his chair. I left them with relief and made my way across to where Leech was idly sketching on the floor with one of Dickens' pieces of chalk.

'Here lies the body,' I said light-heartedly, though I took care to keep my voice down.

'A terrible loss to mankind,' he said with an air of mock seriousness.

'Indeed,' I said, but thought it unwise to venture any further

along that line. The policeman positioned at the corner of the
stage might well have sharp ears. 'What's this I hear about
you being an accountant?' I asked. 'Last man in the world
that I would have guessed to be one of that ilk.'

'Who told you that?' he said, and there was an angry tone
in his voice.

I was about to say, 'Mr Young Charles Dickens', but then
thought I would stir up a little mischief. 'Lady Rosina,' I said
with an innocent air.

He was taken aback at that. 'Long time ago,' he muttered.
'Didn't enjoy it much.'

'I'd keep your hand in if I were you,' I said. 'You never
know, the spring of inspiration might dry up.' He was a gifted
man, though. Those few lines he had sketched on the floor
gave such an impression of a catastrophe; a group of men,
just heads and shoulders, but heads together, a certain rigidity
about their postures, covert glances over shoulders, staring
ahead, apprehension sketched into lined foreheads and several
bitten lips. Nevertheless, I pursued the track that Lady Rosina
had sketched out for me. 'Perhaps you do,' I continued with
an innocent air. 'Somebody told me that you do the books for
Punch magazine. Come to think of it, I seem to remember
that it was Tom Maguire who told me that. Was he right?'

He tried to look unconcerned, but I could see a flush dark-
ening on his cheekbones. He tossed the piece of chalk in the
air, caught it neatly and shoved it into his pocket.

'Don't know what you're talking about,' he said, the tone
of his voice light and unconcerned, but his eyes were angry.

'Careful,' I said, and then allowed a pause to develop before
adding with an innocent air, 'Dickens has every single one of
these pieces of chalk counted and he is not a man to be robbed
with impunity.'

He laughed at that, but I could see that his eyes were still
uncomfortable and that he had guessed that I meant a warning
to him that his secret was out. I felt a slight thrill, the thrill
of a hunter after his prey. I didn't – hadn't – liked the dead
man much and felt no crusading zeal to capture his murderer,
but on the other end we – all of us: me, Mr Young Charles,
Mark Lemon and his wife, nice old Clarkson Stanfield,

Augustus Egg (that very good egg, as Dickens called him), not to mention little Nelly and her dignified mother, Frances Jarman – all of us were in a position where we might have been able to shoot that unpleasant man, Maguire. And, of course, there was Lady Rosina. I had wondered about her earlier; had remembered her great dislike of the secretary and his malice towards her, but then had dismissed the thought. Lady Rosina, though she lurked backstage, had gone nowhere near to the revolver lying on the table. Now, however, another thought had come to me.

Lady Rosina possessed her own pistol! Of course she did! She had taken it from her bag and brandished it in the dining room, aiming it at her husband. Would the police know the difference between a bullet fired from one revolver or from another? I thought not. Their function was purely to keep order on the streets. A country policeman like this sergeant would make sure that no dangerous criminal or lunatic was at large and then would see the body coffined and retire to his police station, unless a very obvious murderer presented himself. Death by person or persons unknown would be the verdict of the coroner's court and the body would be released for burial.

Unless the owner of the house insisted on calling in Scotland Yard. He, and only he, would be in a position to do this. But would he?

Perhaps. If he thought that he knew who it was had fired the shot.

I looked across at Lord Edward and caught a look of malevolence directed at his wife who was gaily chatting with Frances, discussing the scene in *Hamlet* where the young prince kills Ophelia's father. 'Another murder on stage,' I distinctly heard her say, and oddly I thought that Lord Edward, despite his deafness, had heard her say it also. Perhaps he could lip-read, had learned to read her lips, in any case, when they were living together. Certainly, the angry, malevolent look on his face, became more marked. He leaned across to the policeman, touched him on the arm to get his attention and then took from his pocket a small leather notebook and scribbled a few lines with its attached pencil, which he then proffered to the sergeant. I had seen him do this on occasion. Given his disability, the possibility of holding a whispered conversation was completely impossible for him and the notebook fulfilled a need and avoided raised voices. I had seen him do this when Dickens sat beside him and had wondered whether anyone had thought about preserving the dialogue between the two most famous writers in the country.

The policeman nodded respectfully. He did not make use of the pencil, though, but held it indecisively for a minute before returning it to its owner. There was a slight pause and then, making an effort to appear casual, the sergeant sauntered across the stage to where the two women were discussing whether Hamlet had intended the murder of Polonius or whether it was a pure accident. He ignored Frances, her lowly status had already become known to him, but he turned his full attention upon Lady Rosina, bowing respectfully and speaking in a very low voice.

Lady Rosina, however, did not copy his discretion. Her voice rang out loud and clear. 'Yes, Sergeant, I always carry a pistol in my handbag. For an unfortunate woman like myself, living without protection and liable to be attacked and to be raped, it is a necessity.' She glared across the room at her husband and I hoped that she would not bring up the story about his biting her on the cheek when she was heavily pregnant and had rebelled against climbing a ladder in order to fetch him a book from the top shelf in the library. She didn't, however, relate that or any one of her other numerous stories about his lordship's atrocious behaviour to his wife, but held the pistol in her hand, examining it and then, instead of handing it over to the sergeant, she suddenly pointed it directly at Lord Edward, aiming at his heart. He flinched, visibly. Dickens looked distastefully across at Lady Rosina. She returned his look with a charming smile, but she spoke to Frances. 'What is it that Shakespeare says? "Cowards die many times, but the brave die but once." Something like that, is it not? Look at that husband of mine, shaking his shoes.'

'May I examine your pistol, my lady?' To give him his due, the sergeant's hand was steady. No doubt he had broken up many a riot on fair days and this middle-aged, elegantly dressed lady held few fears for him.

'Certainly, Sergeant. And I'm sure when I relate for your private ear my reasons for bringing a gun into this house, you will return it to me, so that I won't be without protection.' She said the words so graciously that he gave an embarrassed bow. His hand remained outstretched, though, and she placed the pistol on top of it.

There was a great silence on stage. The dozen or so people still present made little noise and there was a feeling of tension in the air. The sergeant examined the gun, held it to his nose and then broke it and looked into the barrel. We all, I think, expected him to produce a bullet, like a rabbit from a hat, but he didn't, just stayed very still for a moment, perhaps wondering what to do next. No one moved, and no one spoke. There was dead silence and a feeling of tension in the air.

And then the sergeant spoke. 'There is no bullet in this pistol, my lady.'

She had been expecting this. I could have sworn to that. She didn't hesitate, but shrugged her shoulders with a charming smile and said, 'Should I quote Shakespeare, again, Sergeant? "Cowards die many times . . ." When you are dealing with a coward, the trappings of danger are enough. I have no need to load this pistol. Just the outward appearance of it is enough.'

Each eye stole surreptitiously towards Lord Edward's face and he stared impassively back. The sergeant raised the pistol to his nose, and he sniffed, loudly and vigorously. Nelly gave a nervous giggle and then subsided after a glance from her mother, who stood, charming as ever, with her eyes fixed upon Dickens. He, I noticed, observed her scrutiny and to my surprise gave a reassuring nod in her direction. There was, I thought, quite a bond between these two. Not surprising, really. The actor Macready was one of Dickens' best friends and Frances had played opposite Macready on many occasions. I mused about the pair of them for a few moments. She'd be older than he, of course. Her stage career was long and distinguished and went back to the early years of the century when she was an accomplished child actress. Nevertheless, she would have kept her looks and I wondered, seeing that intimate look, whether they had been good friends when he was a young man and when she still bore the appearance and carriage of a young woman. She was worried now, of course. Worried about Nelly. Her hand was protectively placed in the centre of the girl's back. Her youngest child. But even with that careworn look, one could see that she had been a great beauty in her youth and that beauty of eyes, bone and expression would never leave her.

'Two empty pistols,' said the sergeant aloud. His voice was speculative, and his eyes darted around the assembled company.

'The pistol on the table is, naturally, empty, Sergeant,' said Lord Edward. 'I checked it myself before giving it to Mr Dickens to be used in our play.' That was true, but I had understood that for the performance before an audience, the pistol was to be discharged into a cork panel, specially inserted into Clarkson's backdrop. I looked across at Dickens, but his expression did not change.

'That is correct, Sergeant. And I have formed a habit of checking it every day before rehearsals begin.' Dickens was quietly assured and once again I saw how his eyes went to Frances and how she responded with a sidelong glance. She had an air of great composure about her and I felt that it was a pity that her pretty little daughter, Nelly, could not have taken a cue from her accomplished mother. Not much of an actress, Nelly. Her performance of Pauline in the play was, thanks to her mother's coaching, quite adequate, impossible to criticize really, but it lacked fire and spirit. The two older sisters were very much better. I had not seen the eldest girl, Fanny, though I knew of her reputation, but I had seen Maria in a play at Haymarket Theatre and she was excellent. Nelly, however, had a sweetness about her which the competent Maria would have lacked.

I saw Young Charles look at her protectively and a moment later he stepped forward. 'Excuse me,' he said to the sergeant with a surprising air of confidence. A moment later he had taken Lady Rosina's pistol from the sergeant's hand and turned it over meditatively, lifting it towards his nose and then inserting his little finger into the barrel. A sudden silence fell upon everyone on the stage and all eyes were upon him. And then, as everyone watched, he held up his finger. For such a shy young man he seemed surprisingly assured and

I thought to myself that his schooling at Eton, financed by the wealthy Baroness Coutts, his friendship with the hunting and shooting classes – all of this formed a solid background to his own diffident personality. Now he stood there, quite confident, quite at ease, and held out his finger towards the sergeant. I was short-sighted and I pushed forward to see properly. Not much of a mark, but a distinct smear, a dark-brown stain.

'This gun has been fired recently,' he said, and again his voice was assured. I looked towards Dickens, but he had not moved, and his face was inscrutable. And then I looked at Lady Rosina. This was a damning indictment of her. How could she explain the recent firing of her gun?

'That pistol is not mine,' she said, and I ventured to think that no one in the room would believe her. We had all seen it when she had taken it from her bag on the evening before. She moved a little closer, bent over and looked at the pistol. There was not a tremor in her voice when she repeated the words, 'That pistol is not mine. Someone has taken my pistol and replaced it with this one. There are a lot of pistols in this house, Sergeant. You should examine the gunroom. Anyone can go in and out and help themselves to one as the keys hang in the butler's room. My husband has a collection of derringer pistols. My pistol originally belonged to the gunroom in this house. I took it from a box of a pair of derringer pistols. This one is probably its original mate.' She paused for a moment and then said decisively, 'I thought I heard something in the night. I thought I heard a sound in my room. Someone came in and replaced my pistol with this one.' Dramatically she picked up the pistol and raised it to her nose. 'No, it's not mine,' she said, holding it out towards the sergeant. 'Everything that I own smells of my perfume. See for yourself.'

Rather gingerly, he took it from her and turned it over in his hands. I watched him with suppressed amusement. Could a pistol really smell of perfume? I didn't know and wished that I had my mother here. Helen Lemon was a plain woman who dressed plainly, and I had never smelled perfume from her. Frances Jarman might know, but she was a woman of great discretion and I could not imagine her being willing to venture an opinion. The sergeant looked embarrassed and obviously wondered what to do next.

I scrutinized the faces. No one believed her. Embarrassment on most faces, relief on Nelly's and no expression at all on the face of her mother, Frances. It looked bad for the lady of the house, but the sergeant was in a quandary. Lady Rosina might have caused huge embarrassment when she had abused her husband in public during the hustings, but that had been discreetly dealt with by her husband. The lady had been removed from circulation, placed in a private asylum and no complaint was made to the police. In any case a public order offence was a very small matter compared with murder. I could see by his face that the sergeant found himself facing a dilemma. If the noble lady was guilty of murder, it would be his duty to take her into custody. And then all hell would break loose. Every newspaper in the country would descend upon this village in Hertfordshire; there would be questions asked in the House of Lords; Scotland Yard would send someone down, one of the detective inspectors like Mr Whicher who had been recently in the news. I could see the thought passing through the man's head and guessed that he feared that he would be held responsible for the whole matter. Desperately, he looked around him and then went across the stage and snatched up the gun from the table where Nelly had been standing. Imitating Mr Young Charles Dickens, he thrust his little finger into its barrel, raised it to his nose and declared decisively, 'This pistol has also been fired recently.' He looked directly at Nelly and asked, 'Did you fire this pistol, miss?'

He had not asked anyone to verify the stain on his finger and had rapidly wiped it clean on the edge of his coat. I wondered whether there had, in fact, been any stain, or whether he had set himself to find an alternative suspect to Lady Rosina and he was determined that no one should check upon him. Nevertheless, it would be hard to accuse the girl without some evidence.

Nelly's reply to this was a frightened stare and then she burst into tears. Young Charles began to move towards her but then stopped after a quick glance at his father. Frances took a step forward so that her daughter was partially hidden from view. Lord Edward frowned heavily and to my surprise said, 'You are frightening the girl, Sergeant. Don't be ridiculous. That girl wouldn't hurt a fly.' His voice, harsh like the voices of the deaf always sound, made the sergeant take a step backwards. I could see how he opened his mouth to retort, but then shut it again. Lord Edward's family, the Lyttons, had owned the stately home and its surrounding parkland for almost four hundred years. His word was law. I was surprised, though, to find the noble lord standing up for a mere actress and thought more of him. Nelly swallowed back her tears and looked timidly hopeful. I studied the sergeant's face with interest and wondered what he would do next. Who in this gathering of the famous and the titled might have shot the secretary of a most famous lord of the realm? I could see his eyes going dubiously from face to face and his worried expression made me guess that he was thinking of his superiors at Scotland Yard.

And it was probably the thought of criticism from above which prompted his next move. Lord Edward's intervention hadn't worked. I could see that the sergeant had made his calculations. The easiest solution, the solution that would cause the least notoriety, must be to blame the young actress. Actresses, in the sergeant's mind, were an unstable and reckless crew.

He said abruptly, speaking not to Lord Edward, but in an undertone to the valet, 'Would Lord Edward permit me to have the use of a small room in order to interview everyone?'

The valet discreetly took a notebook from his pocket, scribbled a few words on it, then held it and the pencil out to his master who scribbled a reply. And then he turned back to the sergeant.

'Lord Edward suggests that you could use the Oval Anteroom. I shall take you up to it. Who would you like to interview first?'

The sergeant nodded at Nelly and crooked a finger at her. It was hardly polite, but she came obediently, crossed the floor and stood by his side. Her face was very white, but her step was steady, and she held herself upright and did not look back at her mother.

'Come along, miss,' said the sergeant and both followed the valet on their way up to the Oval Anteroom.

EIGHT

The clouds had gathered, within the last half-hour. The
light was dull; the distance was dim. The lovely face
of Nature met us, soft and still and colourless –
met us without a smile.

Wilkie Collins, *The Moonstone*

'I wish that I knew this castle better,' I said impulsively to
Dickens. Half an hour had elapsed and there was no sign
of little Nelly, nor of the sergeant. The bell from the Oval
Anteroom, where she was being interviewed, had been rung
once. I had lingered in the hallway, seen a servant go in, come
out and then return with the constable. That was all that I saw
as I joined Dickens who was smoking a cigar on the terrace.
Both of us were restless and both paced the ground in front
of the building, looking up at the windows from time to time.

'Knebworth is not really a castle,' said Dickens showing
his usual zeal for instructing me. 'You should have studied
that *Book for Visitors* that our host displays in the library. Most
interesting. Knebworth is just a very old manor house that
was added to, built on to over the centuries and then trans-
formed into this magnificent Gothic mansion not so very long
ago.'

'Bound to be secret passageways,' I went on, ignoring this.
'It's old, isn't it? Looks old, anyway.'

'My dear Wilkie, be precise,' said Dickens. 'What is old?
Old is comparative. My children think me old, because they
are so young. I think myself young, but am forced, when
interrogated, to use the word "middle-aged". However, looks
can be deceptive. What you regard as looking old in this
building in front of us, is not old at all. All these Gothic cren-
ellations, these towers and turrets, these gargoyles and stained
glass, all of these were added to the original façade by our

friend, Lord Edward, and his talented mother. Made a
wonderful job of it,' said Dickens with enthusiasm.

I didn't agree. I thought it ugly and overdone, but I had
more important matters on my mind than an argument over
architecture. 'But the original building was old,' I persisted.

'Yes, as buildings go, this one is old, medieval, about three-
hundred-and-fifty years old, to be precise,' said Dickens in his
instructive way.

He had said nothing much up to now, but I knew that he
was troubled when I saw him smoke one cigar after another.
Now he seemed to be glad to talk about something else other
than this girl, not much older than his own Katey, who seemed
to have spent a very long time being interrogated by two
policemen. He went on to give me a short lecture on the origins
of the house and of the Lytton family and the antiquity of the
banqueting hall.

'Bound to be secret passageways,' I went on, ignoring this.
'I'd like to creep along one and eavesdrop on what is going
on in the anteroom.'

He looked at me with a raised eyebrow. 'You sound like
my Charley,' he said. 'First thing he wanted to do when we
arrived here. Went off looking for secret passages, came back
just before dinner, covered in cobwebs and all excited about
his discoveries, wishing that one of his brothers were with
him and thinking of what a splendid time they could have had.
I wish that boy would grow up! They are such a responsibility,
boys of that age.'

I looked at him with interest. He had spoken like a man
who was deeply worried. And yet why should he be so worried
about Charley? His son was a nice fellow. He had expressed
a love of journalism, of a literary career, but he had been
docile enough to accept his father's opinion that he was unfit
for such a career and had meekly gone off to Germany to be
instructed in the German language and then had taken up the
Baroness Coutts' offer of a place in her family bank. A model
son in some ways.

And yet, I thought that I knew the reason behind the look
of intense worry on my friend's face. A boy, or young man of
Charley's age, feels very intensely. Nelly may have been his

first love and now she was all to him. His father may have reasoned with him, may have ordered, pleaded, coaxed him to give her up, but in this matter, he was adamant and refused to fall in with his father's wishes. An intense and high-minded young man with all the sensitivity that went with his age and with his loving temperament as his mother's son. Dickens might find it hard to sway his son from this, his first love.

And then something else occurred to me, something which might also have occurred to his father. What if young Charley had been so harrowed, so angered by that attempt of the secretary to attack and to rape the girl with whom he was deeply in love? The sergeant suspected that Nelly might have taken the opportunity to kill her assailant, but surely it was more plausible that a hot-tempered, emotional young man, deeply in love for the first time in his life, might have been overcome with rage and detestation of the villain that he decided to put an end to his life – vengeance, but also as a way of keeping a pure, young and fatherless girl safe from a villain who was determined to rob her of her virginity. First love, I thought, looking back at the feelings which I had deliberately stirred up within myself in order to give authenticity to my words when writing my first book, *Basil*, was an immensely potent emotion. In *Basil* my hero just stopped short of murder but had maimed a man for life. When I had been writing that book, I had felt that every word of it could have been true and now looking at Dickens' troubled face and knowing how deeply he loved his children, I wondered whether the terrible thought had crept into his mind. He ground out the last inch of his cigar on the wall that surrounded the terrace and stared at the deer in the park. He had a very anxious expression. He had stared at me angrily when I had first mentioned the possibility of a secret passage and I wondered whether he had been thinking of Charley, or of something else. I did not hesitate to bring my thoughts into the open. There were more important matters on my mind than the maturity or otherwise of Dickens' eldest son.

'If there was a secret passage, I think that I would crawl along it and listen through the ceiling in order to find out what that policeman is saying to Nelly.'

'Unlikely to find one,' he said with an absent-minded expression. 'The anteroom is probably just a part of the original landing that was cut off to prevent draughts coming into the drawing room. Anyway, why should you eavesdrop on the police? It's not your business. You'd be better off studying your lines for the play. Remember half the country-side will be coming to watch it in another few days.'

I was taken aback at his words. Surely the wretched play would be cancelled now! Or, at the very least, postponed until the murdered man was in his grave. There must be relatives to inform, a funeral would have to be held, unless the relatives removed the body. Despite myself, my lips twitched, and I bit back a smile. The play, I thought, would be a sell-out and repeat performances be demanded as everyone, even the London crowd, would want to see a drama enacted upon the very stage where a man had been shot dead. That chalk mark, made by Dickens, would have to be preserved and perhaps crowds would be taken up into the roof in order to look down upon it. But then I thought of Nelly and the smile faded. Poor girl, not much more than a child.

'Dick,' I said impulsively. 'Don't you think that you should interfere? After all, that girl is very young, just about the same age as your own little Katey.'

He did not answer, just stared ahead, the line between his brows deepening. I wondered whether he was still thinking about his son and his worries about the boy's future. But I didn't think that was the problem. He had the look of a man to whom an unpleasant and frightening thought has just occurred. I said no more. Perhaps it was my words about Katey which had brought that expression to his face. Though Dickens always declared that whichever child was the baby was his favourite, privately I had always thought that Katey, so like him in so many ways, was his real favourite. And Nelly, born in the same year had, with her heavy-lidded eyes, a certain resemblance to Katey, though the one was dark like her father, and the other, probably taking after Frances, was prettily blonde.

'The sergeant would take notice of you,' I said. 'You are such a famous man. Everyone has heard of you. And, after all, you have written about how you went around London with Inspector Field; everyone who reads the newspapers and magazines will know that you are on excellent terms with Scotland Yard.'

Still he said nothing, and I lost my patience. 'Well, I'm going, if you won't,' I said angrily. I didn't wait for a reply. There wouldn't be one; I knew that. Dickens was very obstinate, and he would not be moved from a course of action by someone as lowly as myself. In any case, there was something on his mind. I knew him well enough to have observed all the signs in him and he would not turn to this matter until he had come to some conclusion. He followed me indoors but did not ascend the stairs towards the drawing room with me. When I reached the first flight and looked back, I saw him standing in the hall, and oddly, he seemed to be studying his own reflection in the mirror of the Gothic, carved hallstand. I paused for a moment, looking back, feeling, despite the seriousness of the occasion, a slight amusement. Dickens must have taken our conversation about age and the appearance of age seriously and was now endeavouring to be impartial about his own appearance. On the one side of the scales would be his immense amount of exercise, his horse-riding, his thirty-mile walks, his vigour, his punishing regime of the work – work on his books and work on the periodical *Household Words* – but against that had to be placed the heavy pouches beneath his eyes, the lines in his cheeks and the receding hairline. I smiled to myself and then, without giving myself a moment to think, I tapped upon the door of the anteroom and entered it without waiting for a summons.

'Excuse me, Sergeant,' I said, with what I hoped was an easy manner. 'I was just checking on whether Miss Nelly was still here. I had promised to take her to see Bruno, the dog who saved her from an unpleasant experience the other day.'

Not the most sensible of remarks, I thought as soon as the words were out of my mouth. Nevertheless, the sergeant would not have been questioning the girl for over half an hour unless he knew all the details of the scoundrel Tom Maguire's attack upon her. 'He's a lovely dog,' I went on hurriedly. 'Have you seen him, Sergeant? I've never seen a dog so big before now.

A gentle giant,' I summed up with an eye on Nelly's tear-stained face.

A very sweet girl, I thought, and felt even more strongly that I had to do something.

The sergeant looked at me first with annoyance and then with a certain level of interest. 'I understand that you released the dog, Mr Collins. Is that correct?' He looked back at the open notebook on the desk before him. Over his head, placed in the centre of an ornate, gilt-edged triangle, was the oval portrait of Sir Rowland Lytton, depicted after the visit of Queen Elizabeth to Knebworth. I wondered whether there might be a secret hinged panel beneath it that would lead to the roof. In a house this old, anything was possible.

'That's right, Sergeant,' I said in an easy manner and turned to the girl. 'You took quite a fancy to him, didn't you, Miss Nelly?'

She had been weeping; that was obvious, but she pulled herself together with a magnificent self-control which I had to admire. I told myself that if I ever had children, I would insist on them having stage-training. The ability to act a part, to cover up one's feelings, to present a chosen face to the public – what a start in life to have that skill at your fingertips!

'He's lovely,' she said with girlish enthusiasm. 'He's as tall as that, Sergeant,' she said, holding her little hand up somewhere near to her own chest. 'I'd love to go and see him again, Mr Collins. That's if I can't help you any more, Sergeant,' she said with a stage politeness and an actress's bob, not quite a curtsy; that would have been overdoing it, but a sweet, little lowering of her head and shake of her blonde curls.

He melted for a moment. I could see how he hesitated, but then there was an interruption. Lady Rosina called something down the stairs to one of the maids and the sergeant's face hardened as he brought himself back to the grave situation.

'I'm afraid that there are a few more questions that I need to ask of the young lady,' he said. He got to his feet, went and opened the door and held it open until I reluctantly passed through it. I had barely set foot on the landing when I heard it close behind me and then I heard the key turn in the door.

The sergeant was making quite sure that he would not be interrupted again. I had done no good by my intervention. I should have known that I did not carry the weight of my famous friend.

I would have to go and seek out Dickens and persuade him to take an interest in this girl. I was sure that she was innocent. But I had begun to read the sergeant's mind. Someone would have to be arrested for this crime in such a well-known place as Knebworth. There was going to be huge interest throughout the nation in this murder. I had heard Lord Edward give instructions to the butler to have a message sent to the lodge. The gates were to be locked and any stranger seeking admission had to be detained until permission was given for access. This would keep out reporters for a while, but it wouldn't work for long. The park was fenced, but more to keep deer in rather than to keep intruders out. Young agile reporters would scale those wooden fences with great ease and then we would all be under attack – none more so than the police. Results, progress, court appearances would be demanded. I drafted out a plan of action as I moved swiftly down the stairs.

'Dickens,' I began as I went through the front door and on to the gravel beyond it, but then I stopped. Dickens was not alone. The constable was with him, red-faced and mopping his brow.

'Mr Collins will show you up to the room where the sergeant is,' said Dickens. He had a satisfied look on his face, and I could see that the anxiety he had shown earlier was wiped away. 'Apparently, our old friend, Inspector Field, is on the way from London, sitting in a railway carriage at this very moment. Scotland Yard have taken over the case,' he added in a lower tone of voice and I nodded, wondering whether he had despatched a letter to London. The post from Knebworth to London would take less than an hour due to the excellent rail service.

'Certainly,' I said aloud. 'I have just come from there. Through this door, Constable. He's up here. Very beautiful house, this, isn't it, Constable?'

'Yes, sir,' said the constable politely, but I could hear an uneasy note in his voice. He feared, I guessed, that his master, the sergeant, would not be pleased by the news that he was bringing.

I rapped on the door and as soon as I heard the key click in the lock, I threw it open with a flourish and announced, 'The constable has news from London for you, Sergeant.'

Poor little Nelly, he had doubtless been bullying her again as her small handkerchief was clutched in her hand and there were marks of tears in her eyes. I perched on the table by her side and waited while the two men went outside the door.

'Is he giving you a hard time?' I whispered. If she had been a couple of years younger, I could have given her a kiss, but as it was, I just patted her hand and tried the effect of an encouraging smile.

She nodded, tried to say something, but then swallowed convulsively.

I said nothing more, though, as I was straining my ears to listen to the conversation outside the door. And then I heard something that brought a smile to my face. The sergeant rapped out an oath. The news wasn't good. He would have to hand over the investigation to the man from London. He said something, then, something too low for my ears, but I clearly heard the sergeant's reply to it, perfectly respectful but very slightly smug. 'I've heard tell that them London men like to start from scratch, sir. So, I've been told,' he added, detaching himself from his opinion.

There was a short silence before the sergeant threw the door open.

'That's all, miss,' he said. He didn't read back her statement to her. I thought of demanding that he do so, but told myself that it was none of my business and probably a mistake to antagonize him. His face was very red and there was an angry look in his eyes. He held the door open and once again his gesture was less that of politeness than a strong hint for the room to be vacated.

'Come, Nelly,' I said, with dignity and followed her from the room. She paused at the top of the stairs and I wondered whether she wanted to go to her mother, but then she began to go down into the entrance hall.

'Let's go and see Bruno,' I suggested, and she slightly

quickened her steps. I thought of finding Charley Dickens to go with us but decided that the less she was in Charley's company, the more eager his father would be to assist her.

I took her through the front door and then hesitated for a minute as I saw Dickens was there on the terrace, smoking a cigar, his face troubled as he paced the length of the ornate building. It was only when we had come through the porch that I realized that he was not alone. Sitting on the edge of the wall, also smoking a cigar, was Clarkson Stanfield. His face, too, bore a troubled expression.

Dickens' eyes went instantly to the tear-stained face of the girl and he ground out the cigar on the wall, holding the remnant in his hand as he glanced over towards Clarkson. Both men were silent, and I gave them a minute. I could guess what they had been talking about, though. Clarkson had made very clear his admiration and devotion to Lady Rosina and his memories of her as a girl were vivid in his mind.

Two women, two pistols. The one in the handbag of Lady Rosina had been fired recently. Young Charley Dickens had proved that when he had inserted his finger into the barrel – at least, he probably had done, I amended. It was a fleeting second, but I think that I did see a smear on his little finger, and no one had contradicted him. But the sergeant had done the same test with the pistol from the table in front of Nelly and no one had contradicted him, either, when he had asserted that it had been fired, though in that case I was fairly certain that there had been no mark on his finger. I could see that Clarkson looked troubled and I guessed that he was worried about Lady Rosina. I hardened my heart, though. Lady Rosina was tough and resourceful and could manipulate men like Clarkson who remembered her from her youth. Despite her quarrels with her husband, she was still a member of the peerage and a person with powerful friends.

Nelly, on the other hand, had no one except her mother to care for her.

'We are going to see Bruno,' I said to Dickens. 'He'll cheer Nelly up.'

'Good idea,' he said in an absent-minded way. He looked at Nelly with concern and I knew that he saw the tear stains

on her face. I looked towards Clarkson, wondering whether
he might ask what was wrong and give Nelly an opportunity
to tell her story, but he avoided my gaze.

'Come on, Nelly,' I said. 'Let's go to the stable yard.'

I picked some stems of lavender from one of the flower
beds to present to her and her face lit up with pleasure. 'I
never knew that it grew in gardens, grew like a weed,' she
said naively. 'It's my mother's favourite perfume and she gives
me some, too.'

'What did the sergeant ask you?' I put the question with
hesitation. I did not want to start her weeping again, but I
needed to know whether she was in danger of being arrested.

'He was trying to get me to confess,' she said in a low
voice.

'To confess!' I echoed the words with an air of incredulity,
but, in reality, I was not surprised.

'To confess to murdering the secretary, Mr Maguire. He
thought I had done it because I was frightened of him.'

'But no one knew that it was Maguire. Everyone thought
that it was Lord Edward. Did you tell him that?'

She didn't reply to that question, but after a minute of
walking down the avenue towards the stable yard, she said
very quietly, 'I knew it wasn't Lord Edward.'

'How?'

'There was a creak from the floorboards overhead, when
he was onstage. I saw him look up. I knew it wasn't Lord
Edward, then. He was much too deaf to have heard that. I
suddenly realized that it was really Mr Maguire. Don't tell
the sergeant, though, Mr Collins?'

I didn't reply. As we turned in the direction of the stable
yard, my mind was busy. Yes, it was a strong plea in favour
of Nelly that she could have no possible motive to do any
harm to Lord Edward who was host to herself and her mother,
and probably paying their wage. In view of Dickens' praise
of the earl's generosity, I thought that was quite likely; but,
in any case, I had noticed that he treated the pair of actresses
with the same courtesy as he showed to Mark Lemon's wife
and other ladies. Certainly, if Nelly had thought the man
playing the part of the marquis was Lord Edward, then she

would have no possible motive for murdering him and unless that could be proved, any evidence against her was bound to fail if brought to the court. The sergeant, I guessed, hoped to frighten a confession out of her and once that was signed and witnessed, he would be held to have solved the case.

So, Nelly had to stick firmly to the story that she had not known that the man on stage was in fact the secretary, not his master. 'Don't tell anyone else, Nelly,' I warned.

I was glad that she had told me. The story of the footsteps overhead, this was a valuable piece of information. The banqueting hall was in the ancient part of the house, the original medieval hall. The ceiling was formed from the original blackened oak beams with some uneven and warped pieces of board between them. Someone walking up there would have made the boards creak. And if someone had been up there it would have been very easy to lie on the boards and to fire through one of the numerous cracks, to fire down upon the man standing mid-stage, on the chalked mark, and to hit him in the heart. Almost easier, I decided, than to aim from behind stage or through one of the window or door openings in Clarkson Stanfield's cottage backdrop. As so often these days, I decided to confide in Dickens and to ask him what the best thing might be to do.

Bruno was delighted to see us and so was the stable boy and his master. Both came towards us as we entered the yard. They had both been present during the dramatic killing in the banqueting hall and both were mainly anxious about the fate of Bruno.

'Least said, Mr Collins, what do you say?' was the man's contribution.

The boy chimed in with: 'It was that Mr Maguire that wanted the poor fella shot.' He stroked Bruno's nose and Bruno wagged his tail gratefully. 'Never did a moment's harm, did you, Bruno?'

'He's the most beautiful dog in the world, and the cleverest and the kindest,' declared Nelly, depositing a kiss on the dog's broad head between his ears. I saw a tear drop, too, and felt intensely sorry for the girl. I wished that Dickens were with me, witnessing the poor girl's misery. It would have touched

Dickens' heart to see this girl, so near in age to his own
Katey, to be bearing her troubles so gallantly. There was no
equality in the world, I thought. While Katey Dickens was in
the nursery and later with her governess in the school room,
this girl was earning her living on stage, sleeping in cockroach-
infested lodgings, working until late at night, learning new
parts, dancing on stage until collapsing with exhaustion; these
young actresses had no real childhood. They were often more
in demand than adult actors and actresses and, indeed, often
were the major breadwinners in the family.

And if Nelly was accused of murder, there would be no one
except her mother to help her and the word of an actress, the
lack of money to employ a lawyer and the prejudice of juries
might be enough to bring her to a sentence of hanging or at
least of deportation. I resolved to do all I could to protect her.

'Let's take him for a walk in the maze, Mr Collins,' she
said, and I was surprised to hear the note of girlish enthusiasm in her voice. I would have thought that the memory
of what had almost happened to her in the maze would have
made her shudder at the idea of going near to the place, but
I made no comment, just handed Bruno's lead to her and
allowed her to lead him along the pathway. She was trying
to forget her troubles with thinking about the dog, I guessed.
She cross-questioned the stable boy about where the dog
could find water to drink, about where his food was stored
and listened to the tale of how, since he had been bought,
no one needed to lock the stable yard at night because Bruno
would bark his deep-throated warning if a stranger was within
a hundred yards of the place. 'Never says a word if it's
someone he knows,' said young Jim with the pride of an
owner in his voice.

She was only a child, really, I thought, as Nelly delightedly
joined in the game of 'find the correct path' and then allowed
Bruno to lead her out of the maze. I was sorry that I had not
asked young Charley to come with us but was glad to see a
little colour come into her cheeks and animation to her eyes.
When I brought her back to the house, she was reassured to
hear that the sergeant had gone back to Hertford and just the
constable had been left to represent the law in the stately house.

I left her in the library writing a letter to her sister and I went in search of Dickens. My mind was made up. I, Wilkie Collins, a man who had no cause of umbrage against either secretary or master, would be the one who had heard the footsteps overhead in the loft above the ancient ceiling of the banqueting hall.

Dickens and I would investigate the place and would ascertain the possibility of a shot from this secluded place. There was a problem: the person who could have been walking overhead may well have been Dickens' eldest son – Charley had a small part in this play and was not on stage until the third act. However, I could see no possible reason why Charley should want to murder his host, Lord Edward Bulwer-Lytton, and so I would shelve that concern for the moment.

NINE

We neither know nor judge ourselves; others
may judge but cannot know us. God alone
judges and knows us.

Wilkie Collins, *Basil*

The dust of centuries lay thick upon a motley collection
of outmoded furniture and trunk-loads of centuries-old
clothing and cushions stored in the attic spaces of
Knebworth. I was tempted to rummage, but Dickens kept me
firmly to our task. He had placed a covered oil lamp downstairs
on the floor of the banqueting hall, next to the chalked mark
that had been the place, appointed by Dickens, for the marquis
to deliver his soliloquy and then to stretch himself out upon the
floor. We had to see whether it would be possible for an
assassin to put a bullet into his victim from this height.

The trouble was that the place was in excellent repair. The
floors of the attics were boarded as well as though they had
been rooms within the house. Not just that, but most of the
space had been partitioned into small rooms used for storage:
some used for storing of cleaning materials; some filled with
furniture; some with trunk loads of clothing; and others with
games paraphernalia: old tennis rackets, cricket bats, hockey
sticks and masses of indoor occupations, chess sets, old packs
of cards and stacks of well-worn books. We visited each
section, each room. From time to time, we found small cracks
in the floorboards – once, and once only there was a glimmer
from the lantern downstairs, but no place from which a shot
could accurately have been fired to hit a man in the chest.

Then we came back to the place where the young and active
members of the cast who were mainly in the last act of the
play had stood or sat during most of the play. Augustus Egg,
John Leech and Charley Dickens had, I remembered, been

smoking cigars, hidden from the audience and from the stern eye of Dickens, by sitting behind the railing of the minstrels' gallery, some forty feet above the hall floor.

Hastily I climbed back down again, but my face betrayed me. Dickens said nothing but he, in his turn, climbed the steps. I saw him stop at the same place as where I had stood and I saw him stare down at the hall, as I had done, through the perforated wood of the minstrels' gallery.

'Some of the players in the third act stood there during the first act, didn't they?' he asked when he returned. His voice was meditative, and I made no reply. He knew as well as I did who they were: Augustus Egg, John Leech and Charley Dickens, enjoying a surreptitious cigar to alleviate the boredom of listening to the often-repeated lines. He had probably made a note to tell them not to do it again during the final performance.

'Let's go down to your room,' I whispered in his ear and led the way back down the endless flights of stairs, along the red passage and to Dickens' room, known as the Falkland Room. I, as a quite unimportant person, had a chilly room beside the back passageway, but Dickens, as an esteemed guest, had been given this wonderful room, which because of the valuable antiques it contained, was always kept at a constant heat.

'Should have called it the Chinese Room – I know that it belonged to the wife of the fifth Viscount Falkland a couple of hundred years ago, but Chinese would be more appropriate,' I said on the first occasion of surveying the glowing red of the wood framing the metal Chinese images, the magnificent bronze cauldron and the little Chinese pagoda.

'I'm always given this room when I visit Knebworth. I love the place and I used this pagoda in my book *David Copperfield* – David and Dora bought it for Dora's dog, Jip.' Dickens touched one of the tiny bells affectionately and I gave him a moment to reminisce. Dickens, I had often noticed, had a sentimental attachment to *David Copperfield* and every detail of it and of his inspiration for it seemed to be engraved upon his memory. But I had heard that story often, again and again, and I had more serious matters on my mind now.

And so, I gave a perfunctory nod and then sat on the edge

of the canopy bed, enclosed with carved wood, stained a warm colour of red. I almost felt like stretching out upon it while Dickens fiddled with the fire, tossing some more logs on top of it. Still, I had something of importance to say and so I sat up very straight and eyed him with affection, thinking that he had a thousand faults, but he had a brain as sharp as a well-honed, carved knife.

'Dick,' I said, 'let's not take the sergeant into our confidence. It's not as if your friend, Lord Edward, has been killed. The only death is that of the secretary. Let the police handle it – and I think they might find it a very difficult task. They know how he was killed – a shot from a revolver . . . one of two or even three possible revolvers, perhaps,' I amended, before going on in as emphatic a tone of voice that I could conjure up. 'Remember, Dick,' I said earnestly, 'this is going to be a very complicated matter. None of us know who the intended victim was. Speaking for myself, it never crossed my mind to doubt that Lord Edward was the man sitting on the stool, walking on stage, lying down after his soliloquy, dressed in the wig and costume of the marquis – the man who was shot. But some people, some with quicker ears for a voice, more curiosity, better eyesight than mine, may well have known that it was the secretary, while others were sure that it was our host. We have no real means of finding motive or finding evidence against anyone.'

I stopped and hesitated for a minute. He had a stubborn look on his face, and I knew that mood. Dickens would see himself as an upholder of law and order. He was willing to use his brains and his observational powers, and, of course, his knowledge of the people who had gathered here in Knebworth; but it would all be in the service of the police and in order to help them arrest a guilty man. I, on the contrary, had an uneasy feeling that we should keep any findings to ourselves for a moment.

I thought about Charley, about little Nelly, and about the unfortunate Lady Rosina and then burst out with the rest of my inner thoughts. 'Come on, Dick,' I said impatiently. 'Let's face it. He was a most unpleasant fellow that Tom Maguire. Look how he behaved to Lady Rosina – how dare he treat a

lady in that fashion! And look at that attack on poor little
Nelly. If it wasn't for that dog, the man could have raped her
before anyone could have come to her assistance. Even as it
was, he frightened the life out of the poor little thing. She's
looked so pale and anxious ever since. And I know that she
has gone to sleep in her mother's bed because she is so terrified. Give it up, Dick. Let it go. I hope this murder is never
solved. As far as I am concerned it was good riddance.' I did
not look at him, but fiddled with the oil lamp, pumping some
more oil into the glass globe and peering at the Chinese fertility
symbol behind it.

'You forget,' said Dickens quietly, 'that Tom Maguire might
not have been the designated victim. It could have been Lord
Edward himself. And if that is so, the murderous villain may
try again.'

I said nothing for a moment. In view of Dickens' long
friendship with Lord Edward, it would be tactless to repeat
my comment of 'good riddance'. Nevertheless, his statement
had to be answered so I gathered my courage.

'If it were Lady Rosina who shot the man lying on the
stage, shot him in the belief that he was her husband who had
treated her so badly, well, I for one, would not want to play
any part in having her hanged.' I stared at him belligerently
and resolved to warn the lady if enquiries seemed to be leading
towards her. But at the back of mind was the picture of that
carved and perforated screen of the minstrels' gallery and of
three men: Augustus Egg, John Leech and Charley Dickens
coming and going from that set of steps as they disposed of
cigar butts through the hall door.

'I think that you are being unnecessarily melodramatic. It
is obvious that Lady Rosina is slightly insane. The worst that
would happen, if it were found that she was the guilty
person, would be that she would be very rapidly returned to
the place from which she insisted on leaving. Don't forget
what an asylum is, Wilkie. If I remember rightly, I believe
that asylum comes from the Latin word for a sanctuary or a
place of refuge. Lady Rosina would be cared for and her every
need met if she were within the walls of the asylum where
her husband placed her.'

'Don't give me that nonsense, Dick,' I said hastily. 'You know better than that. How would you like to be placed in an asylum where your every need would be met?'

'I'm in full possession of my senses and have never, to the best of my recollection, murdered anyone. And I've never thrown dinner plates at anyone, despite frequent temptation when after-dinner speeches go on for too long.' Dickens pulled the fringes of his moustache and stared at me defiantly.

'You can't agree with her husband that she should spend her life locked up,' I said hotly. Then added, 'He's an abominable man, Dick. You can't defend him. You heard what she said about him. There's no excuse for that sort of behaviour. I was struck by what she said about slaves, weren't you? Every right-minded man or woman must deplore what happened to those unfortunate Africans over there in America, but we should also deplore what is happening to women inside their marital home.'

Dickens traced the curves of the bronze medallion on the bed panel near to his chair. He did not reply for a moment, but I could see that he was thinking very hard.

'He loved her intensely, you know, Wilkie,' he said unexpectedly. 'You have heard what Clarkson said of her, about her beautiful dark eyes, her intensity, her talent, well, all of these things, and more, have been already said to me by Bulwer-Lytton, many, many years ago when we first became friends, and later on, too.'

'Including,' I said, and then with an effort of memory, I quoted Clarkson's words, '"I loved her then, and I would have killed anyone who injured her". Could Lord Edward have echoed these words?'

'He loved her so much that he did almost kill his mother who adored and worshipped him. He was her whole life and she begged and pleaded with him not to marry this girl. She foresaw all the unhappiness that would come of such a marriage. She even did, what I am persuaded, must have broken her heart, she cut off his income when he married that woman.'

I said nothing. Lord Edward's mother had, I seemed to remember, lived a good twenty years or so after the marriage and a triumphant ten years after the separation and divorce, so I was sceptical about the danger that her son's marriage caused to her health. I was willing to admit that the married couple may well have loved each other at one stage. I had seen such outcomes of passionate adoration and it was one of the reasons why I had resolved never to marry but to have a mistress – a mistress in every street, Lady Rosina had advised and I suppressed a smile at the thought of my conversation with her. The memory of it, though, gave me courage to go on battling with Dickens who was so much older, so much wiser, and so much more experienced in the ways of polite society.

'But how did they fall out of love?' I asked the man whose every written work ended with a 'happy ever afterwards' conclusion.

'You don't know much of the world, Wilkie, if you can ask me a question like that.' Dickens, unlike his usual quick-fire delivery, spoke slowly and seriously. 'The hotter the fire burns, the less ash remains in the grate once it has burned itself out. They loved each other, but then the rubs of married life came between them. She was not a good wife to him,' said Dickens sadly. 'She would not make allowances for him. She competed with him. He wrote a book and wanted her to admire it. She didn't. She wrote her own book and declared it was better than his. It was the same with his poetry. He poured his heart and soul into a poem; showed it to her. And she laughed at it!' Dickens stared sombrely into the heart of the fire and rubbed his mouth, moustache and beard vigorously before he resumed.

'She did not play the part of a wife, so I've been told,' he said. 'I met him soon after she left him, and he was a man in mourning. He couldn't get her out of his head. I was a very young man at the time. Dear old Clarkson introduced us and Bulwer, as he was known then, was very kind to me, invited me down to Knebworth, showed me his books, but he couldn't stop talking about Lady Rosina, quoting her, telling me what she had said, even when it was obvious that her words had left wounds in his soul. She had ridiculed him from the start, ridiculed his home, his pictures, his books, his mother; her sharp tongue had made deep wounds. He couldn't get her words out of his head. He had to keep on repeating them. It was then quite some time before I met Catherine and I must say that I made up my mind that I would never marry anyone who fancied herself more talented than I,' said Dickens grimly.

'And yet, he had loved her; you felt that, even then . . .' I let the rest of my thought hang unfinished in the air.

'He loved her; but he feared her.' Dickens said the words very slowly and almost under his breath.

I stared at him in astonishment.

'Feared her?' I said and the image came to me of Lady Rosina with the pistol in her handbag. 'And yet, according to her, he beat her and kicked her and even bit her on the cheek.' That last image would haunt my dreams, I thought. I could never imagine anyone doing such a thing to a girl that he had loved.

'Yes, loved her and feared her. He feared her power over him. He feared that she had taken possession of his soul, and of his mind; that she dominated him, made him doubt his own genius, made him lose his whole confidence in himself. She threatened the life of his soul and of his mind. If they had stayed together longer, he would have lost the ability to write and about twenty great books would have been lost to the English language.'

I looked uneasily at Dickens. 'Couldn't he have made some allowances for her?' I asked. 'If he had truly loved her couldn't he have just smiled to himself if she criticized his books, his pictures, just shown a bit of forbearance. You surely cannot make excuses for him, excuses for his brutality. You would not treat a woman like that.'

'Certainly not,' he said sternly. 'I would never allow myself to get into that position of dependency upon a woman.'

It was not exactly what I had meant, but I supposed that it fitted with his personality. And perhaps, I thought, he was right. My own decision never to marry, but to have mistresses, was born of the same impulse.

'"In time, we hate that which we fear",' I said. 'Wasn't it Shakespeare who said that in some play or other? Lord Edward feared her sharp tongue and then came to hate her.' Suddenly another thought came to me. 'Do you think that *she* fears him?'

Dickens did not hesitate. 'No, indeed. She is an indomitable woman. She despises and hates him, but she does not fear him.'

'So, you don't think that she would have tried to murder him?'

'I didn't say that,' said Dickens. 'I was talking about men who have a different make-up to women. You must ponder on why people murder a relative or someone known to them. My friend, Inspector Field, tells me that money is the first and foremost motive for murders committed by people of our class, in this great city of ours. Jealousy comes somewhere in the list, but very far down compared to money, robberies, legacies; the murderer wants to gain from his crime. But, of course, yes, the relief of a hate that has haunted a man until he is almost out of his mind, yes, of course, that has to be a gain; has to be a motive that can drive a man to murder, as well.'

'Or a woman,' I said, and then, when he looked at me with surprise, I said, 'What about a woman killing a man for pure hate?'

He dismissed that idea. 'Women, Wilkie, do not feel the emotions as deeply as do we men. But they like money, they like possessions, these things are very important to them.'

'And Lady Rosina.' I put a query into my voice. 'Do you see a motive for murder there? Would her husband, hating her as he does, leave her money in his will? Surely not.'

'My dear Wilkie, she may not figure in my friend's will, but with her husband out of the way, Lady Rosina would resume her natural place here, in Knebworth, as mistress of this splendid house. Her son will inherit all; her son, Robert, now in his thirties, a man who has always stood up for her, is unmarried and lives abroad – is it Vienna, or is it Paris? In any case, he has a glittering career ahead of him as a foreign diplomat. India next, perhaps. He is unlikely to return here to Knebworth for many years to come and in the meantime, it would suit him very well to have his mother ensconced here, looking after the house and the estate. Foster tells me that he has hated the scandal. Lummy, Collins,' said Dickens with an attempt at adopting a playful tone, 'Lady Rosina, being a woman, would probably do anything to get back to living here amidst all the splendour, all those towers, those battlements, those turrets, those gargoyles, all of these servants, not one little untrained maid. But not if the price was to live with the man who was her husband. She despises him more than she hates him.'

I thought he was wrong. I thought that Lady Rosina, though a woman, was filled with a strong feeling of hate. But, undoubtedly, the prospect of regaining her position as mistress of this splendour would certainly be a strong motive. But strong enough to kill? I found that hard to believe, but then I was a man who cared little for the external appearances and the ostentatious trappings of wealth. Moreover, Dickens knew the family situation better than I did and what he said about the son restoring his mother to her rightful position in society certainly made sense to me. I sometimes found the thought creeping into my mind that my own mother was jollier, more at ease, certainly suffered from less illnesses and had no trouble whatsoever with her nerves, since the death of my father; attached and all as they had seemed to be when I was young. Being mistress of the house and suiting herself about mealtimes, visitors, being able to decide for herself about the purchase of new items certainly suited my mother and I could just imagine Lady Rosina being extremely happy and hospitable if she were left in charge of this splendid house and estate. But murder? Would she murder a man, shoot him dead in the presence of a roomful of people, take that terrible risk, just in order to be mistress of her son's house? It didn't seem feasible.

I yawned and got to my feet. 'When it comes to it, Dick, I don't really give a damn who killed Maguire and I don't even give a damn if you tell me that the true situation was that someone tried to kill Lord Edward. I don't feel like giving any assistance to the police or troubling my mind anymore about it.'

I had reached the door and had my hand upon the knob when he stopped me in my tracks with a single sentence. 'Not even if they were to hang little Nelly.'

I came back then and sat beside him. 'You're right, of course. I would care if the wrong person was accused. But I don't want anyone to be accused. I want to let the police simmer in a brew of uncertainty, I don't want to give them any clues or evidence which they may twist and manipulate. I think,' I went on, speaking with all the passion of which I was capable, 'that a lot of innocent people, people that you and I care for, may have to suffer some suspicion and so I would want to distance myself from it. Unless, of course, some innocent person is accused. And it may not be Nelly, it may be someone that both of us cares for, someone who is near and dear.' I did not look at him as I spoke but rubbed my finger along the carved rosewood of a bedside table.

'Are you thinking about Charley?' Dickens, in hunting men's parlance, never flinched from a fence, no matter what the consequence.

'No, of course not,' I said hastily and untruthfully, but I knew that he did not believe me, and I despised myself for my cowardice. 'But since you mention his name, well . . . I wouldn't want any suspicion to fall upon him,' I added weakly. 'So, let's not stir matters. Let's not put possibilities in the sergeant's head. Let's keep our trip to the roof and our findings about the screen to ourselves. You don't want to get Charley into danger,' I added.

'I would want any suspicion cleared from his name and as I know that he is incapable of such an act, the matter should be easily resolved,' he said and I trembled for him despite the note of utter confidence in his voice.

'And little Nelly,' I ventured to say.

He allowed a silence to develop there and then said, rather slowly and rather hesitantly, 'I don't know her so well.'

I was surprised at his words and the undertone of almost regret that ran beneath them.

'But you know her mother, you have known her mother for a long time,' I ventured. And then added, 'Before Nelly was born; Clarkson told me that.'

For a moment I caught a strange look in his eyes – almost as though some thought had struck him and then he leaned over and touched a china model of a dog that lay upon a cushion. He stroked the glossy surface for a moment, but did not, as he would normally do, give me a lecture on its provenance and its value, but stared absent-mindedly ahead. He had the look of one who is nerving himself to come to grips with a matter which has frequently troubled him.

'I suggest that we say nothing to anyone about our trip into the roof space,' I repeated. 'Let's not put any ideas into the sergeant's head. Already he seems convinced that Nelly shot the man – it would be an easy shot from where she stood, almost impossible to miss as he lay there in the centre of the stage with his arms outstretched and his chest exposed to view. If it were known that she and Charley – I suppose from what I've seen of the pair, where he went, she went also, I would lay a bet on that – had been prowling around in the roof space the day before, a clever lawyer could suggest to the jury that looking down and seeing the chalk mark, might have given her the idea that the man who menaced her might easily be got rid of with a shot from the pistol provided by Lord Edward and lying so close to her hand for much of the play. The sergeant has been grilling Nelly, but if he picks up any hint of a relationship between her and Charley, he may well then turn his slow mind towards your son.'

Oddly, Dickens didn't question me about Charley, or follow this up. Perhaps, as he had already said, he had utter confidence in his son. I didn't feel the same confidence. Charley, as far as I could judge, was deeply and passionately in love with Nelly. She may well have been the first girl that he had loved, and young men of that age can, I had noticed, feel intensely about their first love. Nelly had already been attacked by the loathsome Tom Maguire, and he had continued to pester her – and she may well have confided her fears to the young man who loved her. If Charley had realized that the man in the costume of the marquis was not Lord Edward, but his secretary, he might have decided to get rid of him. And if both Egg and Leech had gone out to throw away their cigar butts at the same time . . .

'Though, currently, the sergeant's chief suspect seems to be Nelly; we have to bear in mind that he might move on to considering Charley,' I said seriously. 'But he feels that Nelly is the one. Let's face it. If it can be proved that she knew the identity of the man playing the part of the marquis, that it was Maguire, then she could be in serious danger. It's not just a matter of hate; I saw that man; I saw her clothing; I saw how he had manhandled her. He would have raped her if the dog had not turned up.'

'She's so young.' Dickens said the words thoughtfully.

I did not spare him.

'Terrible, isn't it?' I said. 'Think of your darling Katey in a position like that without a father to protect her against false accusations. They're near in age, aren't they?'

Dickens, himself, had told me that Nelly was about the same age as Katey when he had first proposed engaging two professional actresses to take the parts meant for his wife and daughter. Now, however, he hesitated. There was certainly an odd look in his eye, and I looked at him curiously. 'That's right, isn't it?' I added.

'Katey was born in 1839, in October of 1839,' he said and left it at that.

'And Nelly was born in March. I remember her saying that the other evening. She and your son were talking about birthdays and he was telling her about the celebrations of his birthday in January, on New Year's Day and how Baroness Burdett-Coutts sent an enormous cake that could barely fit through the front door.'

Dickens smiled at the memory, but I did not miss the flash of anger that passed over his face at the mention of the conversation between his son and the young actress and the implications of such an intimate subject as birthdays to be discussed at the dinner table.

'Mary was born in March 1838, so just one year older,' he said slowly.

I waited. Mary was his second child. I remembered my mother's strictures about Dickens and how he put his wife through incessant childbearing. A bare fourteen months between Charley and Mary despite a miscarriage brought on by the sudden death of her younger sister; a longer gap then between Mary and Katey and then another miscarriage before the birth of Walter and so on.

'Catherine was not at all well after Mary's birth. For a long time afterwards.' He said the words thoughtfully with the appearance of one who is looking into the distant past. Impatiently, he shrugged his shoulders. 'Nerves! Women's problems,' he said explosively. 'Don't ever get married, Wilkie. It's never worth it.'

I said nothing. Nelly, of course, born in March 1839, was in between his two daughters and the thought of that obviously troubled him. I hoped that it would lead him to intervene once Inspector Field arrived on the scene. I might have good news to give Nelly and I was pleased at that thought.

'What happened to Nelly's father?' I asked the question idly and was surprised to see a startled look in his eyes.

'Why do you want to know?' His voice was irritable, and he rose to his feet, walking restlessly around the ornate room. He had the air of one who is trying to banish an unpleasant thought by physical exercise and I was not surprised when he said, 'Let's go for a brisk walk; never mind the fog – it's country fog – it will wash the dust from our lungs.'

I got to my feet. The idea which had just occurred to me was so momentous that I needed some time to absorb it and to test it against any known facts.

'You go, Dick,' I said. 'You'll do better on your own. I'll only slow you up. I've just remembered something. I promised to look at something for Clarkson Stanfield. He was asking me about the details in one of my father's pictures. He is worried that the picture he is working on now may be too like one of my father's in subject.'

As an excuse it was a good one and though one picture of a stormy ocean looked very like another, both of us knew Clarkson well enough to make it possible that he would worry about stealing another man's ideas. I would go and see him and put some questions to him. Dickens took his caped overcoat from the stand in the corner of the room. I watched him for a moment, rather undecided as to whether to go now or to wait until he was ready and then went hesitantly to the door. He had said no more to me, but had gone over to the chest of drawers, opened the top drawer and taken something out of it. I had been about to say something else, but when I saw what he had in his hand, I quietly closed the door behind me and went quickly down the stairs.

Dickens, I knew, carried a revolver with him always when he walked the streets at night, but I had not realized that he had taken it with him when staying at a friend's house in rural Hertfordshire.

Clarkson's scruples were soon put to rest. I had a private belief that one painting of a seascape looked like another but was soon able to reassure him that no one could accuse him of plagiarism and that my father would be the first to appreciate his latest painting. 'He had a huge admiration for you as a painter,' I said with sincerity. 'I remember very clearly, when I was a young lad, that he was telling me about the magnificent backdrop that you were painting for Macready for his production in Drury Lane – must have been in the summer of 1838. I would have been about fourteen years old at the time, not very interested in painting, but my imagination was captured by the size of the diorama which he described in such detail to me.'

The kind old man looked at with an admiring smile. 'What a memory you have. Yes, that's right,' he said. 'It would have been 1838. Our friend, Dickens, was writing *Nicholas Nickleby*, Macready was playing Macbeth in Drury Lane . . .'

'And Frances Jarman was playing opposite to him,' I said. 'I was too young to remember her, but my mother was an admirer of hers.' I had no idea whether that was true or not, but it certainly fitted in with my mother's personality that she would declare that the female actress was every bit as worthy of applause as was the male.

'That's right,' said Clarkson slowly. He did not stop to question my assertion or search his memory or even contradict me. The fact that Frances Jarman had been part of that circle was fresh in his mind.

'Heard some story about her husband . . .' I stopped as though from diffidence.

Clarkson nodded sadly. 'Ended in an asylum,' he said. 'Not then, but certainly later. Nelly was a tiny child. Bethnal Green. Insanity, they say. Brought on by syphilis, of course.'

'His wife?' I hinted.

'They had separated, lived apart for some time before,' said Clarkson. 'He had gone back to live with his brother in Rochester. She had little contact, I think and who could blame her.'

There was, I thought, at the back of both our minds, the terrible risk that Frances would run if she had lived as a wife with a man riddled with syphilis. I wondered when they had separated.

'But the child, little Nelly?' I was treading on dangerous grounds here, but I felt that I had to know the truth. Something did not ring true about this separation.

'Well, that was years before,' said Clarkson dismissively, but I saw by his eyes that his thoughts had followed mine. I had not known Dickens back in the last years of the 1830s; in fact, I had not met him until recent years, but I imagined that he with his kindness, his enthusiasm, and his entertaining companionship, may have been devastatingly attractive to a lonely woman who had been betrayed by her husband in the bitterest and most dangerous fashion.

Daniel Maclise had painted a portrait of Dickens in 1839, the year of Nelly's birth. It hung in his house and I had often admired it and privately contrasted the glowing young face, and the smooth glossy hair with my friend as he was now: grizzled hair, lined face, pouches under his eyes. His unceasing toil had stamped age on his features and his grey hair and beard made him look older than he was, in fact. But in 1838 he had been a most handsome young man.

'She must have been very beautiful then – Frances, I mean,' I said calling to mind the perfect oval of the face, the very lovely eyes and the pale gold of the hair.

'Yes,' admitted Clarkson. 'We all admired her immensely!' He said the words in a low voice, almost to himself and I could see that he was visualizing a picture that I could only guess at.

I gazed absent-mindedly at his painting while I conjured up the scene of those days long gone by. Dickens, now and for the whole of his life, from what he had told me, had been fascinated by the theatre, loved to smell the greasepaint, to stand before the limelight, absorb the atmosphere of make-believe. Add to that the vision of a lonely woman, weighed down by responsibilities, but caring for her two little girls, earning a living for them and bearing her burden with dignity and acting with all the grace and the charm which she still possessed, but which, almost twenty years ago, would have been enhanced by the patina of youth. A devasting temptation to a young man in his twenties whose wife was incapacitated by post-natal problems.

'And Nelly?' I watched his face and saw him start. I could have sworn that a fresh, new thought had entered his mind, the thought which had already sprung into my mind.

'You are turning into a gossip, young Collins,' he said with an attempt at humour. 'Now, tell me what is happening upstairs.'

'It's a pity that Nelly doesn't have a father. That policeman was frightening the life out of the poor little girl,' I said, still watching him carefully. I thought that I could guess what thoughts were going through his head. If anyone understood Dickens, I had often thought, it was not Foster who made such a play of being Dickens' oldest and closest friend, but this unassuming man who had once been a sailor and was now one of the most successful artists in London. He and Dickens had been friends for over thirty years.

I gave him a nod and then went in search of my friend Barrymore the butler. By now I was enough at home in the social world into which Dickens had plunged me, to know that in one of these houses of the rich, the man who knows what is going on will invariably be the butler. I ran him to earth in the cellar, where he was thoughtfully sipping some claret.

'What do you think, Mr Collins,' he said, 'the Bordeaux or the Burgundy? Try a sip of both, but chew on a piece of bread in between. The cook tells me that the master has ordered a beefsteak pie to please Mr Dickens. Not something that we have too often in this house so I've been trying to decide which wine will go best with it.'

'The Burgundy,' I said after taking somewhat more than the recommended sip.

'I was more inclined towards the claret myself, but you could be right,' he said, pouring us both some more of the Burgundy, murmuring, 'Steak and kidney,' and then nodding gravely. 'The Burgundy it is, then,' he said.

'I'll drink to that,' I said, and he kept me company with a couple of generous glassfuls.

'What's going on with the police?' I asked after we had both managed to finish a decanter between us.

'New man coming. Down from Scotland Yard. Put this fellow's nose out of joint,' he confided. 'Name of Inspector Field.'

'He's a friend of Mr Dickens,' I said. Whether it was the news or the wine, but I began to feel very enthusiastic. Inspector Field had a great opinion of Dickens.

The butler absorbed that information without comment. He had drunk enough of the Burgundy wine to mellow him, though and so he gave me a wink.

'Thought something like that would happen,' he said. 'Don't want any scandal involving a lady, do they? Not that lady, anyway. Mark my words, sir; they'll work something out.'

'You're a man who knows how these things are done,' I said. I wasn't quite sure what I meant, but I was sober enough to know that the butler was referring to Lady Rosina, not to a young actress when he used the word 'lady'. I began to feel a little more optimistic and decided to do my best to relieve Nelly's mind when I saw her at dinner.

TEN

Nothing in this world is hidden forever . . . the laws of
nature: the lasting preservation of a secret is a miracle
which the world has never yet seen.

Wilkie Collins, *No Name*

She wasn't there, though. Her mother came down to
dinner alone. When I came into the dining room, late
as usual, I heard her tell Lord Edward that her daughter
had a headache and had retired to bed with a few drops of
laudanum. Discreet and gently spoken though she normally
was, Frances was forced by Lord Edward's deafness to
raise and project her voice as though she were on the stage.
Everyone, including the servants, heard every word of the
excuse. There was a moment's silence as she made that
announcement and most people exchanged looks with neigh-
bours. There was an uneasy atmosphere at the table and most
people, I guessed, wished that *The Lady of Lyons* was over
and done with.

'Why not cancel this bloody play?' I said in a whisper to
Mark Lemon as I passed him in order to take my place beside
his wife.

He looked at me uneasily. 'I did suggest it to Lord Edward,'
he said and then said no more, just crumbling his bread and
waiting for his soup plate to be filled.

'Don't eat too much of that bread; there's a very substantial
steak and kidney pie coming,' I warned him. 'and Dickens
has requested double helping for everyone. I heard him
myself.' I had heard nothing of the sort, but, oddly, as a
friend of Dickens, I usually felt bound to uphold his reputation as the warm-hearted author of 'Pickwick' and of 'Oliver
Twist' who wanted all of his readers to eat copious meals
and drink draughts of warming punch, winter and summer,

at all available opportunities. The fact that he, personally, ate very little and drank sparingly of any alcoholic beverage generally passed unnoticed.

As usual, we were eating in the oak dining parlour, not a big room, barely large enough to fit the rosewood, satinwood-banded table and the twelve chairs, made from apple wood, as our host had informed everyone on the first evening. We all had to take his word for the apple wood, though, as the red velvet cushions hid all but the ornately twisted legs, stained an un-apple-like shade of murky black. They were, I had told him on the first day of my visit, some of the most comfortable chairs I had ever sat upon, but he had stared at me coldly and said something about Jacobean embroidery.

Not a good host, Lord Edward, I had decided days ago. Despite the intimacy of the room, the beauty of the furniture and of the gilt, carved candelabra that lined the centre of the table, there was an atmosphere of awkward feeling among the guests. The plight of a fatherless girl who had been grilled by a policeman and was now lying on her mother's bed with a sick headache caused almost all to swallow their soup in an uncomfortable silence.

But Mark Lemon's wife, Helen, was made of sterner stuff. 'I'm so glad that we are sitting together, Mr Collins,' she whispered with that air of roguish flirtation which, for some reason, middle-aged and overweight women seemed invariably to adopt with me.

'Oh, so am I; so very glad,' I whispered back, wondering whether I was supposed to elope with her.

She giggled mischievously. 'I've got a little gossip for you.'

'Have you, indeed!' I said and this time my enthusiasm was not feigned. I leaned eagerly towards her and she cast a surreptitious glance at her husband on her other side.

'Mark tells me not to gossip,' she said in my ear, 'but I overheard something, Mr Collins, and I am dying to pass it on.'

'It would be your duty,' I told her with a sort of mock seriousness that seemed to fit the occasion. Nevertheless, despite my light tone, I listened eagerly.

'Well, you know I have a passion for statuary,' she said, and went on without a perceptible pause. 'I was just admiring that amazing statue of Diana when I heard our host's voice. Well, Mr Collins, I was in an awkward position: if I withdrew, I would encounter the maid polishing the hall table and she would wonder what I had been doing and so I stayed where I was and did my best not to listen.'

'A very difficult thing to do, since his voice is so loud, so penetrating,' I murmured with a glance up at Lord Edward.

She beamed at me. 'You are so right. Almost impossible to shut one's ears, is it not?'

And with that out of the way, she leaned over towards me and whispered loudly, 'It was Dr Hill that he was talking to.'

'Dr Hill,' I repeated.

'Yes,' she said impatiently. 'Do you remember the talk of Dr Hill? Do you remember what Lady Rosina said?'

'Yes, of course,' I said. 'Yes, Lady Rosina mentioned him, did she not? He was one of the doctors who had been responsible for her treatment, isn't that right?'

'You remember what she said, don't you?' Mrs Lemon was impatient with me and my slowness. 'I can just hear her saying it,' she went on. 'Don't you remember her words? "I'm sick to death, worn to a thread and so would everyone here be if they were incarcerated by two such scoundrels as Dr Hill and fat old Dr Connolly."'

'And so Dr Hill turned up here, at Knebworth,' I said, and my eyes went to Lady Rosina, telling a theatre anecdote to John Foster. She seemed lively, animated and in a very good humour. I wondered whether she had heard of the visit.

'That's right. They were talking in the hall and I heard every word of it,' hissed Helen Lemon. 'Of course, *he* ' – she cast a contemptuous glance at Lord Edward – 'of course, *he* was making a big fuss about his concern for his wife and his certainty that she needed treatment, but Dr Hill interrupted him and this is what he said.' She had a quick look around and then whispered in my ear. '"I'm most sorry not to be able to help you, Lord Edward, but I do not feel that Lady Rosina's case is one that I can handle." Turned him right down,' said Mrs Lemon with an air of satisfaction before she swallowed some of her soup. 'Of course,' she resumed after dabbing her mouth with a napkin, 'he was concerned for his job, and for that new "asylum" that he has put so much money into – after all, Lady Rosina had made a great fuss, had caused questions to be asked in high places. Disraeli, I heard. Her son had to join in the controversy, then. Had to talk with his father.'

'And it worked,' I said, seeing that she expected a response. I had a poor opinion of 'high places' – government circles, she meant, I thought. Surely the people in charge of a country should be concerned about justice for all wives. Nevertheless, these sorts of questions could get into newspapers and governments dreaded the scrutiny of newspapers.

'Caused a lot of trouble and, of course, a man running a business, running an asylum for ladies with "nerve" problems, an asylum which would seem worth the high fees to the husbands, certainly his name in the papers was the last thing that he needed, but, of course,' she said in a knowing fashion, 'of course, Dr Hill laid it out in the usual medical language, felt that "the dear lady might be better off in familiar surroundings" and he could "recommend a local practitioner, someone in whom Lord Edward could have complete trust". And so,' completed Mrs Lemon in a tone of satisfaction, 'our host will have to think again, won't he? What do you think that he will do with her? It's obvious that he hates having her here in his beloved house.'

Mrs Lemon stopped and looked around. Lady Rosina was talking across the table to Frances Jarman, enquiring about her daughter. There was something about the lady, an unusual loudness of voice, perhaps, that seemed as though she were permanently on stage, acting the part of mistress of the house when she was aware that the master of the house would do anything to get rid of her. What did she really want, I wondered? Yes, it was obvious that her husband did not want his wife in the house, but it was equally obvious that she loathed and detested him.

'Money,' I said in Mrs Lemon's ear. 'Money will solve the

problem. That's why she came here. He makes her an allowance, has made it since she got free of that asylum, but she
thinks it's not enough. Says that she can only afford to have
one servant and to rent an unpleasant few rooms for herself
and the servant. She came here to make trouble – enough
trouble to make him long to get rid of her as soon as possible.
You mark my words, Helen – either today or tomorrow he
will offer her money and then she will go.'

'No, she won't! Look at her face, Wilkie! She's really
enjoying herself. She wants to be back here; she wants to
be the lady of the manor again. She won't allow herself to be
turfed out again. She's got their son on her side. He protested
to the father, you know. You mark my words, Wilkie. By hook
or by crook she'll hang on here, she'll revolutionize this house.
Put her own stamp upon it. He'll have to shoot her to get rid
of her.'

'Won't be much fun for her, though, will it? Not with him
glaring at her and trying to oust her and denigrating her in
the presence of his servants and his employees. No,' I said,
beginning to enjoy this conversation, 'no, my dear Helen,
you've got the story all wrong. You must permit me, as a
novelist – well, I've had a couple of books published, anyway
– no, I must insist on writing the end of this story of *Man*
versus *Woman*. *She* shoots *him*. That would work well as an
ending to the story, wouldn't it? She'd be a good mistress to
this house. Her son, Robert, won't interfere. He has his own
career in the diplomatic service. Ambassador out in Vienna
at the moment, so I believe. No, that's the way that the story
will go. She'll make a wonderful hostess. Look at the way
she manages the conversation at the table – wheresoever she
sits there is animation among the guests.' I swallowed another
glass of the excellent Burgundy wine which I had chosen
earlier and, feeling rather drunk, more with the exuberance
of my own verbosity, as Disraeli put it once, than with the
amount I had consumed, I filled her glass as well as my own
and declaimed, rather more loudly than I intended. 'She
stands at her window and shoots him when he takes his
evening stroll!'

I suddenly realized that my voice had reached far beyond

its intended recipient, so I waved my glass in the air and said, 'New book! Title: *Who Killed Him?* Drink to its success.' I gave an apologetic glance up at Dickens who, good fellow that he is, threw his hands up into the air, gave a hearty laugh and raised his glass in my direction.

'And now a toast to the steak and kidney pie, my favourite dish!' he said as a footman came in bearing on an enormous dish the biggest steak and kidney pie that I had ever seen. My indiscreet remark was lost in the chorus of exclamations and toasts were drunk in a more abandoned fashion than normally happened at Knebworth. The whole table benefitted from that giddy moment of indiscretion and the rest of the dinner passed in a buzz of conversation. So animated was the discussion between myself and Mark Lemon, leaning across his wife to engage me in a controversy about the latest *Punch* magazine that I did not notice that Frances Jarman had slipped from the room and only became aware of it when Lady Rosina got to her feet.

'I must go and see if the poor little girl is well,' she said in a loud and very clear voice. 'She is a visitor in this house, a very young girl, and she should have been protected by her host and shielded from the bullying of a police sergeant.' She stared at her husband with a contemptuous gaze and then smiled at everyone around the table. 'I'm sure you will forgive me if I go and see that all is well,' she said, and this time she did not include Lord Edward in her glance.

The biscuits and the cheese proved to be ideal with my Burgundy discovery from our host's wine cellars and so, deep in a rowdy conversation with Augustus Egg, I did not notice some empty places until Dickens came behind my chair and touched me on the shoulder. He handed me a cup of strong coffee, but no sooner than I had swallowed it down, his hand was beneath my elbow and I found myself on my feet.

'Let's have a stroll by moonlight,' he said and firmly steered me from the table, through the door, down the entrance hall and out into the moonlit night. We paced the terrace in silence. The fog had lifted, and the air was cool. I had the early beginnings of a headache, but the air improved it.

'I wasn't particularly drunk,' I said resentfully to Dickens.

'No, it's not that. I wanted to talk to you.' His voice was low, and I saw that he glanced at the upper windows of the ornate pile of stone beside us.

'What's wrong?' I had been enjoying myself in there. Had felt as though I were the life and the soul of the party. The wine had robbed me of a slightly uneasy feeling that I usually experienced at Lord Edward's table and I had a vague memory of uttering some very witty remarks and making some good jokes.

'It's not that,' he repeated. His voice was quiet, but it held a serious note that helped more of the alcohol to evaporate from my bloodstream. He gave me a moment and it was only when I stopped and turned to look at him, that he spoke again.

'Nelly has disappeared,' he said.

'Disappeared!' I said stupidly. 'She can't have. I saw her earlier. I handed her a letter just before dinner.'

'Her mother has searched everywhere.' His voice was quiet. 'We went together through the house and even out into the park. Went to the stable yard, also. All was peaceful there. Your friend, the noble dog, was fast asleep in his kennel. You know nothing about this, do you?'

'Of course not,' I said. I shook my head. The fumes of the drink were making me still a little light-headed.

'Who was her letter from?'

'How on earth should I know? Oh, I know. I remember now. She said something. She was pleased when I handed it to her. Her face lit up, she felt the envelope and then she smiled. She said something – what was it? A girl's name – but I can't remember what name.'

'What letter did it begin with?' Dickens believed strongly in his powers to hypnotize people and now he was staring intently at me.

'How would I know?' I repeated.

'A – Angela, Amy; B – Beth, Belinda—'

'Stop,' I said. 'You are confusing me. Give me a minute to think. I handed her the letter. She stood there. She felt the

letter, squeezed the envelope and then she said something, just
to herself, I remember that she smiled. Yes, I know now. She
said "Maria" and then she smiled as if she was pleased.'

'Maria is her sister, one of her sisters. And she squeezed
the letter. That's very valuable information.'

'Why?' I asked. My brain still felt fuzzy and I was conscious
of a feeling of resentment. He was always so clever, always
so sure of himself, always treating me as though I were not
at all as intelligent as he was. And then it came to me. 'Money,'
I said. 'Her sister sent her money.'

'I think that we should take a walk to the railway station.
Can't have been too many people getting a train in the evening.
Wait here while I go and have a word with Frances and tell
her that we are on the trail.'

He was back within minutes. A sensible woman, Frances
Jarman. She would not have detained him or wanted to come
with him. She would have known that the least said the best
and that two men, having eaten a large dinner, could stroll off
down the road without exciting any interest or without it
coming to the ears of an inquisitive police officer. The longer
that Nelly's absence could be concealed, the easier it would
be to avert suspicion.

'Why have the police picked upon her, poor girl?' I asked
as we walked at Dickens' brisk pace down the road to
Knebworth station.

He looked at me sideways without slackening his strides.
'Can't you guess?'

'No,' I said, concealing my irritation. Dickens, good fellow
though he was, always had to be quicker and cleverer than
anyone else in his company. The easiest way to get along with
him was to allow this to be the cornerstone of our acquaintance and not to rebel against it. 'Tell me,' I added
invitingly.

I expected him to make a joke, to jest about himself being
the fountain of all knowledge. But he did not. He had been very
sombre since he had returned from his meeting with Frances.
He had one of those very focussed looks on his face, the expression he wore when he was determined to achieve a goal, even
though that goal might seem to be impossible to most men.

That was the right approach. Any attempt to appear knowing, or even any attempt to guess would have irritated him even more. Now he just nodded at me.

'Who would be the main suspect otherwise?' he asked, and then, when I didn't reply instantly, his impatience mastered him. 'Think about it, Wilkie. You're a decent, hardworking girl, reliant on the good opinion of others in order to earn your daily bread. Not only that, but you have been brought up by a decent, hardworking mother, who, also, was dependent on goodwill, and she, in her turn, was brought up by her mother, who was also on the stage and also reliant on goodwill for her bread. What do you think the life of those girls are like, in reality?' he enquired. 'I know I wrote some sort of nonsense, glorifying their profession, but one of the first things they are taught is to avoid rape, not to make a fuss because that might alienate their employers, but to be clever, to be adroit, not to be alone with a man whom they can't trust, but if any situation arises they have to get out of it as well they can and then – and this is the important point, Wilkie – they are trained by their mothers, their aunts and their sisters, not to make a fuss afterwards, just to treat it as a learning process, and resolve not to place themselves in this situation again. Do you seriously think that little Nelly, having escaped from the obnoxious secretary's attempts to rape would then shoot him as soon as she had a gun near to her hand? Of course she wouldn't. She would have been brought up to tell herself to avoid being near to him again, unless she had protection. She would have been brought up to tell her mother or her sisters, but, otherwise, to keep her mouth firmly shut on the matter and I would say that it would be a chance in a million to think that she would shoot him.'

He said nothing about his son, I noticed. Young Charley was not brought up like that. He was the son of a famous writer, was educated at Eton and lived in a beautiful country house with horses and dogs and everything that a boy might want. I said nothing about Charley, either. I was fond of the boy. In any case, Dickens, I knew, was building up to the climax of his speech. He swiped at a clump of cow parsley in the ditch and neatly decapitated it with his stick. And then he stopped and looked at me.

'But when you come to Lady Rosina, well this is a very different female with a very different upbringing. In the first place,' he said, resuming his rapid walk and swinging his stick with an eye for more prey in the roadside weeds, 'in the first place, my dear Wilkie, the woman is Irish and we all know that the Irish are hot-tempered and impulsive. In the second place her mother was a radical feminist, one of these women that think they are better than any man and she brought up her daughter to despise the other sex. In the third place, she was educated in London by another feminist and a poet, if you please. And when she was there her best friend was the wife of poor William Lamb, that notorious Lady Caroline and goodness knows what she didn't do to alarm polite society. More Irish blood, there,' concluded Dickens with a strange note of admiration in a voice which he strove to make sound censorious. 'So,' he said briskly, 'when it comes to taking a potshot at a man who has offended her, which, if you were a policeman, would you chose for a suspect: a gentle, well-brought-up little actress, used to concealing offences against her and making the best of everything, or a woman like Rosina Bulwer-Lytton whose life has been a long rebellion against all the values which polite society holds good?'

Dickens did not wait for my answer but supplied it instead. 'Well, the police of this country are not stupid. Of course, if anyone were to take a potshot at a man whom she assumed was her husband, it was going to be Lady Rosina. She was there, standing there behind stage, a revolver in her handbag – and you can bet that it was a loaded one. She was brought up to be wild, galloping through the countryside on horses, shooting foxes from a young age! All her dangerous passions aroused by the hated presence of her husband who has treated her badly. Well, of course, she would have been the first to be suspected.'

And with an air of triumph, Dickens spotted another yard-high, defiantly flowering, stalk of cow parsley and snapped its hollow stem in half. 'Very bad for cows, that stuff,' he said by way of explanation. 'It's hemlock, you know. Poisons the beasts. A farmer told me that once and I've been trying to destroy as many as I can ever since.'

'But Lady Rosina?' I stammered. I had a feeling that there was a difference between hemlock and cow parsley, but I never argued with Dickens about matters to do with the countryside. Ever since he had bought Gad's Hill in Kent, he had adopted the mantle of a country squire, born and bred.

'Well, if you are a policeman, liable to be criticized in the newspapers or in Parliament, would you accuse a titled lady, wife of a lord and mother of an ambassador, would you accuse her of murder? Not unless you caught her in front of a hundred witnesses with a smoking gun in her hand.' With a satisfied air, Dickens twirled his stick in the air and scanned the hedgerows for any more cow parsley.

I took his word for it. It was unfair, but this was the country, not London, and from what I could see, the nobility was treated with far more respect and deference than they were in the capital city. A matter of rarity, I supposed, with each town having just one stately home and one revered owner.

'So, you think that the police are harassing poor Nelly because they dare not tackle Lady Rosina, but in reality they think it was Lady Rosina who fired the shot,' I said. I thought about the matter for a moment. 'Could she do it? A woman? At her age?'

'Bet she shot rats when she was a girl; she had that sort of upbringing. Someone told me that she boasted of not learning to read until she went to school in London when she was fourteen. She said that she had lived as a tomboy and was seldom indoors and that no governess would stay with her.'

'I can imagine her shooting her husband, and shooting him in public,' I said, 'but I don't think she would bother to conceal any act like that. She is hot-blooded and impulsive. Look at the way that she hurled the plates at Lord Edward. Nothing furtive about that, was there?'

'So, you think that little Nelly did it,' he said, looking at me keenly.

'No,' I said. 'I'm convinced by what you say about her upbringing, I'm convinced that Maguire's loathsome behaviour was something that she would have been warned about by her mother and her sister, and I'm convinced that she probably would feel the threat was over if she made sure not to go alone into secluded spots – but I still don't believe that Lady Rosina did it. I think she despises her husband too much to bother shooting him. I have been thinking about what you said about the money aspect, but don't you think that she is the kind of woman who would go to the law to get back her rights, go to Parliament, even, make a huge fuss. There's even talk of presenting a bill to Parliament which would give the same rights to married women as unmarried women possess. You've heard of that, I'm sure, Dick.'

'Good point,' said Dickens with the air of a generous man. 'No, all I am saying is that the police, I feel very sure, fear, and I say *fear*, that it may be Lady Rosina. They will remember her turning up at the hustings when our host was about to make his bid for Parliament, and they will remember her violence and lack of womanly reticence on that occasion. Finding her here, finding that she was present behind the stage when the man was murdered, hearing, no doubt from servants, about her violent outbreak the day before, I would venture to assert that she would immediately become the focus of suspicion. But then, the sergeant, a cautious man, would shudder at the thought of the newspaper coverage, shudder at the questions to be asked by his superiors in Scotland Yard, would imagine that he would be regarded as being slow with his investigations. He has to find a suspect, has to trick Nelly into some damaging admissions, arrest her with enough evidence to convince a jury and then hand the matter over to the lawyers.'

His words, measured and reasonable, made me shudder with apprehension. 'She's only a child,' I said.

'She's a young woman. She's seventeen years old. Young children, and I mean young children, have been hanged before now. Good God, Wilkie, I've seen children condemned to death and they were so small that they had to be lifted up so that the judge could see them before he passed sentence.'

'I shudder at your words, Dick,' I said, and felt glad that I had abandoned the law and was now, like himself, a writer. 'But Nelly,' I said diffidently.

There was a long pause. He had quickened his steps so much that I found it hard to keep up with him and pounded along behind, hoping for some reassurance. He said nothing, just looked straight ahead of him and ignored a patch of wickedly flowering cow parsley or deadly hemlock.

'You believe that the police think it was Lady Rosina but are diverting attention by trying to fix suspicions on an obscure young actress like Nelly,' I said breathlessly. I managed to catch hold of his sleeve forcing him to halt and to face me. 'But, Dickens, we can't allow that to happen. She and her mother would have no money to pay for a lawyer – she might hang. If Lady Rosina is brought to court, it will be a *cause célèbre*. Her husband will be forced by the weight of popular opinion to find a lawyer to defend her. The verdict of the court, if they find her guilty, will be to pronounce her insane and Lord Edward will get his way and put her back into that cosy little asylum where she is allowed to go for drives and to walk in gardens. But Nelly,' I concluded, 'Nelly will hang.'

I saw his jaw set and was satisfied with the effect of my words. Dickens would be a formidable opponent for any village policeman. He said nothing, though, but went on walking fast towards the station of Knebworth and I toiled behind him.

The ticket office wasn't manned when we reached the station, but a uniformed railway man came out instantly when Dickens rapped on its window. He recognized the famous author, of course. Opened up the office, instantly! Aghast and wondering what to do!

'Oh, Mr Dickens,' he said. 'I'm terribly sorry. The last train to London has gone half an hour ago. There won't be another until morning.'

Dickens was quick to reassure him. 'Just wondering if a

friend of mine, a young lady, managed to catch it after all,' said Dickens, who was never at a loss for a story.

'No young lady, Mr Dickens. The only one who got on the eight o'clock train was Mr Hobbs, the butcher.'

'And the train before that?'

'You mean the lunchtime one, Mr Dickens, do you?' And then when the man saw that the famous author looked baffled, he pointed at the timetable on the wall next to the booking office. 'Only three trains in the day, Mr Dickens. All of them going to London. The nine o'clock in the morning – that's the one sitting in the station just now. And then there is the one at lunch time, the shopping train, we call it, and then the eight in the evening train. That's the lot, Mr Dickens.'

'You must have made a mistake, Collins. She must have said tomorrow. That's good, I can return her signed book to her before she leaves.' Dickens, as usual, invented a little story around our enquiry and I was to play the part of the absent-minded man who got things wrong. I had almost begun to believe in this mythical fan with her copy of his latest book by the time that he had finished.

'Wonderful having you here, Mr Dickens,' said the railway man. 'Puts us up in the world, having a famous author like yourself visiting the village. My wife won't believe me when I go home and tell her that I spoke to you yourself.'

'Let's convince her, then, shall we?' Dickens by now was an old hand at this publicity game. He took a stray ticket to London from the board behind the window and scribbled his name and the date and even managed to fit his famous flourish beneath the signature. 'There you are,' he said. 'Proof positive. There is not a living person in the world who can reproduce my flourish, isn't that right, Collins?'

We left amidst the admiration of some porters and clerks who had all emerged from their last cup of tea of the day, refused offers to summon a taxi and set off on the walk home. The fog had completely disappeared, and the moon was full. A lovely evening and very little chill in the air. I wondered where little Nelly was, and whether, despite the booking clerk's denial, she had managed to slip on to the train when he wasn't looking.

If she hadn't gone to London, and she wasn't with her mother, where could she be? I thought of Charley and wondered whether he knew.

ELEVEN

Death takes the good, the beautiful, and the young –
and spares me.

Wilkie Collins, *The Woman in White*

Charley was waiting at the gate when we arrived back. 'Any sign of her?' he called out when we approached. 'No, she didn't take the London train, apparently,' said Dickens. He had a slight note of disapproval in his voice. Almost as though he were about to say to his son: 'What is your concern in the matter, young man?' but he suppressed a further comment with a visible effort.

'Her mother is very anxious.' Charley was a sensitive boy and had picked up the nuance of disapproval from his father's voice. 'I've been thinking. I wonder whether Wilkie's dog – I mean Lord Edward's dog, Bruno – might be able to track her down? Would it be worth a try? I asked Mrs Jarman for something belonging to Nelly and she gave me this glove.' He took from his pocket a small pink glove and held it out to us.

'What a good idea.' I spoke quickly in order to forestall any objections from Dickens, who I knew would not like his son to display any undue anxiety or connection with a young actress. I took the glove from Charley, put it in my pocket and turned to Dickens. 'Don't you bother coming, Dick,' I said. 'The more strangers around, the more the likelihood of the dog being confused.' I left him, rapidly, and jerking my head at Charley made my way towards the stable yard.

I had, I must say, very little hope of this succeeding. A Great Dane was not a bloodhound. I had never heard of these dogs being used for tracking. As far as I knew they were not bred for anything other than size. Their function was to run beside a carriage and deter highwaymen. Nevertheless, I sympathized with Charley's desire to do something, rather than to wait for his little love to turn up. He would have a sleepless night, in any case, I guessed.

I was getting very worried by now. The obvious thing for Nelly to do was to get the train to London and to seek refuge with her sisters. There would be a network of young actresses in the big city, all friendly with each other, and it seemed to me, from what I knew of actresses, that they changed their place of abode with great regularity. Nelly could be found easily by the police if she went back to Park Cottage beside Northumberland Park, but if lodged in some back street near to Drury Lane or Haymarket, she would be impossible to find and the acting community would be most unlikely to think that it was their duty to help the police to seek out one of their own.

If she hadn't gone to London, where was she now? I strode along the well-raked gravel paths as quickly as I could and was aware that Charley was making his way through the gardens not far from me.

He arrived at the stable yard before me, and it was lucky that he did because the stable manager and the boy, Jim, were shutting up the stables for the night and minutes later they would both have been gone. All the horses were locked in, heads still looking over the doors and the yard was swept clean. Bruno was lapping loudly from his water plate and Jim was washing another plate under the tap.

Charley was explaining all when I arrived, and the stable manager was listening to him. Even by the uncertain light of the moon I could see a sceptical expression on the man's face. He greeted my arrival with relief.

'Just explaining to the young sir that this here dog ain't trained to tracking,' he said to me. He gazed sceptically down at the small pink glove. 'Don't think that he'd know what he was supposed to do, sir,' he said to Charley.

'Yes, but we can try. Walk him around the park.' Charley wasn't as upset as I would have expected; perhaps he had anticipated this response. He was probably more used, than I, to dealing with these country people and their stubbornness as he spent a lot of his time at his father's country estate at Gad's Hill. Also, he had more knowledge of large dogs than I as his father kept several.

'I'll go too. And then I can put the dog back in his kennel and lock up everything,' said Jim enthusiastically. 'You can trust me.'

'And I'll make sure that everything is safe,' I said reassuringly. I fingered a coin in my waistcoat pocket but did not produce it. This was a man responsible for the safety and well-being of a lot of valuable animals and I did not want to appear to bribe him into doing anything which he felt might imperil his charges. 'We shouldn't be more than a half an hour,' I added. Someone had told me that Knebworth Park was about 250 acres. I had no idea how long it would take to walk around it, but I felt that if Jim ran up paths with the dog towing him, and Charley, also running, following him, that the place could be searched fairly quickly without undue exertion on my part. After all, a dog should be able to smell a human from a distance. Surely, he would bark or something if he scented Nelly. I didn't know, but I wanted to back up Charley and to help him to do something which would relieve his anxiety for the moment. Poor lad! He faced a sleepless night, I feared.

The dog was puzzled. I could see that. This was out of his normal routine. He kept looking up at the boy as if to ask why he was not, by now, bedded down in the straw and sleeping off the effects of his dinner. It might be a bad idea to allow him to run. I suddenly remembered my father telling me never to exercise my dog after he had eaten his evening meal.

'We'll keep together until he shows signs of scenting something,' I said to Charley and he agreed. Dickens had a couple of Newfoundland dogs and Charley, like me, had probably remembered that these large dogs who had just eaten a meal should not be exercised. It was easy enough to walk up and down the paths at a steady pace and to keep an eye on the dog to see whether he showed any interest.

We had been out for about a quarter of an hour, I reckoned, when I saw a light appear in the window at the top of one of the towers. A shadow of a man, appearing just like a silhouette against the panes. I knew who it was instantly. I had been in that high room close to the roof, and the long nose, high forehead and straggly beard made it certain that Lord Edward

Bulwer-Lytton looked down upon us. I wondered whether he had seen us on the moonlit path and decided, more for Jim's sake than for my own, that I did not want to have to explain what we were doing to the master of the house.

'Let's take him into the maze,' I said in a low voice to Jim, and he turned readily and found a shortcut across the grass to the entrance to the maze. Bruno wagged his tail enthusiastically as I took his lead from the boy and led the way in. It was a good decision, I thought. The tall yew trees and the hawthorn hedges which surrounded the maze would hide us from any gaze from the top of the house and it was very probable that Nelly might have sought a hiding place there if she were trying to escape from her tormentor, the police sergeant.

Bruno and I paced the paths and the other two followed in silence. The night was very still, except for the odd hoot of an owl and one shriek which probably signalled the death of a rabbit. No one spoke and I reckoned that the boy must be getting tired of the expedition and probably wished that he were back in the snug house of his adoptive father and mother. Bruno, I thought, was puzzled. From time to time he turned his large head and looked back at me as though waiting for instructions. A sort of dread had crept over me. I remembered the dead body of the secretary, Tom Maguire, and I wondered whether we would find another body tonight. Nelly, I thought, might well know who had taken that pistol from the table in that dark space; may have seen it replaced amid the chaos and confusion when everyone dashed on stage and stared at the dead man, some kneeling, some looking around helplessly. Looking back at that moment in the dark, I could not for the life of me be sure that everyone had been there, and even less could I be sure of what anyone did or from which direction that they approached. The shock of that dead body lying in the centre of the stage was so great that it acted on my memory like a damp sponge erasing all chalk marks from a surface.

'Seek, boy, seek!' I said once again in desperation to Bruno, and once again he turned his head and stared at me with his large eyes. No, as far as the dog was concerned, there was nothing to be found within the maze – no being, other than we ourselves, walked between those clipped hawthorn hedges. I would have to go back. Jim should be in his bed by now and his adoptative parents might well be worrying about him.

'Home, boy,' I said then, and the dog's ears drooped, catching the note of disappointment in my voice and he turned to go back. Charley said nothing. I had thought he would try to persuade me to go on trying, and was ready with my arguments, but he said nothing and we followed the sagacious dog as without hesitation he turned left and right and threaded his way through the confusing twists and turns and led us out from the enclosure.

'Home, boy, home, Bruno,' I repeated, and felt that the dog responded more enthusiastically this time. Dogs, from my experience, always liked their routine. As far as Bruno was concerned, his heavy evening meal should have been followed by a sleep on the straw in his kennel and he was now pleased to be heading back into that safe world of routine.

We had just turned on to the last avenue leading towards the stables when I heard a gasp. The dog heard it, too, and for the first time this evening, he gave a short, sharp bark.

'Who's there?' The voice was high-pitched, but steady. 'Stand still or I shoot. I have a pistol here in my hand and I can assure you that I never miss my aim!'

There was a flash of light before our eyes. I stood very still and said, 'Quiet, Bruno, quiet, boy!' I had recognized that voice. I was sure of that. 'It's Wilkie Collins, Lady Rosina, just myself and young Mr Dickens and the stable yard boy. No need for you to worry.'

The lantern came nearer, one of these kerosene lanterns with the shutter pulled back.

'Goodness, Mr Collins, what in the world are you doing out here at this time of the night?' she said coolly.

'I thought of asking you the same question and then I thought that I dare not,' I replied, and she laughed.

'Night-time, darkness, animals that prowl by the light of the moon, none of these hold any fears for me,' she said, and her voice was still quite steady and quite matter of fact. 'But what are you doing out of your bed at this time of the night, Mr Collins?'

'We're looking for Nelly,' said Charley and the note of desolation in his voice rang out.

'Poor boy,' she said. 'And poor little Nelly. This house is full of wickedness. You should leave it as soon as possible. Leave it, all of you.'

And with that she turned on her heel. By the light of her lantern I could see that she still held the pistol in her hand, and I wondered whether she had it cocked and ready to fire. A dangerous woman.

'Let's get you and Bruno back to bed,' I said reassuringly to Jim as I felt him grab nervously at my sleeve. I wondered whether Lady Rosina was completely sane. After all, what woman wanders by midnight around the grounds of her husband's estate brandishing a pistol?

'Quick march!' I said as cheerfully as I could when she had disappeared in the direction of the house. I still felt Jim's nervous grip on my sleeve, and I took his hand.

'Don't let me fall off this path,' I said in order to save his pride, but I was glad to feel the warm little hand in mine.

The lights of the stable manager's house were still on when we came back and I had a moment's compunction about keeping a hard-working man up so late.

'No, no sign,' I said as he came to the door. I slipped the coin into Jim's hand and handed over Bruno's lead.

'She'll turn up. Never you worry, sir,' said the boy's foster father to Charley and I guessed that the little love affair was known to all on the estate as well as to the servants and guests in the house.

When we were walking back, I repeated to him the man's words about not worrying and added, 'I reckon she has gone to London, to the house where she and her sisters live with their mother. These fellows at the station are probably quite unreliable.'

He said nothing and I looked up at his face as we emerged from the moonlight. Oddly, he didn't look worried. He was walking very fast, almost too fast for me to keep up with him and I thought that he almost wanted to put the memory of that useless search behind him.

'Your father will think of something in the morning,' I said as we parted, and I saw him smile for the first time that day. It was, though, a very odd smile. Not the smile of one who has been reassured. I often wondered what their relationship was, the diffident, mediocre son and the rich, immensely talented and immensely successful man, famous from the length and breadth of the country, famous too in America. What did Charley think when his father took everything out of his hands and always proved to know best? Did he ever yearn to get away from him, to make his own decisions and to marry where he wished to marry?

Dickens himself was sitting upon my bed, reading a slightly salacious magazine, lent to me by a young poet of my acquaintance. He lifted an eyebrow at me when I came in and allowed a half smile to part his lips, but said nothing, just returned his eyes to the magazine and deliberately read to the end of the page. Then he rolled it up and tossed it into the wastepaper basket beside the bed. I retrieved it, smoothed it out, placed it upon the bedside table, carefully weighing it down with a paperweight and a couple of books. And then I looked at him in an enquiring fashion.

'Well,' I said. 'What can I do for you, my dear Dickens?'

'Where's that boy of mine?' He, as he so often did, answered one question with another. 'In bed, I hope.'

'That's right,' I said. 'I gave him his bath, cleaned his teeth, brushed his hair, checked his fingernails and then I heard him say his prayers and popped him into bed.'

A glint from the eyes beneath the bushy eyebrows acknowledged a hit, but he did not deign to reply or to make any enquiry.

'You worry too much about Charley,' I said giving way to the temptation of handing him some good advice. It made a nice change in our relationship as he was forever bestowing advice upon me. 'When I was Charley's age,' I said warming to my task, 'I had been desperately in love with dozens of girls and the most respectable of them all was a young actress.'

'You're different,' he said. 'Charley is a sensitive boy. He takes these things seriously.' And then he said nothing else, just gazed broodingly into the fire.

'We couldn't find her.' I was the first to give way in this game of poker.

'Most likely she's gone to London.'

'But the ticket-seller . . .'

'Didn't go by Knebworth. Guessed the hunt for her would start there. Stevenage station is only a few miles down the road. Easy for her to walk, could even have got a lift. Country people are like that. Always offer lifts. They plague the life out of me when I'm going for a walk. Got into the habit now of just waving them on when I hear wheels grind to a halt behind me.' Dickens rapped out the sentences in a staccato fashion and looked at me to gauge how impressed I was.

'You may be right,' I said rather dubiously. It certainly did make sense. 'The only thing is that somehow I can't imagine Nelly having the sense to think of something like that. She's a sweet girl, but she doesn't seem too bright.'

'That's a part she plays,' he said briefly. 'She's fooled you, Collins. She's clever enough to know that she's not much of an actress so she puts all her efforts into portraying the sweet young girl. Works well with managers of theatres. She gets parts because she makes people sorry for her. Has her mother and her two sisters running around her. But she'll never be the actress that her mother was – was and is.' Dickens stared ahead of him for a minute and then, in his usual fashion, changed the subject.

'So, who shot the secretary, then?' he asked, eyeing me keenly.

'Who do you think?' I retorted. I had played this game too often with Dickens. He would ask my opinion, allow me enough time to twist myself into knots and then tell me roundly that I was completely wrong and that he, Dickens, knew the answer to the question and without any doubt in the world, his answer had to be the right one. He joked about it, of course, called himself the inimitable, declared that he was always right, in a tone that betrayed amusement at his own pretensions, but, deep down, he was, in fact, convinced that his opinion should be the last word on any question. It would be less fatiguing, I felt, if he came out with his own verdict before asking for my view.

He gave a nod now, as though acknowledging my good judgement and without any hesitation at all, said, 'Lady Rosina, of course.'

'Really?' I was betrayed into astonishment and he smiled kindly upon me.

'You're surprised.'

'I always think that when people do a lot of talking and utter a lot of menaces that they seldom perform what they have threatened,' I said, thinking that sounded quite wise.

He shook his head at me. 'Sane people, Wilkie, sane people. Lady Rosina is mad and therefore she doesn't care what she does or what she says. She's so full of hate that her only desire is to have vengeance.'

'Upon her husband,' I asked.

He grimaced. 'I can't make up my mind which one she meant to kill. The secretary, that unpleasant Tom Maguire, had laid hands upon her, was, she probably considered, instrumental in stirring up her husband's bad feelings towards her, but on the other hand these are all trivial matters compared to the deep well of hate which she has cultivated over the years—'

'Hatred of her husband, hatred of Lord Edward, is that what you are saying?'

Dickens nodded. 'They should never have married. His mother knew that. She was devoted to her son, but when he proposed marrying Miss Rosina Doyle Wheeler, she was so appalled that she did everything she could to stop him, even to the extent of threatening to halve his allowance.'

'But it didn't work.' I had heard this story so often and so often had thanked my lucky stars for the gift of a loving mother who was devoted to her two sons and who felt that everything they did was the right decision. 'What was her objection?'

'Bad blood,' said Dickens. 'Lady Rosina's own mother was a rebel, one of those women's rights protesters, contraception for women, all that sort of thing. Left her husband, said he was an abusive alcoholic and took her two daughters to stay with her own relations. And then there was this business of sending Rosina to that school in Kensington. Gave her ideas.'

'Shocking!' I said and waited for his reaction. He had strong views about a woman's place in the home: as a goddess on a pedestal, a warm presence in the kitchen, someone who was mistress of all domestic arts, who supported her husband and made no demands upon him. And as for contraception, well, I didn't think that as a father of about a dozen children, that he would have much truck with a woman who spoke of such matters in public.

'Oddly enough,' he said, ignoring my comment, 'that marriage was the making of him. Had his mother continued financing him completely he might well have sailed through life, making the odd speech in Parliament, doing his bit for his constituency of Ives and then of Lincoln, but when he found himself short of money and was still absolutely determined to marry the lady, why then he turned to writing novels in order to support them. If his mother had never withdrawn her support of him, or if Lord Edward had not married Rosina Doyle Wheeler, then the world would have lacked many fine books.'

'Hm.' I contented myself with the monosyllable. I had more important matters to discuss than my views on the popular books by Lord Edward. '"The deep well of hate", that's what you said, didn't you? And I agree with you. If Lady Rosina fired that shot, then I think that she thought that the man acting the part of the marquis was, as expected and as we all believed, her husband, not the secretary who was wearing the costume, wig and hat. I must say, Dickens, that I had no suspicion at all, not even when he began his speech.'

Dickens scratched meditatively the lower part of his little finger with his thumb and stared ahead. 'She is a quicker thinker than most; I would say that about her, the sort of woman who takes advantage of an opportunity. She was there in the dark, no one's eyes upon her, a loaded pistol in her handbag, the man that she desperately hated there on stage, lying prone on the floor. An easy shot for anyone used to handling a gun and remember that her childhood was, in her own words, that of tomboy, over there in Ireland: chasing foxes, shooting animals, hares, rats; nerve-racking cliff-climbing; even, I've heard the story, acting the part of a highwayman and holding up her own grandmother's coach;

everything that most women could never experience. No, indeed, Rosina Wheeler had the upbringing which would make it feasible that she could kill a man who had disgraced her and robbed her of her house and of her children.'

I had a feeling that Dickens was rehearsing something, that his words, which as he went on, carried more and more conviction, were meant not just for my ears but for the ears of someone of far greater importance. I was not surprised when he got to his feet, patted the cover of my bed and said, 'Well, Inspector Field will be with us first thing tomorrow morning.'

'And you "will open your poor mind to him",' I said, quoting Sir Thomas More. Dickens, I thought, was not familiar with the learned man, and his writings, as he looked at me with a slightly startled expression.

'I shall, of course, give any desired help to the forces of law and order,' he said in his most pompous fashion. 'Good night, Collins.' He sent the wish in a most perfunctory fashion, over his left shoulder, as he opened the door and closed it quietly behind him.

When he had gone, I did not go straight to bed but sat by the fire and stirred up its remains, casting a few handfuls of fire cones on the top of the embers and then adding some slim logs of an aromatic wood. My mind was concentrating intensely upon that murder. After all, I had been there. Surely, I could trace the trajectory of the bullet. I allowed my mind to wander over the scene on stage. Dickens' carpenter had built the set, built it so that it could be taken apart for storage and for conveying to different places, and then quickly reassembled again. The waiting place for the actors was at either side space, behind the stage and at a slight height above the stage. The backdrop was at the back of the stage, hanging from a pole, on a height reached by steps on either side of the back of the stage. There was a space behind the backdrop where the actors entering or leaving the stage could cross over to the other side so that players entered or exited either from the right or from the left, down a slope and on to the stage. High up behind all, behind the minstrels' gallery, on some steps and a narrow platform were positioned some of the lads from the stable and wood yards, standing poised, ready to roll up and roll down backdrops under the supervision of Clarkson.

The shot, I was almost sure, had come from on high, but how high? I thought back to the wooden screen of the minstrels' gallery and the perforations carved into it and tried to remember my view of the stage. It was hard to cast one's mind back exactly, and probably impossible to be sure, but I had a distinct impression that the man on stage had looked up in a startled fashion before . . . well, before his death, I supposed. Had he seen something on high, a flash, a face, even a pistol?

It was, I thought, a damnably complicated matter as there was no true way of knowing which man, Lord Edward, or his secretary Tom Maguire, was the intended victim. Almost everyone there would have thought, as I did myself, that it was, as planned, Lord Edward, but I had to bear in mind, and so, in all probability, would the police, that there was a possibility that Tom Maguire had been recognized and that he had been the intended victim. It had taken me aback to hear that Nelly had guessed that it wasn't Lord Edward when the man had glanced up at the creak of a board in the ceiling, thereby showing that he certainly was not deaf.

Nevertheless, I decided, I would pick Lord Edward as the intended victim. The murderer was Lady Rosina – so had Dickens declared. I would start with her. She had the opportunity. She had a pistol in her hand, and she was behind stage. I was not too far from her, but it was dark there, almost pitch black with just a glimmer of light from the closed lantern at the prompter's feet. Dickens had a good opportunity to look down over the stage, but knowing how conscientious he was, I knew that his eyes would have been fixed upon the script, following word by word the speech uttered by the actor on stage. And in this case, since he was the only one there who knew that Lord Edward was ill and that his place was taken by his understudy, Dickens would have been especially careful to be ready to prompt at the slightest hesitation.

Odd, I thought, allowing my mind to drift for a moment, that Dickens had such a high esteem for Lord Edward. Especially since he knew all about the treatment of the noble lord's spirited wife. And there was his treatment of his daughter, also. Neglected her. Had put her through painful and useless procedures to straighten her spine, to make her more of a prize on the marriage market. Had condemned her to a life-long dependency on laudanum. Surely Dickens knew all of this.

And now I was back to Lady Rosina again. Dickens had instantly plumped for her as the person that fired the shot. Yes, she had a pistol; yes, she was in a position where she could have aimed and hit her mark; yes, she was used, from an early age, to guns, used to firing to kill. Myself, I thought, if I picked up a gun and aimed it at someone, my hand would probably shake so badly that I would end up by shooting my own foot. But Lady Rosina, given an opportunity where she was in the dark and surrounded by others, might have taken a chance to have her revenge upon her husband for his bad treatment of her; might have gambled on doing the deed with impunity. It was well-known that juries hated to convict a woman of murder and it was unknown to have a titled lady convicted in the courts of such a crime.

And then I thought of Lady Rosina's words. 'This house is full of guns,' she had said. 'Anyone can go in and out and help themselves to one as the keys hang in the butler's room.'

TWELVE

We had our breakfasts – whatever happens in a house,
robbery or murder, it doesn't matter, you must have
your breakfast.

Wilkie Collins, *The Moonstone*

I slept well and once awake, got up and dressed quickly. No
sign of Nelly, said the girl who brought me my hot water
but, she told me, there was a crowd of young lads searching
the grounds for her. I was relieved to hear that, but somehow,
I thought that it was more likely that the girl had made her
way to London and would have been hidden by her sisters
and her sisters' actress friends. I shaved carefully and then
went to get my breakfast.

On time for once! Dickens was ahead of me, though. I saw
him on the bottom landing when I emerged from my room
and I hesitated and waited for a moment until I was sure that
he had gone into the breakfast parlour and had shut the door
behind him. He would eat his breakfast rapidly, I guessed, and
then he would set off to walk to the station in order to meet
the inspector arriving on the London train, taking the route
along Park Lane and Old Knebworth Lane at a fast stride. I
didn't propose to join him. Let him talk to Inspector Field on
his own. Both men would be more at ease if I were not there.
Dickens, I knew, could handle the inspector.

And so, I did not follow him into the breakfast parlour, but
turned back towards the servants' hall and knocked on the
door of the butler's pantry.

He looked slightly startled, but then pleased to see me. He
was, I noticed, treating himself to a nice, full breakfast, relying
on the more junior staff to see to the guests and to the master
of the house.

'Don't get up,' I said hastily. 'I just came in to say how

much I enjoyed that wine. So good! I wanted the full name
of the wine so that I can order it from my wine merchant.'

It worked, of course. He was delighted. Poured me a cup
of excellent coffee, swallowed the rest of his sausages, bacon,
and egg while we chatted about various wine merchants in
London and he insisted on sharing his toast and scones with
me. While we argued amiably about the relative merits of
individual wine merchants, the different virtues of Thomas
Gray and of the Berry Brothers, my eye wandered to the board
on the wall. Keys to everything, cellar, tea chests, linen room
. . . and the gunroom. Quite a small key, hanging there on its
hook and clearly labelled. It took a lot of self-control for me
to avert my eyes from it and to continue to chat in an easy
fashion. Unfortunately, he didn't go away to fetch the wine,
didn't even have to look at its label in order to refresh his
memory, but wrote the name and its vintage on a card in an
elaborate copperplate script which put my own untidy hand-
writing to shame. I was in a quandary. Even if I got the
opportunity to pocket the key, even if managed to get him to
leave the room for long enough, I had a feeling that this shrewd
man might well miss it instantly. There was one key missing
on the board, but there was a piece of paper in its place and
it was signed with a woman's name. No, I thought, I was fairly
sure that Lady Rosina's assertion that anyone could just walk
into the butler's pantry, take the key and help themselves to
a pistol, all without being found out, was quite untrue.

Nevertheless, I was keen to look at the room, to see the
guns, to look for the sets of derringer pistols. I wondered how
on earth I was going to be able to manage it and then I got
an inspiration.

'I wonder whether you could possibly show me the gunroom
at some time when you are not too busy,' I said to my new
friend, mopping my mouth with the starched linen napkin
and getting to my feet. 'You see, I'm a writer, and I have a
scene to describe where the villain breaks into his host's
gunroom and steals a gun.' I gave a little laugh. 'Of course,'
I said, 'I'm a Londoner – I've never fired a gun in my life.
I'm blind as a bat, anyway.' I touched my glasses and told
him that I was sure I could not hit the side of the barn, but

an author had to appear to be an expert in everything which he describes.

'No time like the present,' he said, obliging man that he was. He rang the bell, detached the key to the gunroom, popped it into his pocket and ordered the kitchen maid who came to clear the table to tell the housekeeper that he would be with her in ten minutes.

The gunroom was not, as I had imagined it to be, situated on the ground floor, but was high up in the building at the side of the house. Well out of the way of passing guests, and, according to my friend the butler, well out of the way of any stray burglar.

'You'd want to have a map to find this place,' he said as we toiled up stair after stair.

'Lots of guns, I suppose,' I said, and reminded myself to make a few notes when we got there eventually. I had a small leather-bound book which Dickens had presented me with and ordered me to use whenever an idea came to me. This would fit with what the butler would imagine a writer doing and would allay all suspicion.

'I'm sorry to be taking you away from your duties,' I said to him when eventually we ceased to climb the endless sets of stairs and Barrymore led the way down a narrow corridor.

'That's all right, sir,' he said. 'It's good to come up here from time to time. I was showing young Mr Dickens the place a few days ago and I noticed that the window was very dirty. Had to have a tactful word with the housekeeper about it. A place this size, sir, well, it's no good just having a routine that everyone knows, you need to keep your eye on everything from time to time when there is an opportunity and pop in unexpectedly, or the junior staff take advantage.'

And with that wise saying, he produced the key and opened the gunroom. No doubt, because he had had a word about that window, everything was meticulously clean and tidy. Row upon row of guns on shelves, barrels of ammunition on the floor and on a long table, in the centre of the room, were shining boxes.

'Ah, derringer pistols,' I said, making a quick guess. 'That's what I need for my book.' Quickly I produced the notebook,

and hurriedly opened it at the centre so that he would not
notice that it was bare of notes. I measured a random one with
the span of thumb and little finger and saw, by a quick glance,
that he looked impressed at my business-like demeanour.

'Like to have a look, sir?' He was able to open all the
derringer pistol cases with no trouble. None were locked.
Once within the room, a would-be murderer could choose a
gun or pistol of his choice. It would, though, I reckoned, take
months of practice before one could hit a target so small as
a human heart. Another good point in Nelly's defence, I
thought and resolved to mention that to Dickens. The inspector
would take more notice of him than of me. I wondered whether
it would be possible to steal a gun. Not that I wanted a gun,
but I was curious to know how easy it would be to abstract
one of those small pistols from its satin nest within the box.
I cast a quick glance at Barrymore. He was not looking at
me, nor was he looking at the guns. After a quick glance
around to make sure that everything was spick and span, he
had gone over to the window, thrown it open, letting in the
smell of mown hay and a waft of something else which might
have been gardenia.

'Look at this, sir. They're dragging the lake,' he said with
a note of intense interest in his voice and immediately I lost
all interest in guns. I closed the lid on a pair of slender-barrelled
pistols and joined him instantly.

'Why?' I breathed and then remembered the search party
looking for Nelly. I turned a shocked face towards him, but
his mind was on other matters.

'I must tell the housekeeper; the men will be wet, will need
hot drinks,' he said moving away from the window and closing
it down carefully. 'Now, sir, do you think . . .?'

'Yes, of course, I've seen everything that I want to see. That
was perfect, many thanks.' I no longer made a pretence of
writing in my notebook, but thankfully slipped it into my
pocket. 'I'll leave you to lock up,' I said hurriedly and made
my escape, but not before I noticed that the man, probably a
creature of habit, was checking all guns and all derringer pistol
boxes. If they were dragging the lake to find the body of little
Nelly, then I needed to find young Charley and do my best to

reassure him. And her poor mother. I hardly could bear to think of Frances. What must she be feeling?

It didn't make sense, I told myself as I went through the door and along the passage to the stairs. The corridor was lined with small windows and from each one of them I had a vision of the lake. Not policemen, I thought as I narrowed my eyes and wished that I had better sight. The boats, and there were three of them, looked like ordinary dinghies, the sort of boats that were there for the pleasure of the guests. And the men and boys, gesticulating to each other, looked more like estate workers or farm workers than uniformed police.

Nevertheless, I went down the stairs as fast as I could go.

'What's happening?' I snapped at Foster when I reached the hall. He had come out from the smoking room and was standing there, holding his pipe in his hand, standing just by the opened front door and appeared to be listening. He didn't respond to my question and so I repeated it with a note of exasperation in my voice. He looked at me coolly and I caught a look of dislike in his eyes. It puzzled me for a passing moment, but I had more things to think of at the moment and so I pushed past him and ran across the lawn towards the lake. Charley was there and to my enormous relief he did not look too upset.

'What's going on?' I asked, and wondered why Dickens and Inspector Field were not present.

'Lord Edward ordered the lake to be dragged,' said Charley. And then, I suppose he read my fears from my expression, because, kind boy that he was, he gave me a reassuring pat on the arm. 'A man thought he saw something in the water. The levels have gone down very low after all the dry weather. It's probably a deer that got himself drowned. It's not Nelly. Don't worry. She wouldn't do that. She knows that I'd look after her.'

'Yes, of course,' I said hastily. 'A very level-headed young lady,' I added. Though I didn't know whether to believe my own words, he obviously did.

'That's right, Wilkie,' he said seizing my hand and squeezing it rather painfully. 'She's so sensible, so full of good ideas.

We have such plans, the two of us. We don't want much, just each other. My father has to agree. He must! We don't want to wait until I am twenty-one. I'm old enough now to know my own mind. We plan to live with her mother for a while until I start earning better money. Fanny, her eldest sister, you know, well she is going to Italy. Nelly says that we can have her room and Maria can move in with their mother.' He beamed at me and I thought sadly how young he was, and how little he knew his own father.

And then my heart sank. I caught the words 'the girl'.

Someone, someone on the lake, in one of the boats, had shouted it. Why on earth was Charley planning a happy future with his Nelly if the estate workers were dragging the lake for a girl who had not been seen for almost a day? I looked over my shoulder once again and this time, to my relief, I saw Dickens coming. Alone! I thanked goodness for that. I didn't want Inspector Field taking over. Dickens, in his competent way, could care for his son if some tragedy occurred.

Abruptly I left Charley and went back towards his father. 'Dick,' I said urgently, 'Dick, something terrible has happened. One of the estate workers saw something in the lake – something . . . a bundle . . . a . . . a . . . They've dragged the lake and . . .' I stumbled over my words. I could not bring myself to say 'body', but I saw from the look of alarm in his eyes that he had understood my meaning instantly.

'Oh, my God, poor Frances!' he exclaimed, and without saying another word, he turned decisively and quickly and made his way at a rapid pace, back towards his house. I looked after him feeling frustrated. He had not given me any time to say something about his son. I stood, unsure and indecisive, for a moment and then Charley turned his head and looked back at me. I waited, did not go to him and so he came back to me.

'Where's my father gone?' he asked, and I replied to him almost instantly. There was nothing that I could do now to disguise the truth.

'He's gone to see Nelly's mother,' I said.

He stared at me and to my amazement there was a look of incredulous anger on his face.

'Oh, no!' he exclaimed impatiently. 'Trust him to jump to conclusions!' And then he started to run.

I toiled after him, endeavouring to move my short legs to a pace which they had never yet achieved. I was lucky that he met Mark Lemon and his wife on the stairs, and they detained him for a few minutes with questions. And then he was off again but by now I was at his heels and I grabbed the tail of his coat.

'Wait, Charley,' I said, but he took no notice, wrenched his coat from my grasp and by the time that I had followed him to the second storey, he had thrown open a door and was standing in the entrance.

I had suspected something like this and so I was not as taken aback as he at the sight of Frances, the discreet Frances, in Dickens' arms. I gave Charley a slight push and managed to close the door behind the two of us. Explanations had to be made, but there was no need for the whole house to know them.

'It's not Nelly, Mrs Jarman,' stuttered Charley, his face turning a very bright shade of red. 'It's definitely not Nelly. She's safe and sound. Don't worry about her. I've made a hiding place for her in the roof. I bring her food and she's nice and comfortable . . . blankets . . . a pillow . . . and books . . . and . . .' His voice tailed to a finish as he looked from one to the other. The woman looked as though she were about to faint, and it was only Dickens' arm which kept her from collapsing down on the floor.

'Well done! But you should perhaps have told her mother.' Dickens' voice was quite cool. He did not move his arm but supported Nelly's mother still. I carried over a chair, but both ignored it. 'Or, indeed, your own father!' pronounced Dickens but Frances said nothing.

Charley had run out of words. He stared at his father and I could see that a puzzled expression had come over his face. I should leave, I told myself, but I didn't. I stayed. Dickens, typically, wore a defiant expression upon his face, and I wondered how the drama was going to end. Now that I knew Nelly was safe, I was rather more amused by the whole situation. How was Dickens going to get himself out of this?

'Well, I don't care, anyway,' said Charley resentfully. 'It was up to me to keep her safe. She's my intended wife. I'm going to marry Nelly. We've worked it all out and we know our own minds.'

He was answered, to my surprise, not by his father but by Frances.

'You can't do that, Charley,' she said, and now that she had recovered from her fright, there was a note of sympathy in her voice. She had no sons of her own, but she had probably seen many young actors and stage-struck young men in the throes of first love. 'It's impossible,' she said firmly.

He was a little taken aback at that. He looked from her to his father and was disconcerted, I think, by the look of compassion and embarrassment on the face of the man, whom he always reverenced and obeyed. And then love gave him courage.

'Why not?' he said in a truculent voice. 'Not that I care what anyone says. I'm going to marry Nelly.'

'You can take my word for it; it's impossible.' Dickens was regaining his usual self-confidence.

'Why?'

The fatal question, I thought, and I waited for the reply. It wasn't Dickens, however, who answered, but Frances who had a working woman's courage and ability to face facts and to take action. 'Because it is impossible, Charley,' she said earnestly. And then when he mutely shook his head, her voice hardened. 'Nelly is only seventeen,' she said firmly. 'Both of you are too young to marry without your parents' consent and neither of us will ever give that consent. A marriage between the two of you is impossible and will always and ever remain impossible.' She said the words without emphasis, without even a glance at Dickens, but in a simple and matter-of-fact voice and Charley stared back at her with an air of incomprehension. He looked from his father to the actress in a puzzled fashion, but Dickens said nothing, just got to his feet, jerked his head, went towards the door and Charley followed him.

I held my breath. I was left alone with Frances. My instinct was to mutter an excuse and to go, but the sight of her face, and the realization of how alone in the world she was, made me more compassionate. I waited. I would ask no questions, but I would wait and give her the opportunity to unburden herself.

'He'll get over it,' I said to her, meaning to offer consolation.

'I hope he doesn't retain any hopes,' she said in a low voice. 'You are friendly with him, Mr Collins. Impress upon him that it is impossible, that neither his father nor I will . . .' There she stopped and then when she resumed there was a note of determination in her voice. 'Impress upon him,' she said, 'that marriage between the two of them is now and always will be impossible.'

There was little point in pretending to misunderstand her. 'You and Dickens were close in the spring and early summer of 1838,' I said slowly. 'Forgive me, but dear old Clarkson has been reminiscing about your performances in those months and I could not help but think . . .'

She gave a gesture that was so redolent of sorrow, regret and pathos that it brought tears to my eyes.

'Don't feel that you need to explain anything to me,' I said hurriedly.

'It is as you have guessed,' she said with a simple dignity. 'I was lonely, frightened of the future and he was . . . well, he was a man whom anyone would be proud to call a friend.' She stopped and I could see tears in her eyes before she added, 'I trust you for everyone's sake, to keep the secret.'

I couldn't help it. I took her in my arms as though she had been my sister and I kissed her cheek. 'You can rely upon me,' I said. 'I see no fault on either side.'

Very simple words, awkwardly spoken, but they brought tears to her eyes. 'Clarkson will have told you the whole story of my sad marriage,' she said quietly. 'It does not excuse, but it may explain.' She turned away from me then and went across to lean upon the mantelpiece hiding her face from me.

'You can rely upon me,' I repeated. 'I will do my best to reconcile Charley to the ending of his first romance. There is talk of him going to Germany again or perhaps the Low Countries and I will suggest to Dickens that the sooner the boy leaves England, the better.'

She bowed her head but did not speak, and I guessed that she would wait until she had control of her voice. I respected and admired her immensely and, in order to give her some minutes to herself, I walked across to the window.

There was something more happening out there on the lake. I shaded my eyes with both hands in an effort to see what was happening and then opened the window. There were shouts from the boat to the shore. Another boat took off with a man carrying a large metal hook. A terrible thought came to me. Rapidly I closed the window. 'I'll leave you now,' I said.

She came to the door with me, and I heard the click of a key in the lock as I went down the stairs and when I came out on to the terrace and looked back up at her room, I saw the curtains had been drawn.

I walked rapidly down to the lakeside to see what was going on. Something had been found; I was sure of that.

I watched, fascinated, but despite Charley's assurance I was still feeling apprehensive about Nelly. By now, I thought, the object that had surfaced due to the low levels in the lake must be recognizable. The men must surely know whether it was a human or not. There was a sombre air about them. Even the boys were very quiet. There was no excitement, no encouraging shouts as attempts were made to throw the heavy weight of the metal grappling hook. Time after time, there was a splash but no result. For some reason, perhaps stones, the boat could not go near to the object. I reached the edge of the lake and stood there watching. A couple of boys stripped off and prepared to go into the water. A few of the guests were there, also. I saw the heavy form of John Foster and at some distance, on the south side of the lake, the leggy silhouette of Augustus Egg.

All were silent there now – everyone was waiting. And then there was a brief, but immediately silenced, shout of triumph. The grappling irons had hit their mark. One man held the rope while the other pair handled the oars and turned the prow of the boat towards the shore. There was a movement beside me, and I saw that Dickens had joined me. I wondered where Charley was, but he said nothing and so I said nothing. Now was not the time for a discussion of his family affairs. The boat was carving its way through the surface of the water, dragging behind it an untidy bundle, festooned with water lilies and dead vegetation and leaving a wavering track cut into the green scum of the algae that coated the surface of the lake. There was a dead silence. Even with my poor eyesight I could make out the ominous shape of the bundle that was being towed to the shoreline of the lake. Without a word to each other we both began to walk down to the lakeshore.

The boat came to land quite close to where we stood, Dickens and I. Making no noise, but anxious to see all, the rest of the bystanders gathered swiftly at that spot. Nothing was said when the boat arrived, but several eager young boys waded into the lake and, seizing a firm hold upon the stern, they pulled it on to the shore. The oarsmen got out, still in that rather eerie silence, and all eyes were fixed on the bundle that had been towed ashore.

Not a deer, nor a girl as far as could be seen. A man, I thought, and quite a tall, well-made man. Just a carcass, now, of course, probably just a skeleton. It had spent long months, if not years, in the lake, but the body, even the hooded head, was clothed in heavy leather and that had kept the bones together. And dragging behind the trunk of the body there were heavy, leather, thigh-high boots. No word was spoken, but an enormous dragnet was produced, slipped beneath the body parts and the corpse was deftly towed to the sandy shore.

'A gamekeeper. Look at the boots and the leather clothing. Must be the missing gamekeeper.' Dickens' clear, decisive voice broke the silence, and all looked towards him. Instinctively I looked amongst the workers for young Jim, but he was not there. These were the farm workers and the estate workers; one man who was probably the replacement gamekeeper was dressed in leather and I guessed that it was a custom that these men, out in all weathers, were provided with warm and protective clothing.

''That 'ud be 'e,' said one man eventually.

'Jim's father?' I asked and the man beside me gave a nod.

'How dreadful!' I was appalled and must have betrayed my feeling because he looked at me compassionately. 'Don't take it on too much, sir,' he said. 'Happen, it'll be a consolation

to the lad to know what became of him. Always felt bad that
his father had deserted him and never came back for him. Very
fond of his father, that lad.'

'We'll go and tell the stable yard manager, Collins. And I'll
go up to the house and tell Lord Edward.' He looked around
and pointed. 'You, and you, come with me and you can give
all the details.' Dickens, as usual, took charge and all did as
he had appointed, the designated men following as he crossed
the lawns, making for the house ready to break the news
to the master of the house. I stood, slightly taken aback,
wondering what the right thing to do was. It looked as though
I was going to be the one who should go towards the stable
yard and break the news to Jim's foster father and then to Jim,
himself. Not a task I relished. I had told myself, earlier, that
Dickens would be the right person to handle it. I dreaded the
thought of breaking such terrible news to the young boy.

'I'll go and see the stable manager; he'll be the best person
to tell the boy,' I said to a man who seemed to be ordering
the men in the boat. There would, I knew, be various tasks to
do. The body had to be towed ashore, laid on a bank, a coffin
would have to be made; however hastily makeshift, there had
to be a coffin and then the parson had to be alerted, and a
quick service arranged when the body, long since reduced to
a skeleton, would have to be perfunctorily laid to rest. It would
be best if Jim did not see the sodden remains until the corpse
was neatly arranged in the coffin.

Without waiting for an answer, I went off towards the stable
yard.

Bruno gave a perfunctory bark when I arrived and then
wagged his tail. I waited for a moment, standing there in the
summer sun. Life, I thought, was not easy for some. This boy,
by all accounts, had loved his father very deeply. No one had
made any allusion to his mother, and so, I fancied, that she
was not of the same importance to young Jim. He had witnessed
the shooting, had witnessed his father going forth from the
house, had seen him cast his gun into the well, or so he said.
But after that? What had happened next? There was a strange
gap in the story, then. Had the watching boy, and his frantic
father, held any communication then? Had the boy really made

any effort to see whether his mother still lived? Or had he, like a faithful hound, dogged his father's footsteps to the very last moment. Would the discovery of his father's corpse, hauled from the depths of the deep lake, come of any surprise to him?

I did not, I thought, know the answers to these questions but I plodded along the path to the stable yard and hoped that I would deal with this matter correctly.

He was there. Not the boy. Just the master. But one look at his face told me that he had heard the news. Had sent the boy indoors, was now ready to deal with any questions that arose.

'Mr Collins,' he said, and then said no more. Bruno, from his kennel, gave another perfunctory bark of greeting and then wagged his tail. For once, I paid no attention to him.

'They've recovered the body,' I said.

He did not make any pretext of misunderstanding me. 'So I've heerd tell,' he said.

'It looks as though it might be young Jim's father,' I said. 'He was wearing a gamekeeper's leggings, jacket and boots. The leather was preserved where cloth might have decayed. Most of the men thought it was the gamekeeper.'

'Very likely,' he said in a guarded manner.

'And Jim?' I put a note of query into my voice.

'I've told him,' he said, and he cast an eye back at the lighted windows in his snug, little house.

'What did he say?' I asked, and his reply to this was short and uninformative.

'Not a lot,' he said.

'Doesn't he want to see his father . . .?' I had begun bravely, but then when I remembered the appearance of that inhuman lump of leather clothing, I heard my voice falter.

He gave my words the tribute of a minute's silence and then he spoke.

'Is there anything for the boy to do, sir?' he asked and somehow that one word, that ironically respectful 'sir' make me realize how stupid I was being. No, of course, poor Jim should not be dragged over to see the remains of one whom he had loved and who had been gone from him for all that time. It was not for me to play judge here. Not for me to declare that a mother should be sacred and that a shot fired in a fit of terrible anger should be enough to condemn a man to the gallows. Jim, I realized, might know far more about this matter than I did. Might have, in a far more mature way than I could possibly have summoned up at his age, have forgiven his mother for her infidelity and his father for his fit of passionate anger.

'No,' I said in answer to the stable manager's sensible question, 'no, you are right. No, there is nothing for the boy to do.' The estate, I thought, could bury the man. And, perhaps, later on, Jim might visit the grave. I had a quick hope that the clergy might be kept out of the matter for the moment, that some compassionate local magistrate might declare the drowning to be one of 'death by misadventure' and that the unfortunate gamekeeper should be given a service in the church and a burial in the estate church yard and that he and his wife should, perhaps, after a stormy and unhappy married life, lie in peace within the grounds of St Mary's Church where their son and only child could visit them from time to time.

'You are a good man,' I said with approval. 'You've done a charitable deed in sheltering this boy and I hope that you are rewarded for it.'

'Thank you, sir,' he said, but there was a note of reserve in his voice, a worried look on his face and I thought that I knew why when I thought back over the boy's story and wondered whether it had any link with another death on the Knebworth estate.

'The secretary, Mr Maguire, did he have anything to do with it – with the affair of the wife?' I asked, and I bent down and stroked the dog, so that he did not feel pressurized to answer immediately.

There was a very long few minutes of silence. Eventually the man named Dick gave a sigh.

'They were friends; him and the fellow she hung about with,' he said eventually. 'Not equal friends. After all, Mr Maguire was a gentleman, a secretary to Lord Edward. I don't know if anyone could tell you why they were friends, but friends they were.'

'Who was he?' I asked. I almost said the words in a whisper. I had the feeling that I might be about to uncover something of great significance.

'A nobody,' said Dick decisively. 'He was a Londoner, name of Jenkins, had moved here, first to a bank in Stevenage, just a doorman, you know, and then he got another job, same thing, in the bank at Knebworth. They were friends, he and Mr Maguire, but you could see that they came from different backgrounds. They say that Mr Maguire was a university man, but this, his friend, well, he was a strange fellow. Quite rough. My wife didn't like him, no, not one bit. She said that she didn't trust him. I pressed her, you know. Asked her whether he said anything, had done anything, but no, she wouldn't say – just that she didn't like him or didn't trust him. And he had a grudge against the gamekeeper, young Jim's father. I did hear tell that the gamekeeper told Sir Edward that his secretary's friend was in with a crowd of poachers, but I don't know whether that was true or not.'

'But this fellow, Jenkins, he hung around the house and the grounds, is that right?'

'That's right, sir. He seemed, a' purpose like, to take up with the gamekeeper's wife. Flattered her, I'd say. Probably brought her little presents. She was lonely, I suppose, on her own most of the time. The boy was off at school, doing well there, so I've been told, and her husband spent every day and every evening checking on the young partridges and making sure that the game was preserved and so this Jenkins got in the habit of dropping into the gamekeeper's cottage and paying court to his wife.'

I waited. It was like watching a play where you knew that it would end in tragedy.

'Bound to happen, eventually, sir,' said Dick at last. 'I don't much listen to gossip myself, but my wife brings plenty home when she does a couple of days' work in the castle kitchens. Everyone was talking about it, according to her. Would be murder done? she said once. She came home one night with these words on her lips and God be my witness, I hushed her. "Don't say that," I said to her. "You never know but that God will fulfil a prophesy!" She said no more, and I tell you, sir,

I stood there with an icy chill running down the back of my neck.'

'And you think that poor young Jim heard this sort of talk?' I said.

'Bound to,' he said. 'A very bright young fellow, Jim. Got a great brain. The schoolteacher said that to my wife a few weeks ago and she was that pleased, was my wife. Didn't hesitate to tell me about it, either. "You was right and I was wrong," she said to me. "He'll do us credit. You mark my words." That was what she said to me, sir.'

'So, you think that the boy knew what was going on?' I asked once again. 'And perhaps that Maguire had something to do with it?' I added.

Dick got an odd look on his face when I said these last words, almost as though, quite suddenly, he had seen what was behind my last words.

'I couldn't say, sir,' he said then.

THIRTEEN

'Some people call that picturesque,' said Sir Percival,
pointing over the wide prospect with his half-finished
walking-stick. 'I call it a blot on a gentleman's
property. In my great-grandfather's time, the lake
flowed to this place. Look at it now! It is not four feet
deep anywhere, and it is all puddles and pools. I wish
I could afford to drain it, and plant it all over. My
bailiff (a superstitious idiot) says he is quite sure the
lake has a curse on it, like the Dead Sea. What do you
think, Fosco? It looks just the place for a murder,
doesn't it?'

Wilkie Collins, *The Woman in White*

The dragging of the lake went on throughout all the
afternoon. A couple of boats, the grappling irons, some
young lads who'd stripped off and were diving into
the water again and again. It puzzled me, but Dickens, of
course, guessed instantly.

'Looking for the gun,' he said. 'These men would love to
find a gun. Will be rusty, but there again, who knows, it might
be cleaned up. In any case, it would be the last piece in the
jigsaw if that were to be found. Makes sense, when you come
to think of it. The man throws his gun in the lake and then
himself after it. I'll go and have a word with Lord Edward.
All of this must be most upsetting for a man who is not in
good health.'

'I haven't much sympathy for him,' I said hotly. 'He treated
his wife abominably and his daughter, also, I understand.'

I thought he would be annoyed with me. No one was a
better friend than Dickens. His loyalty was immense once
the bonds of friendship were established. He didn't erupt,
though, as I had expected. He merely looked at me sadly,

almost as though he were commiserating some lack of integrity in me.

'Life isn't easy, Wilkie,' he said quietly. 'What is it the Bible says? "Judge not and neither shall ye be judged."'

And then he walked away, and I shrugged my shoulders and went in the opposite direction.

I kept out of the way of Dickens and Inspector Field during the afternoon. In fact, I saw little of either of them once lunch was over. I then took Bruno for a walk. Not to the maze, but for a wander around the parkland, past the mausoleum and to the edges of the woodland. The gamekeeper's cottage was there. A snug and well-built house. And not far away from this was the school. I was in luck. The children were just pouring out of the door, shouting happily. The boys had a shabby ball, a good quality leather rugby ball originally, I guessed, a relic of the big house, and the girls had some worn pieces of rope which they used to skip with. I lingered to watch them, glad to see that Bruno had wagged his tail at the pats bestowed upon him and then waited quietly by my side. After a minute, an elderly woman came out from the schoolhouse and I quickly doffed my hat and introduced myself as a guest at the house.

'I didn't expect to see the school at work in August,' I said, after we had discussed the weather for a few minutes. She gazed dubiously at Bruno and he, like the gentleman that he was, didn't force his attentions upon her.

'We always give the children a few weeks' schooling at this time in the summer, sir. You see, they are off in June for the haymaking and then they have most of September off for the harvest, picking potatoes and all that. It's not like town and city children. The parents need their children to help. But the knowledge goes from their heads if they are off for too long and they get idle. So, we do a few weeks' schooling in August.'

I nodded in the direction of the lake. 'Sad business, that,' I said. 'I hope that the children were not too upset.'

She cast a cynical glance at the shrieking children but said nothing. She had the air of someone who was waiting for a question. An intelligent-looking woman with a quiet air of authority. Been a long time in her job, I guessed. Without wasting any more time, I moved on to the subject of Jim.

'I'm very sorry for his son, Jim,' I said. And then, in case, she would think that I was an idle gossip, I said impulsively, 'I know the boy because he looks after this dog and we've made friends because we are both fond of Bruno, here.'

Her face softened and the wary look went from her eyes. 'He's a very nice boy, sir. And a very clever boy. I was sorry when he left the school, but there you are. The Baldocks were good-natured enough to take him in after that terrible business. No one could expect that they would keep him in idleness for another year or two. I don't see anything much of him these days, but I'd say he's happy. He likes the animals, likes the horses and the dogs. He'll do well. He's a hard-working boy. Did very well here.'

'He would have been helping his father, too, I expect. On Saturdays and Sundays,' I added.

She smiled at my ignorance. 'And Monday, Tuesday, Wednesday, Thursday and Fridays. Before school and after school. These farm children work from the time that they can walk,' she said. 'You see children as young as two years helping to herd cows, put standing in a gap. A stick is put into their hand and they are told to block an animal ten times their own size, walking miles to market, lifting bales of hay as big as themselves. They're hard-working children, sir.'

'And Jim.'

'Could do everything that his father did. I've seen that boy shoot a pair of kestrels that were trying to nest near to the young partridges, and he couldn't have been more than about eight years old. The gun nearly as big as himself. But the birds fell stone dead out from a tree forty feet high.'

I nodded. The age of eight for such ability as to be able to shoot a pair of birds from a tree forty feet above the ground was a shock, but otherwise she had said nothing that I had not told myself. My mind went over those hours of drama that occurred in that peaceful-looking house so near to where I stood. A drama as moving as the tale of Shakespeare's Ophelia. *Crime passionel*, the French would have called it, but such a term was unknown in English courts, and Jim's father would,

undoubtedly, have been hanged if he had been caught. I
surveyed the building, thinking of the gamekeeper, gun at his
side, with his son at his heels, coming back and finding his wife
with her lover. A matter of minutes, almost a reflex action to
lift the gun . . .

And after it was all over? What happened then? I stared at
the house as I asked myself that question. A neat house, but
no out-building beside it. Plenty of trees and bushes around,
but . . .

'Must be very damp around here in the wintertime,' I said.

'We keep a fire going in the school right through the winter.'
She had not followed my train of thought, but I listened with
interest as she explained how they stored the wood. 'When
the men are cutting the trees in the late autumn,' she said,
'they always do a supply for the school. They borrow some
of the older children. Bring us a cartload of logs and we stack
them over there, just beside the school. I've got a few girls
here that are great at thatching; I had a girl here about ten
years ago who had learned it from her grandfather, very neat
with her fingers, this girl. And she taught the other girls and
it's been passed on down through the school. The ones who
know how to do it, well, they teach the young ones, and
we usually have plenty of straw for them to work with because
once the harvest is over, we all set to and we gather some
straw from the fields and the hedgerows, and then when the
boys unload the logs, the girls make a roof over them. All
gone now, as you can see for yourself.' She pointed to a well-
swept square of flagstones on the southern gable of the school
and then looked back at her charges. At that moment, the
church bell pealed the hour and all activity immediately ceased.
The school mistress clapped her hands and two neat lines
formed, one shorter line of boys and a longer one of girls.
Another clap and the two lines marched into school.

'You have them well-trained,' I said with a smile.

'They're good children, on the whole,' she said. 'Not that,
when it comes to the summer, I won't be glad to get rid of a
few of these older boys who've been itching to get out to
work. They can be troublesome, these boys at that age. Not
bad boys, you understand. It's just their age. Makes them do

things without thinking of the consequences. Act on the spur of the moment and they're sorry afterwards. That's boys for you.'

And with that piece of wisdom, the schoolmistress went back to her classroom and I went to put Bruno back in his kennel.

The library at Knebworth House was completely empty, to my relief, as I did not want to make conversation and I did not want to have to hide my searches from idle eyes. I scanned the top shelves and then when I had identified the shelves dealing with the estate, I remembered Lady Rosina's story about her husband's cruelty and hunted for the ladder which she'd had to toil up and down in order to fetch his lordship the plans of the house.

It was easily discovered in an alcove by the doorway to the vestibule, but I had to trudge up and down the ladder for about twenty minutes before discovering the bound volume. By then, I, though not heavily pregnant at the time, was so thoroughly exhausted that I was full of sympathy for Lady Rosina that I felt that shooting was too good for that brute of a husband.

Nevertheless, he had a huge pride in his house and the achievement of remodelling it, so I didn't feel either embarrassment or fear about the possibility of being discovered in my nosiness. I took the large book over to a table and settled down to turn pages until I discovered what I was searching for.

Yes, the banqueting hall was the original core of the house. The drawings made that clear and so I turned my attention to the page where that was depicted. A normal house, I mused, would be built from the bottom up and the attic storey would cover the same footage as the bottom floor. Not so here. Here all was higgledy-piggledy and large portions of the attics were inaccessible to others. Stairs led up to various parts, and in some places, judging by the drawings, it looked as though portions of the attic were connected to the lower floor just by a ladder. I wondered how all those rooms were kept clean and remembered what I had been told about how Jim had a job and got paid a small stipend to keep one of the rooms in the roof clean and in good repair.

I followed the drawings as closely as I could until my head was spinning, and then I sat back and began to think hard, sitting perfectly still and looking not at the attic drawings but at the sketch of the finished banqueting hall, paying extra attention to the detailed drawings of the roof, sectioned into squares and oblongs, framing medallions and heraldic symbols. This roof, I read, was designed by Sir Edward Bulwer-Lytton, and his was the decision to dark stain all of the wood and to stud the ceiling with heraldic symbols wrought in bronze. It had been his special care, this room, this magnificent relic of the past and his aim was to pay tribute to his great ancestors of the past, I read, in the typical flowery prose which was the hallmark of this man. I even struggled through his turgid poem that was engraved, at ceiling height, around the four walls of the immense hall. A very accomplished sketch, I thought, and was able to pick out the exact spot where Dickens' chalk mark had indicated that the marquis had to stretch himself out and declare his love. I then replaced the book of plans and carried the ladder over to its niche and left the room.

I could no longer postpone what I had planned to do. I went back upstairs to my ornate bedroom and opened my luggage bag and took out a pair of slippers.

My mother presented me with a pair of slippers every year at Christmas time. Something about me, my idle nature, no doubt, but I love slippers. Not just bedroom slippers, but those wonderful pieces of footwear that have a solid, but flexible sole, and soft, carpet soft, uppers which tie securely and ensure that you don't trip or fall. I had brought the latest pair in my luggage, though I had not dared to wear them coming down to breakfast for fear that Dickens would lecture me on sloppy behaviour.

But now I would wear them. They would be ideal for my purpose. I knotted the laces securely, then put a box of matches into my pocket. Quietly I stole out of my room and began to mount the stairs. My visit to the gunroom had helped as I had noted a door at the end of the corridor where I had reckoned that the front wall should end. I made straight for it, passing

no one on the way and feeling a rush of relief as I found that
it was unlocked.

No room on the other side of it. Nothing but a small landing
and two flights of stairs. One going down to the kitchen regions,
I guessed, noting the poor-quality wood and the lack of
carpeting or balusters. The other, similar in type, led upwards
and I began to climb. Very steep! I was out of breath by the
time that I reached the top of them. I paused for a moment's
rest and then heard a whisper. A man's whisper. And then a
girl's low-pitched reply, ending in a sob. I grimaced. So Charley
had made a snug hideaway up here for his darling little Nelly.
The story should have had a happy ending. Nelly would be
kept safe until the puzzle of the murder was solved and then,
by hook or by crook, Charley would convince his father and
Nelly's mother that by dint of hard work in Coutts Bank he
would make enough money to support a wife and not be a
burden upon his father. It couldn't happen now, of course.
Nelly's mother, Frances Jarman, or Frances Ternan as was her
married name, had been utterly clear and decisive and no one
could accuse a woman like that of not being sure of who was
the father to her youngest daughter. No marriage could now
take place. I had a moment's admiration for the dignified
woman. All through those eighteen years, life had not been
easy for Frances. The sole guardian of three girls. And she
had kept the secret. But now the secret had been told. Charley
and Nelly would have to part. I was not surprised to hear the
heart-broken sobbing. To these two young people it must seem
like the end of the world. There had been obstacles in front
of them but with the resilience of youth, there would have
been hope, also. Hope that the adults in their lives would come
to their senses and see that love must triumph overall. But
now there was no hope and Nelly's voice, incautiously, was
lifted on a cry of pain. 'I must see my mother,' she said, and
I knew that the boy who loved her would not be able to deny
her that consolation.

I hesitated, wondering whether to retreat silently, but then
realized from the sounds that they were going in the opposite
direction. That was a relief to me. It seemed, I hoped, to show
that Charley was not aware of this domestic stairway and that

he had found Nelly's hiding place from the other side of the attics. And so I stayed very still and waited until the sounds of their footsteps had faded.

And then moving very quietly, I entered that space above the banqueting hall, stepping carefully from beam to beam. For a few minutes I felt terrified in case I fell through that modern ceiling. It was pitch dark up there and I wondered how anyone could see their way. Timidly and with slightly trembling hands I struck a match and then saw that, in this well-ordered household, a closed lantern hung from a hook just near to the entrance. Another match, after the first had been carefully extinguished, and now I could see. Surprisingly clean. A few cobwebs, that was all, but the ancient, five-hundred-year-old beams were newly soaked with tar – the smell was perceptible, and I wondered whether that was young Jim's work. Everything looked well cared for. Here and there repairs to the ancient beams were made with metal straps – probably when the alterations were made thirty years ago but since then there had been plaster renewed and a workman-looking cupboard was full of feather dusters, buckets, paint brushes, cans of limewash and well-sealed small buckets of tar.

Between the beams, though, was what interested me. Five hundred years ago these magnificent beams would have been blackened by the smoke from a fire on the stone floor of the original building, but when the renovations were made, the rudimentary attempts at ceilings were replaced and the spaces between the beams were sealed by thin slabs of wood. Downstairs a coat of plaster over the paint made them look smooth and as though they were cut from one enormous slab, but up here one could see how it had been done.

That was not all, though. I raised my lantern almost breathless with excitement. My guess had been correct. The circular and oval heraldic symbols of burnished bronze that decorated the ceiling of the banqueting hall would need to be cleaned and polished. I had worked that out for myself and had wondered briefly whether enormous, sixty-foot-high ladders and platforms would have been brought into the magnificent surrounds of the banqueting hall. However, I hoped that there might be an easier solution and I was right. Each one of these ceiling decorations had a broad rim around it so that it could be prised off by someone up here in the roof space, and then cleaned and polished and clicked back into place again.

I had one other task and that was to find the gun, the missing gun after the tragedy that had occurred in the gamekeeper's house. If it had been thrown down the well in a moment's revulsion after a violent act, it had certainly not remained there. It could, of course, just as easily been dropped on the ground, or thrown, in a fit of passionate remorse, into the undergrowth of the nearby woodland.

But wherever it was thrown before the guilty man put an end to his own life, it was, to my mind, most unlikely that it had stayed there. There had been one silent witness to the killing and the boy Jim, who had loved and revered his father and who had been trained to shoot with that very gun, would undoubtedly have retrieved it. Where had he hidden it? I had checked around the gamekeeper's cottage and around the school. There might have been a temporary outdoor hiding place, but guns, I had a feeling, needed constant care if they were not to rust away. All the guns and pistols in the gunroom at Knebworth bore a sheen of oil. I had wondered whether the gamekeeper's gun might have been placed there, but when I saw the careful tidiness of the place, and heard how the master of the house and his butler supervised the room, I knew that Jim would not have risked putting the gun in amongst all those carefully enumerated guns belonging to the master of the estate and he would not have risked bringing it to the Balcocks' house. The gun, after all, would not have been the property of the dead gamekeeper, but would have belonged to the estate. So, if Jim wanted to keep it, then he would have to find a safe, dry hiding spot for it. No outdoor shed or nook in the wood-lands would do to keep it safe.

How about a small cubbyhole of a room, high up under the roof, and a room which he, and he alone, entered in order to clean? I remembered the story about the master of the house watching him, unknown to the boy and then telling the house-keeper that he was to have sole charge of that room and a few pence a week to keep it in good order and free of dust and cobwebs. A room in the roof to which he, alone, had access. That would be a safe hiding place for a gun.

I found it quite quickly, well disguised in a tall bag filled with feather dusters attached to long canes. Not at all hard to find but would a man like Lord Edward keep silent about the boy's secret?

I thought about the matter very carefully. It had seemed odd that the master of the house, even if wanted to be charitable to an orphaned boy, would find such an odd occupation for him. After all, it would seem more sensible if he had been put to do a couple of hours' assisting the gamekeeper with the feeding of the young partridges or even cleaning guns for the shoot under the new man's supervision.

Still, as I began to think of it, I reluctantly admitted that the boy's secret might have appealed to Lord Edward's novelistic mind. He may have toyed with the idea of getting the true story out of the boy, sometime, not to betray him, but to use it in a book. That would fit with the man's rather odd personality.

I made sure that all was as I had found it and went from the room and down the steep, ladder-like stairs. I had a lot to think of.

FOURTEEN

'If you will look about you (which most people won't
do),' says Sergeant Cuff, 'you will see that the nature
of a man's tastes is, most times, as opposite as
possible to the nature of a man's business.'

Wilkie Collins, *The Moonstone*

'Well, you're honoured, Wilkie,' said Dickens when
he met me coming down the back stairs which
led to the original medieval house. 'Inspector Field
wants to have a word with you. Thinks you are a very good
man at understanding people. At least,' said Dickens, with one
of his verbal flourishes, 'I told him that no man in the world
is better at probing the human mind and he said, "I'm sure
that you are right, Mr Dickens!" Come in here, Wilkie. We're
down here, down the red passage, in the little room at the foot
of the back stairs.'

This place is like a rabbit warren, I told myself as obediently
I followed him, still thinking hard. In my mind I enumerated
all those shadowy figures who had perched up in the gallery,
high above us, ready to lower the second screen, or those in
the third act who were surreptitiously smoking cigars. What
had they all done afterwards, once the backdrop was in position? Had they stayed there, waited through the long and
boring monologues? Would anyone have noticed, in the darkness, whether someone had slipped away, even if it were
Clarkson himself?

I resented having to waste time listening to the inspector.
I doubted that he wanted my opinions. That was just one of
Dickens' ideas. Dickens was a kind man and thought from
time to time that I needed to have my confidence bolstered.
And it pleased him when his friends did well, bolstered his
good opinion of his own judgement. I couldn't resist that

rather mean thought and then felt ashamed of myself. Dickens had been immeasurably good to me and I owed what little successes that I had achieved to his relentless praise of my abilities to all in the literary world of London. It was a small return for all his kindnesses for me to be occasionally at his beck and call.

Still, perhaps I could use the time to good account. Foster, I thought. I would turn the inspector's thoughts towards Foster. After all, if the man was, as I expected, an example of a decadent, why then was he in grave danger? I would enlarge on the character of the secretary, Tom Maguire. I would invite a conversation where he interrogated me about Foster; where he hinted at matters which had puzzled and appalled me. I wasn't a wonderful actor, but I thought that I could play this scene to my satisfaction. And who knows whether it was true or not? The fact remains that this would be an extremely valid reason for murder. A far, far better reason than the little girl Nelly could possibly have had. After all, in the inspector's eyes she was just a little actress, someone who would be used to dealing with importunate men and who would have learned little tricks to avoid them. Why should she kill a man when it would be easier just to avoid ever being alone with him and staying under the shelter of her mother's experienced wing during day and night?

However, Foster was a different matter. Anyone caught in the act of sodomy could be condemned to death. A brutal law, but a law, nevertheless. I had a moment's compunction, but I reassured myself, thinking of the man's immense respectability and of his position in literary and legal London. There was little chance of anything, of any action, coming from my hints, I assured myself. Foster was the epitome of respectability. He held a government office, was an editor, a journalist, a man with influential friends all over London.

And Leech, John Leech, I thought. He could be another candidate for the role of suspect, I had planned. Turning the last corner of the passageway, my mind raced rapidly through the reasons why Leech might have been the one to have fired the shot. Fear of being found out, fear of long-dead matters being uncovered, rumours of embezzlement of money, these were the common gossip of clubs and coffee rooms. There was little danger that the inspector, without help, could instantly sift idle chatter from actual fact, though doubtless, he would soon find out the true position. But any distraction would be good enough to cause a diversion and to stop him from arresting Nelly or even Lady Rosina.

My task now, I thought, as I followed Dickens into the little back salon, was to distract the inspector from the young and the defenceless. And from others, also, who though not young, were nevertheless defenceless. I thought fleetingly of Lady Rosina and found myself feeling intensely sorry for her. For all her bravery and for all that audacious valour with which she had confronted the husband who had tried to silence her, she was as vulnerable as the young people in this sorry mess.

By the time that I had sunk into the depths of the richly upholstered chair and placed my hands on its deeply carved arms, I had hit upon my route. I leaned forward.

'Inspector,' I said, 'you have a very difficult task ahead of you. This Mr Thomas Maguire was a very strange man, a man who got satisfaction out of taunting and terrifying others. And that is not all,' I continued, still eyeing him closely, 'this man had some very strange friends. He cultivated them. Men who came from the gutter, who knew the dark secrets of the underworld, men who had a history of crime and a record of incarceration in prison. He probed them. Fed them with gin and small gifts of money and he found out secrets, whether true secrets or idle rumours, it would be impossible to tell.' I was beginning to like the sound of this and to find that a story had begun to flood into my mind. 'Even into this very house where we now sit,' I said, lowering my voice and leaning forward, 'into this very house, he invited men who told him of shameful goings on, of criminal acts. Not,' I said, warming to my theme, 'because this Mr Maguire wanted to put a stop to evil, not because he was anything to do with the police, not because he had an appointed position in the courts of our land, not because he wanted to prevent evil from contaminating a household, but because he wanted to profit from it. To put the matter in plain words, Inspector, this man, Maguire, was a blackmailer.'

I sat back against the cushion and waited for a reaction.

'Is that a fact?' said the inspector, his eyes slightly bulging as he stared at me before making a quick note.

'God bless my soul,' said Dickens, coming in pat just as though he and I were acting in one of those wretched plays. I looked towards him and saw that he was nodding vigorously in a pantomime of admiration and of total conviction. I hoped that he wouldn't be too shocked at what I was going on to say. After all, the young in my mind included a child of his, or even, perhaps, two children of his. Once again, my mind wandered to Charley and his in-depth knowledge of the attic storey of the building.

I ploughed on rapidly. 'He has made trouble in the past,' I said gravely. 'He has caused tragedies, but this time it was his own life that he destroyed. The man that he tackled had too much at stake and he could not allow his tormentor to live. It was a case of life or death,' I finished dramatically.

'You're talking of Mr Maguire, aren't you, Mr Collins?' The inspector was beginning to recover from the strength of my onslaught. 'But you see, I understand that most people there behind the stage and above the stage thought that they were witnessing the performance of Lord Edward Bulwer-Lytton. Surely Lord Edward was the intended victim.'

I considered that only for a moment. On the one hand it would absolve the young people if it were considered that Lord Edward was the victim, but on the other hand it might result in the life-long incarceration of Lady Rosina. I decided to take the more audacious course and to broaden the field of the suspects.

'Oh, the audience did!' I said this with a light laugh. 'They all believed that it was Lord Edward. They saw only the costume, the hat and the wig and they had all been told that Lord Edward would be acting the part of the marquis. But as for all of us actors, and scene workers, well, it was obvious. Different voice, different manner, different way of holding his head – after all, the man was a good twenty years younger than Lord Edward.' I kept my voice resolutely confident and did not look towards Dickens. The die was cast. My mind was made up. I had decided that the intended victim had to be Tom Maguire. There were plenty who might have wanted to kill Lord Edward's secretary; but only one, Lady Rosina, who might have wanted to kill Lord Edward, himself and I felt, thinking of her face as she stared at the mausoleum which held her daughter's seventeen-year-old bones, that I owed a certain loyalty to that unfortunate woman. I did not want to aid her husband in his resolve to incarcerate her once more with the locked doors and windows of a private asylum, or worse still, see her dangle on the end of a rope. I glanced sideways at Dickens and saw him sitting very still with a grim look on his face, and so I plunged on with my lies.

'No, Inspector,' I said. 'I was quite certain that this was the secretary and not the owner of the house, and I'm sure that no one else was truly surprised when the real identity of the dead man was uncovered.' I went on, hoping that no one would tell the inspector about my astonishment when Dickens had revealed the truth. There was, I had thought, only one of the actors who was certain that the man, not the master, had enacted the part of the marquis and had died from a bullet on the floor of the ancient banqueting hall and that was Dickens. But, when I came to think of it, I realized that the house servants, the valet, probably Barrymore the butler and the housekeeper, Mrs Robinson, all of these would have heard that Lord Edward was ill and in his bed and that it was not beyond the bounds of possibility that some member of staff had told one of the players. And not beyond the bounds of possibility that someone with better eyesight and more interest in the play might have ascertained the truth even if they had heard nothing.

'And, of course, Inspector,' I said warming to my task, 'remember that the door to the back of the hall was wide open and that people filed in and took their seats where they could find an empty space. It was meant, of course, that this dress rehearsal should be for the amusement and appraisal of the workers within the house and the workers out on the estate. No seats were allocated and no one who came to the door would be turned back. Who knows, in that dimly lit hall, what man could have been sitting in a seat with a pistol in his hand and murder in his heart?' I finished with a dramatic flourish and caught a suppressed grin from Dickens.

'You think that someone, that one of the workers might have had a grudge against this man, Maguire, do you, Mr Collins?' The inspector sounded a little dubious. 'Or even against Sir Edward?' he added.

Like an efficient sheepdog, I herded the inspector back to Tom Maguire and away from any complications. 'I don't suppose,' I said spacing out my words in a judicial fashion, 'no, I don't suppose that most of the workers on the estate had anything much to do with Lord Edward.'

'That's true,' said Dickens. 'Lord Edward, himself, told me that was why he kept a secretary and always insisted that the man live in the house. Like myself, he preferred to write his own letters, make his own copies of his day's work at his writing desk, but he hated to have to deal with servants and workers. All of that was left to his secretary. To the estate workers and the house servants, Mr Maguire was the man who gave the orders and who hired and fired the staff.'

I was glad of Dickens' backing as I had merely hazarded a guess. His words, though, made me think fleetingly again about why it was Lord Edward who ordered that only young Jim Baldock was to have charge of cleaning out that cubby-hole above the ceiling of the banqueting hall. To ensure that the boy had a small wage, was that it? Wouldn't he have given another task, something that the boy had been bred to do, something like feeding the partridge chicks or similar? No, I thought there must be a link between the hidden gun and the order which made sure that his secret was safe. Was it a novelist's interest in an unfinished story? Did he, one day, plan to surprise Jim and confront him with his father's gun, find out what had happened to the missing man? I pushed the thoughts from my head and concentrated on my shepherding task.

'A most disliked man, Mr Maguire; I've gathered that during my time here,' I said with a shake of my head. 'It might be worthwhile finding out whether anyone was under notice, or had been accused of theft by the secretary,' I suggested.

The inspector made a note of that, but in a perfunctory

manner. Once he had laid down his pencil, I noticed that his eyes were fixed upon me with a look of curiosity.

'You may have noticed, Mr Collins, that the dead man held a conversation with one of the guests here in the house – a private conversation, perhaps. Something that made you think of the word blackmail.'

'Well, no . . . yes . . . well, I'm not very sure,' I said unhelpfully, and was glad to see that my hesitation had increased his interest.

'No hurry,' he said. 'Take your time, cast your mind back. There would have been a minute when your interest was aroused, when you thought that it was no idle chat that you were witnessing but a clue which roused your memories of something you had heard about this man Maguire and about possible links with blackmail. Just a few names, Mr Collins. You will do no harm to anyone except the man or woman who was guilty of murdering a fellow human being.' The inspector sat back and looked at me benevolently.

'Well, I did notice a few conversations that seemed rather intense, not like the usual remarks about the weather or about the house.' I enunciated the words slowly and carefully and wished that Dickens would disappear.

He didn't, though. He stayed very still and stared at me. I could feel the tension in the air, and it unsettled me. Ever since I was a child, I hated suspense, hated waiting for something bad to happen and always preferred to rush ahead and to trigger the crisis, to release the thunder rather than waiting apprehensively for the storm to break.

'Just a few names, Mr Collins. Won't go any further than this room unless there's a question of hard, solid evidence against someone.' The inspector had, I was glad to see, a very thoughtful and interested expression on his face. I could, perhaps, trust that nothing would ever be said about my guess and that my words would not be quoted.

'Oh, quite a few,' I said with an effort to appear casual. 'I did notice, in particular, that he seemed to be having a very earnest conversation with Mr Foster and with Mr Leech, the caricaturist. Does very clever drawings in *Punch* magazine, Inspector. I'm sure that you've seen them. Odd, really, because he didn't train as an artist, but as an accountant. Used to do the books for the magazine before he started to submit drawings.' I had a strong desire to stop there, but I knew that it wasn't enough. That piece of information was, I thought, worth little. It didn't seem worthy of the inspector's attention. 'Mr Leech didn't appear to be too happy when Maguire buttonholed him and whispered something in his ear.' I finished. And even to my own ears, it all sounded a little lame. The inspector gave a perfunctory nod, scribbled a few words into his notebook and then fixed me with a severe, pale grey eye.

'You mentioned the name of Mr Foster,' he said. He looked down at his notebook, carefully turning over the pages and only looked up when the silence had lasted somewhat too long. 'Tell me about Mr Foster,' he invited.

'A very highly esteemed gentleman and a great friend of mine. If you will excuse me, Inspector, I would prefer not to take any part in a discussion about him in his absence. So, you must excuse me.' Dickens was at his most haughty and was on his feet before he finished the sentence.

I dared not look at him, but there was too much at stake for me to withdraw my hints to the inspector. It will do no harm, I told myself, but I felt bad. I waited, eyes on the table in front of me, until he had left the room with, if it were not truly a slam of the door, certainly a decided snap of the lock.

We were both glad to see the back of him, I suspect. I leaned back in my chair and the inspector hitched his a little nearer to me.

'Now, sir,' he said, pencil at the ready and adding reassuringly, 'everything you say, Mr Collins, will, at this stage of the investigation, be treated as confidential. It will, of course, be a different matter if anything of concrete evidence is mentioned, but if that happens, I will stop you and warn you that what you say may be used in court.'

And with that little preamble over, he and I put our heads a little nearer to each other and I began.

'Absolutely no concrete evidence, Inspector, but as you know my brother is an artist and my mother's house, where he and I live, is filled with artists and poets, and of course, Inspector, you know how such people gossip.'

He nodded gravely, glad to be taken for such a man of the world.

'Strange man, Foster,' I mused, not looking at the inspector now, but drawing circles with my forefinger over the polished surface of the splay-legged table beside me. 'Son of a unitarian minister, of course. Upbringing very strict, eldest son, very close to his mother . . . well, you know.' I really had no idea of what I was trying to explain but the inspector looked most impressed.

'Not that I've ever noticed anything much myself,' I said cautiously, remembering his broad hint to me, 'but, of course, from time to time, well, you know how it is, Inspector. People will gossip and I get invited to lots of places. You'd be surprised what often comes up after the brandy has been chased around the table a couple of times.' And that obscure statement, I thought with satisfaction, could not lead to either myself or Foster ever ending up in a courthouse. 'And, of course, he was so reluctant to marry that he stretched out an engagement for many, many years, pretended to think the lady was unchaste and then broke the engagement.' I told him Lady Rosina's story about her poetess friend and hoped that it bored him. And then managed to shift the conversation to John Leech and was able to drop a few slanderous hints of suspicions of his honesty – all under the sheltering umbrella of repeating stories that I had been told. I thanked my lucky stars for the fortunate absence of Dickens, who valued Leech because of his wonderful drawings in *A Christmas Carol* and because the caricaturist was a rapid and indefatigable artist who could produce three or four talented woodcuts in the time between breakfast and dinner. Dickens would have been wounded and furious at these pieces of gossip about his friends and would, I knew, have hotly refuted them and thoroughly confused the inspector.

As it was, I hoped that I was confusing the picture and so was disappointed when he touched upon Lady Rosina.

'I understand that there was a disturbance at dinner,' he said, referring to his notes. 'The girl who waited at table gave evidence to the sergeant.' He skimmed down the page, reading isolated words and phrases aloud: broken plates, pistol, soup,

Mr Maguire, soup bowl on head, phone call, asylum. And then, decisively, he shut his notebook.

'Between you and me, Mr Collins, what is your honest opinion of the lady? Is she sane?'

I pretended to give that my most earnest consideration before answering.

'To be honest with you, Inspector,' I said, 'I think that she is a bit of an actress.' And then I sat back and looked for the response.

It took him aback. I saw him turning the idea over in his mind. After a moment, he said, in a most reasonable manner, 'What's her game, Mr Collins?'

I was ready for that one, had thought it through in a flash of inspiration.

'Money, Inspector, money. The lady wants money.'

He laughed at that. 'Don't we all,' he said indulgently.

'She more than most.' I persisted with my thesis. 'This is a lady who lived here in this house.' I waved my hand to encompass the glowing Persian carpet, velvet curtains, priceless pieces of furniture and then ended by picking up a small picture showing a watercolour of Knebworth House in all its Gothic splendour. I saw his eye move along the yards and yards of towers and turrets, domes and spires, flying buttresses and carved insignia. 'She was used to living here, to having servants at her beck and call,' I said quietly. 'Of course, she knows that she can never return, would not wish to return, but she wants more than to be living in genteel poverty with just one untrained maid to wait upon her. Shooting the secretary, no matter how annoyed she was with him, would do her no good. She was here to strike a bargain with her husband, to force him into granting her a generous settlement.'

Of course, I thought, as I enumerated all the reasons why Lady Rosina was an unlikely assassin, I was aware that these reasons would have given her a very good reason to shoot the noble lord, himself – she of all those present in the house on that day would be the only one that had such a motive. But when it came to the secretary, Tom Maguire, well, I said to myself, there were plenty who could have wanted to get rid of him. Safety in numbers, I told myself, though I trembled for these young people who might have wanted to get rid of a monstrously evil man like Tom Maguire. I was, though, reasonably certain that the intended victim was Tom Maguire. An unpleasant man, probably a blackmailer, certainly a would-be rapist and, I guessed, an instigator to evil deeds. He may have deserved his killing.

But as I watched the inspector's busy pencil scribble in his notebook, a very strange idea came into my head.

And if I were right, I thought, Maguire was a side figure, an accidental casualty in this strange affair. I would have to see Dickens, not now, but when dinner was over, and we could retire to our rooms and have an uninterrupted conversation. I needed his clarity of mind, his strong moral sense and his knowledge of the world.

FIFTEEN

There are foolish criminals who are discovered, and
wise criminals who escape. The hiding of a crime, or
the detection of a crime, what is it? A trial of skill
between the police on one side, and the individual on
the other. When the criminal is a brutal, ignorant fool,
the police, in nine cases out of ten, win. When the
criminal is a resolute, educated, highly intelligent man,
the police, in nine cases out of ten, lose.

Wilkie Collins, *The Woman in White*

D inner was a sombre meal. Everyone had witnessed
the dragging of the pond and the story of the passionate
gamekeeper and his unfaithful wife had percolated
through the guests. Their thoughts were, I guessed, on the
absent girl. Even Lady Rosina was unusually quiet and from
time to time looked down the table at the white face of Frances,
sitting alone, with the empty space for her daughter at her
side. Young Charles was there, only after a struggle with his
father, I guessed, because he ate virtually nothing and made
no attempt at conversation. Foster and Leech ate thoughtfully
and said little, wearing the appearance of men fresh from an
unpleasant interview. I averted my eyes from them both and
hoped that neither would ever find out the part that I had
played in throwing suspicion on them. Even Helen Lemon
was unusually silent, and from time to time, I could see her
look across at her husband with a surreptitious and slightly
questioning air.

At the head of the table, Dickens was holding an animated
conversation with Clarkson about the wrecking of a brigantine
at Lowestoft in Suffolk and they were arguing about whether
the ship was on its way to Galway or to Cork in southern
Ireland. The master of the house, Lord Edward, sat in silence

for most of the meal and glared malevolently down the table at his wife. After the table was cleared of the main course and the cheese platters and the plates of biscuits were arranged in a neat line down the centre of the table, I saw him tap Dickens on the shoulder and then his voice could be heard, speaking into Dickens' ear. I overheard some words: 'Malvern. Waters. Physician' and saw my friend nod thoughtfully. Not pleased though, I thought, as I looked at his face and guessed what was coming. And so, I was not surprised when Lord Edward rose to his feet and tapped a small gong by his plate.

'Ladies and gentlemen,' he said in the loud, toneless fashion of the very deaf. 'I regret very much that this pleasant gathering must come to an end. Our little dramatic production has, of course, been already cancelled as a consequence of the tragedy that occurred in the banqueting hall.' He stopped there and looked at both sides of the table with his inimitably haughty air of slight surprise. There had been a murmur after his words. No one had, I guessed, been told this news; certainly Dickens, who was closest of all to the master of the house and had been the stage manager of the event, had not heard that the performance was cancelled. I looked down the table and saw his lips tighten but he said nothing. There was an air of relief on most faces. Despite the luxury of the surroundings I doubted whether anyone was enjoying their stay.

'The butler and the housekeeper and their staff,' went on the toneless voice of Lord Edward, 'are completely at your disposal to help you in your travel arrangements. The morning trains to London leave at nine o'clock and at twelve o'clock and the carriage and other vehicles will be at your disposal. I myself will be setting off at an early hour of the morning for Malvern as I am forced to seek medical attention, so I will bid you all goodnight and goodbye and hope that we meet again in happier times.'

The noble lord bowed in his stiff, mannered fashion and then, to everyone's astonishment, he left the room.

'What a perfect host,' said Lady Rosina in a loud, mocking tone once the door had closed behind her former husband. 'Shall we all get the nine o'clock train to London, do let's! There should be a couple of wagonettes in the stables so we can all go together. The sooner we are out of this house, the happier we will be. You will, I'm sure, my dear' – she turned with her impulsive grace to Frances and placed a hand on her arm – 'you will find your little Nelly safe and sound tucked up cosily with one of her sisters or one of her friends.' There was a note of deep sympathy in her voice. I looked with interest at Frances but was not surprised when she merely bowed her head and murmured her thanks. A very discreet lady. The fact that Nelly was hidden up in the attics would implicate Charley Dickens and even, perhaps, Dickens himself. And now it was Dickens who interrupted Lady Rosina's plans.

'But what about the police enquiry?' he asked looking across at Foster who usually took command of gatherings like ours.

'We'll steal away at the crack of dawn,' said Lady Rosina gaily. 'Don't worry. Barrymore will manage the police. He's very efficient. Don't frown at me, Mr Dickens. You know that the play is dead, the secretary is dead, but we're all alive and well so let's get out of this house. I'll send my lawyer to Edward, I think. I don't believe that I can stand talking to him, myself.' She stood up and looked all around the table. 'Now, my dears,' she said addressing herself to the ladies, 'let's leave the men to their cigars and brandy and we'll go to the drawing room and I'll ring for Barrymore and for Mrs Robinson and we'll get everything arranged. What fun!'

My eyes met those of Frances, and I raised my eyebrows. Discreet as always, she gave me the slightest nod. No doubt but that she would arrange matters so that if Nelly were still at Knebworth, then she would certainly join them at the station. I saw young Charley try to catch her eye, but she resolutely avoided looking in his direction. Nor did she look in the direction of his father. The secret which had been kept for almost twenty years was still to remain hidden. Both she and Dickens had reputations to uphold and Charley would just have to forget his first love. I avoided looking at him and went to hold the door open for the ladies.

'Wish I was going with you to the drawing room; much more fun than staying here,' I whispered to Lady Rosina in a flirtatious manner, and she blew me a kiss.

'You stay here and organize them into getting rid of the police,' she whispered back. 'We don't want them hanging around and upsetting the servants. Barrymore and Mrs Robinson will manage the place excellently as long as they are left in peace.' And with that she took Helen Lemon's arm and said gaily, 'Let's send one of the footmen down to the station to reserve two carriages on the morning train. And we'll just have entertaining men like Mr Collins, young Mr Dickens and your nice husband in with us. What do you think? Should we have luncheon baskets or is the journey too short?'

I didn't hear Mrs Lemon's reply. I was too busy thinking about the police. This was an extraordinary business. A murder had been committed in the house, the local police had been summoned and then the matter handed over to Scotland Yard and now the master of the house chose to go away and had more or less dismissed all of his guests, leaving nobody but servants to answer enquiries. And no matter how efficient Mr Barrymore and Mrs Robinson were in their roles as butler and housekeeper, it did seem quite extraordinary to leave them to deal with the police, just as though, perhaps, that a poacher had been found dead in the grounds.

I closed the door firmly behind the women and then went up past the chairs and knelt on the floor beside Dicken's chair, impatiently pushing the empty chair of our host out of my way. 'Dick,' I whispered, 'we can't let this happen. Someone must tell Inspector Field. Lord Edward can't walk off like that, surely.'

Dickens shrugged. 'He's already been informed. A servant has taken a letter to the police station. Everyone has made a statement, and everyone has left their permanent address with the inspector. After all, if a murder took place at a race meeting, or in a theatre, you would not, could not reasonably expect people to remain on the spot for more than a day or so. I've had a strong word with the inspector, recalling to his mind that Nelly was under my eye all of the time before the murder occurred. I expressed myself surprised that his men had harassed the girl so much that she had panicked and gone off to London. I left him grovelling for forgiveness and blaming all on the stupidity of the sergeant and his men. Myself,' finished Dickens pensively, 'I suspect that this murder will be one of the great unsolved crimes of the century and I am, as you know, seldom wrong about these matters. And, let's face it, Collins, the man will not be mourned.' He got to his feet and manufactured a stage version of a sleepy man, rubbing his eyes and smothering a yawn, then looked at his watch and made a remark about early rising to catch the nine o'clock train to London.

I looked at him uneasily. It was tempting to bow my head and to give into the certainty in his voice. After all, did it matter? The man, Tom Maguire, was thoroughly unpleasant. I was almost certain now that he was not only a potential rapist, but also a blackmailer. The case had already dropped out of public interest. Yesterday's papers had mentioned the possibility of some former soldier, wandering the countryside after the Crimean War, finding his way through the open front door and into the hall. The newspapers were strong in their citations of such crimes and rather weak on why Lord Edward should have attracted the attention of such masterless men, but a few catchphrases about the lack of moral fibre and quotes from parliamentary debates about the dangers lurking in the streets of London spreading into the peaceful countryside were enough to frighten the well-to-do and to satisfy their curiosity about the murder at Knebworth House.

Nevertheless, if I were right then another shooting might take place . . .

Suddenly I made up my mind.

'I'll walk up with you,' I said, and did not wait for an answer but proceeded him out of the room and up the stairs towards the bedrooms. I kept ahead of him all the way and when he produced his key from his pocket, I waited with him.

'A nightcap?' he queried with a resigned look and I nodded enthusiastically. I knew that Dickens could never resist mixing one of his celebrated nightcaps. In any case, I was inside the door before he could possibly have shut it without appearing rude.

Once inside the room, I ensconced myself upon his bed, beneath the cosy crimson of the Chinese panels. He looked at me with one of his long-suffering glances and then busied himself with the punch, absorbed in mixing potions from the various bottles on a tray and adding a spoonful of brown sugar and sprinklings of spices to his mixture.

I watched him, and despite myself, there was a measure of indulgence in my glance. Yes, he had a hundred faults. Yes, he was bombastic, was overbearing at times, but he was a genius, and, almost more important to me, he was a very good and very faithful friend. He had done marvels for me, had emancipated me from the drudgery of an office situation, had taught me to believe in myself, had given me the tools of the trade, the ability to write so as to capture the mind and the imagination of the reading population of the English-speaking world.

And now I was going to wound him.

'Dick,' I said and then I stopped. I needed to gather my thoughts, to arrange my pieces of evidence, to be as persuasive to him as I had been to myself when I had gone over and over this matter within my mind.

'Yes,' he said, not really paying attention to me, but concentrating on the precise measurements of the spices and of the liquor which would draw forth their aroma.

I sat back. This was not the moment. I would wait until we were both relaxed, both filled with the peaceful state of mind where everything suddenly takes on a clarity and a truth, unknown during more sober moments.

I did not interrupt again and as he went through the mystic process of combining taste and smell and the subtlety of the euphoria wrought upon the brain by the perfection of an alcoholic drink matched with spices and sugars from other worlds.

And so, while Dickens fussed over teaspoons of this and of that, and over glassfuls from an assortment of bottles, I sat back and ran pictures through my mind. There was the arrival of Lady Rosina. The reaction of Clarkson, the fury of her husband. The gun in the handbag, the listening tube, always by Lord Edward's side, the strange puzzlement of watching the man's face and how he scrutinized mine as though he, perhaps, heard far more than he pretended to do. And then there was the worried and – yes, it was anger – the worried and angry face of the cartoonist Leech, the moment of fury upon the face of Clarkson as he recalled the adorable figure of Lady Rosina and his assertion that he would die for her. The reaction of the stable manager, his reserve, the way that he baulked at the idea of the boy, Jim Baldock, being involved in the dragging of the lake.

And then there was my own visit to the gunroom. My observation of the height of the ceiling of the banqueting hall and my idle speculation upon the difficulty of cleaning the bronze medallions. I sat very still and allowed Dickens to talk about the play while he mixed the ingredients for one of his famous concoctions.

'Terrible shame,' he said while busily engaged. 'I'm a good judge of a play and of actors and I think this was going to be a superb production. Superbly directed, of course, by a stage manager at the height of his genius.'

I said nothing. I was used to Dickens. In another man his tendency to praise himself might have become irritating and, indeed, unbearable, but with Dickens such observations were always salted with a humour and a self-awareness so that they never grated. It was as though the character of Charles Dickens was ranged in his mind alongside other such notable boasters such as Bumble and Pickwick and Mr Pecksniff. 'This same extraordinary character', 'the inimitable' – he had a dozen names for himself. I saw him eye me with a slight air of uneasiness, but I was too busy with my thoughts to give him the acknowledgement which he sought.

'Drink this down and then I think that you should seek your bed,' he said abruptly as he put the steaming beverage in front of me. 'You look tired, Wilkie, and we will have an early start in the morning.'

I took a sip from the punch and then gulped some more down. It was hot and strong. I felt the heat run through my veins and it gave me courage. For a few moments I had thought of acquiescing to his unspoken wish: drink my punch, wish him goodnight and retire to my bedroom.

But I could not do it. The name of the murderer was on the tip of my tongue and I blurted out my thoughts.

'Lady Rosina,' I said and then pronounced her maiden name. 'Lady Rosina Doyle Wheeler married Edward Bulwer-Lytton, Edward Bulwer at the time. It was considered a great match for her. You have a very high opinion of him, Dick, don't you? You enjoy coming here and staying with him. You are grateful for his introductions to the great and to the good. You understand the man; you know what a terrible blow it was to him when the marriage deteriorated into public wrangling.'

Dickens said nothing and I knew, in a flash, that he had forestalled me. That the swarm of small clues that swam in my mind had already been ranged up in neat rows within his own superior brain. I looked across at him and waited. Impatiently he snatched the embroidered cover from his bed, folded it neatly and placed it on top of a chair.

'Go to bed, Collins,' he said sternly. 'We'll meet in the morning.'

I think it was the use of my surname, the coldness of his voice, the dropping of the affectionate tone with which he normally pronounced 'Wilkie' which strengthened my resolve. He had tossed back the remains of his punch and now he got to his feet. I did not follow suit. I stayed seated. I put my own unfinished punch aside and ordered my thoughts for a long minute before I spoke.

'I suppose,' I said, 'that murder was in the air from the moment when Lady Rosina came in through the door of the library. She was a woman with a grievance and she, as you said yourself, is an indomitable woman. There may have been faults on both sides, but she had no doubt in her mind but that her husband was responsible for her unhappy situation and she had no compunction about ridiculing him and trying to disgrace him in front of his friends.'

Dickens looked at me keenly. 'And what is that to do with this murder? What are you implying? Be careful, Collins, be very careful! You are meddling with matters which may be injurious to a young man like yourself.' His voice was abrupt and held a warning.

I disregarded his words and the threat beneath them.

'If Lady Rosina had been shot, who would be the suspect?' I asked abruptly.

He looked at me quizzically. 'Tom Maguire, the perfect secretary,' he said lightly, but his eyes were dark with anger.

'Though that might be going beyond the duties that any master might expect from a secretary, it would certainly make the man rise to the top of his profession,' he added lightly, with a smile which I refused to return.

'But you acknowledge that Lord Edward would have liked to be rid of Lady Rosina?' When he made no answer to that, I added quietly, 'You were very eloquent about their relationship, Dick. And I think that you summed him up well when you said, "He is a sensitive man, a man whose place in society is of the utmost importance to him". And being that sort of man, to have a wife who ridiculed him, who pilloried him all over London and in his hometown in Hertfordshire, it would not be impossible that he would toy with the idea of ridding himself of her permanently. He tried to incarcerate her within the walls of a genteel asylum, but that did not work. It led to more criticism of him and more disgrace to his name. I could imagine that a man of his temperament would get to the end of his tether and would resolve to rid himself of her permanently. And so,' I finished, 'a murder was committed.'

I sat back and looked at him, rather pleased with myself and with the drama of my presentation. This should puzzle him.

It didn't, though. There was a flash of anger, and indeed of apprehension in the look which he cast upon me, but he refused to play his part. 'Don't be ridiculous,' was all that he said.

'Yes, of course, you are right,' I said. 'Lady Rosina was, in fact, not the person who was killed; nevertheless, she was the intended victim.'

I waited a few seconds for him to point out that Lady Rosina was not on stage and so could not have been the intended victim, but again he refused me that satisfaction; just sat there eyeing me coldly. I began to feel like an author whose intended dramatic conclusion has been foreseen by all. Nevertheless, I had to go forward.

'Lady Rosina's hatred of her husband was well known,' I said. 'She had demonstrated it again and again during these few past days. She had taken her gun from her handbag and pointed it at her husband, had threatened him on numerous occasions. She was standing backstage, carrying, as always, her handbag. In the darkness, she could easily shoot him. You could say that Lord Edward set up a situation where his own murder could occur, but he cleverly swopped the victim. Everyone, except you, thought that the man dressed as the marquis was Lord Edward. He and his secretary were of similar heights and the costume, wig and hat shaded the face.' I stopped to give him time to assimilate the details and then added, 'But, of course, she didn't shoot him. It was not Lady Rosina who fired the fatal bullet. Lord Edward shot the secretary in the hope that his wife would be declared insane and that she could be permanently shut up in an asylum and would never bother him again.'

Once again, I stopped, but this time I determined to go no further until he answered me. Let him pick holes in my thesis if he wished, I told myself. I had, I thought, an answer to any objection.

When he spoke, his voice was harsh and ironic. 'Is this what you are saying, Collins? Lord Edward, my dear friend Lord Edward, rises from his sick bed, dresses without the help or even the knowledge of his valet, goes downstairs, walks into the banqueting hall and passes beneath my all-seeing eye, lifts a revolver and shoots his own secretary.' Dickens finished and sat back, looking inscrutably at me.

'Wrong,' I said with a certain measure of satisfaction in my voice. 'Yes, Lord Edward gets out of bed, but he does not dress. I suggest that he pulls on a dressing gown as though to go to the bathroom, but instead, once he sees that the coast is clear, he climbs the last set of stairs to the attic and makes his way across to the small space above the ceiling of the banqueting hall, he takes from the broom cupboard the gun belonging to young Jim's gamekeeper father, a gun which I guess the boy kept in good order, and possibly may have loaded with ammunition – though it's just as possible that Lord Edward came prepared – and in any way would have previously checked the gun when he planned the deed.' It was, I remembered from my visit to the gunroom, quite difficult for anyone to remove a gun or pistol, but extremely easy to help oneself to ammunition.

'The deed,' repeated Dickens with a note of sarcasm in his voice. His eyes were shielded from me as he kept them fixed on the ornate Chinese-patterned wallpaper by his side. I leaned back in the chair and with no little pride in my cleverness, I proceeded to spell out the plot.

'It was, you know, quite clever,' I said. 'Lady Rosina would have been deemed to have eventually carried out her oft repeated threat – to kill her husband. Lord Edward would feign an ear infection – though I had noted that he was only pretending to be even more deaf than usual as he heard something that the sergeant said although it was spoken in quite a low voice. But it was a plausible excuse to be ill with one of his chronic ear problems – that, after all, was one of the reasons why he insisted that the secretary should be word perfect as an understudy.' I saw him nod and guessed that he had thought of that before. Nevertheless, I gave him a moment to digest my points before I went on.

'And who knows but that the secretary who, I guess from some other information, was a blackmailer, may well have had some secret hold over his master. So that there may have been another reason to get rid of him,' I added. 'Or, since he managed all of Lord Edward's affairs, he may have cheated him of a large sum of money. Lord Edward is the sort of man who would have winced to have his affairs exposed in a court case and might prefer to be rid of the man in a secret fashion. But, in any case, Lord Edward was not the sort of man to allow something like the death of a mere secretary to deter him once he had conceived the idea and once he had realized that he and he alone knew the secret of how to shoot a man lying on the floor of the banqueting hall stage without anyone seeing him or seeing the gun that he held.'

I waited for a question, but Dickens didn't give me that satisfaction, so I proceeded to enlighten him.

'You remember the bronze medallions in the ceiling of the banqueting hall,' I said. 'It had occurred to me when I saw them first, when you showed me around the house, that it would be quite a job to keep them cleaned and polished since they were a good forty feet above floor level, but once I went into the little room in the attic, I could see how it was managed

– quite ingenious really. They unclipped from above and when
dealt with they were just clipped back into place again. That
would have been one of young Jim's tasks – to keep the
medallions clean and polished. You can see, can't you,
Dickens, how a man with a gun could easily unclip a medallion above the place where you had designated with your
chalk mark that the marquis should stretch on the ground.
The murderer could fire the fatal shot and then clip it back
again within a couple of seconds. No one could possibly have
seen it at that height above floor level. Remember all the
lighting is below ten feet in height. Remember also that Lord
Edward must have been the only one who knew of that. Lord
Edward could have shot the man and then returned to his bed
before there was any chance of being discovered. And Nelly
heard footsteps from the ceiling above the stage and saw the
man acting the part of the marquis look up. She told me that
she knew it could not be Lord Edward there on stage and so
it must be his understudy, the secretary.'

I sat back and after a moment could not resist asking, 'Well,
have I convinced you?'

'My dear Collins, the whole thing is most unlikely, and
the police will never believe it. And if, by any chance, you
do tell this tale to Inspector Field, I can tell you what will
happen.'

I could not resist it. 'What?' I asked.

'Our young friend, Jim, will, without doubt, be arrested,'
he said coolly. 'Remember that he knew of how the bronze
medallions could be unscrewed from above the ceiling. The
police are not going to swallow this far-fetched story that Lord
Edward, a peer of the realm, murders his own secretary in
order that his estranged wife might be found guilty of the act,
declared insane and confined to an asylum for the rest of her
life. My dear Collins, Inspector Field would laugh in your
face. However, that was a clever idea that the man could have
been shot from forty feet up through the ceiling. I imagine
that you are right and that was how the killing was accomplished. And, of course, young Jim would bear a grudge against
the secretary, would be terrified, in fact, that the dog he cared
for would be shot on this man's orders.'

'Surely the boy would not kill a man, just in case a dog might be shot,' I said feebly. 'It wasn't even his dog.'

'Boys, my dear friend, get very attached to dogs. There is nothing,' said Dickens in his usual sweeping fashion, 'that anyone can tell me, a father of eight boys, about the species, so you can take my word for it. And I remember my own house filled with sobs when our dog, Timber, died of old age. That boy, however kind his master is to him, is alone in the world and the dog may have been of more importance to him than anyone could realize. Do you remember how he spoke up when I proposed buying the dog? He wanted you to have him, thought that he would have been happier with you. Very, very fond of that dog. Just think, Collins. He hears that the dog is to be shot because of the malice of one man and who knows he might already have had a dislike of that man. If the secretary had been involved in the seduction of the boy's mother and was known to be a friend of her lover, the boy could have had a previous grudge against Maguire, might have blamed him for his orphaned state. He knows where the gun is hidden, he knows a way of shooting the man without the knowledge of anyone else in the house.'

I stared at him in dismay. He was right, of course. Damn him, I thought, he's always right. I had seen how, on very little evidence, that the police had seized upon the seventeen-year-old actress and had terrified and persecuted her while most of the evidence would have pointed towards Lady Rosina who not only had a pistol in her handbag, but had previously aimed it at the master of the house and had threatened to kill him. An orphaned boy, son of a murderer, would be an obvious suspect.

'So, we must let him get away with it; is that what you are saying, Dick?' I said bitterly. I took off my glasses and cleaned them vigorously with my pocket handkerchief.

He did not answer for a moment and as his face came into focus again when I had replaced my glasses, I could see a thoughtful look upon it. He held up a hand.

'I don't think that we can quite leave it at that,' he said. 'If you are right, then there is a danger that something else might happen and murder is something that I cannot condone. Lady

Rosina may be still in danger. A man who has killed once, will lose a certain inhibition and the next time he kills, he may make sure of his prey.' He got to his feet decisively: Dickens never took long to make up his mind. 'Come with me, Collins. We need to see about this matter before we leave the house tomorrow morning.'

It took me a moment to guess what he was about to do and then I was appalled. 'No, you go, Dickens,' I spoke quickly and even I could hear the note of panic in my tone. 'I'll leave it to you,' I said and rose to my feet ready to disappear through the door.

He stopped me, of course. He never could brook any disagreement with his plans. 'No, damn you; you've started this, so you'll see it through to the bitter end,' he said as he swiftly interposed his frame between me and the door.

'But, Dick' – I rather despised the note of pleading in my voice, but I persisted – 'you're his friend. He'll take it better from you. You can get a promise from him that he will not do anything to injure Lady Rosina again.'

'I need you as a witness,' he said firmly and then he lowered the gas lamp flame, blew out the candle by his bedside, took my arm and in a moment we were both out of the room and were mounting the interminable steps of stairs up to where the master of the house had situated his sleeping place. Dickens, now fired with energy, took them at a pace and I toiled three or four steps behind him. He stopped though, when he reached the top stair, stopped and put a finger to his lips. Voices were coming to our ears, the loud, rather toneless voice of Lord Edward and another – Inspector Field. I recognized the London accent.

Perhaps, I thought, we were too late.

But no, they were at the preliminary stages, the inspector was still talking about Nelly, one of his men had visited her sister's place and Drury Lane management had supplied a list of actresses' addresses. His somewhat monotonous voice was interrupted and just as I reached the door, I heard Lord Edward say, 'You're on the wrong track completely, Inspector. This young girl had nothing to do with the murder of my secretary. I'm afraid that the guilt lies at another door.'

Dickens did not hesitate. He rapped sharply on the door and then without waiting for an answer pushed it open. I was embarrassed as I followed him in, but Dickens immediately greeted Inspector Field and without a blush joined in with the interrupted conversation, giving his strong opinion that it was not Nelly who, he declared, had been under his own eye at the time, and declaring that he had a feeling the shot had come from the other side of the stage. He and Inspector Field discussed this theory in an animated way and Dickens related an anecdote that he had overheard in the village about a group of masterless men, left over from the Crimean War, who made a living by the burglary of houses of the wealthy. I ventured to rest my short legs by perching upon the windowsill while names of places like Alma, Balaclava and Inkerman were bandied between the two men until Dickens, in his forceful way, accompanied the inspector to the door, promised to visit him in Scotland Yard on an appointed day, shut the door upon him and then came back into the room.

And now the atmosphere had changed. Lord Edward had said nothing since we had entered the room. He had not interfered in any way with Dickens, just stayed sitting upon an uncomfortable-looking chair with a deeply carved back and looking intently, it appeared to me, into my guilt-filled face. But now he spoke.

'Well,' he said. 'I hope that I have managed to convince that blockhead of an inspector that the intended victim was certainly me and that there was no earthly reason why that little actress should have shot me. It's obvious that the murderer was someone who wished for my death. The wrong man got the bullet.'

'Inspector Field is no blockhead but I'm glad that you convinced him of Nelly's innocence,' said Dickens. 'Nevertheless, I don't think that the murderer made a mistake. I think that he knew full well who he was killing, when he removed the bronze medallion from the ceiling of the banqueting hall and fired the shot down on the man who lay there on the stage. His aim was true, and he trusted to accomplish his purpose, but his real intent was not that death.' He spoke without raising his voice unduly, but he was an accomplished and an experienced public speaker and it was obvious that his words were heard without difficulty by our host. Lord Edward said nothing, though, just stroked his chin meditatively and gazed across at Dickens. Me, he ignored, and I held my breath, realizing that every word that Dickens spoke was weighted with meaning.

And with a rush of excitement I also realized that my guess had been correct. The face in front of me had all its bland assurance peeled from it and it was the guilty face of a murderer. He himself had said, 'There is nothing so agonizing to the fine skin of vanity as the application of a rough truth,' and the blotched, reddened skin of his face and the panic-filled eyes betrayed that he had heard that rough truth. He said nothing, though, and made no plea, no justification, just sat there, clothed in the sumptuous purple velvet of his dressing gown and stared rigidly ahead.

Dickens, with the instinct of an accomplished actor, left a long minute of silence before he spoke again and when he did so, his voice was friendly and cordial. 'Now, my dear Bulwer,' he said, 'let me talk to you like a grandfather. This sad affair between yourself and Lady Rosina, each trying to injure the other, now this really must not go on. You're a sensible man, but perhaps you are too involved to see the solution. The lady wants money and so she must get money. You're a rich man; I happen to know that you earn a huge income from your forty or so novels, not to mention your plays and your volumes of poetry,' said Dickens with a slight note of bitterness in his voice, but that was lost when he plunged on with his solution. 'Allow me, my dear fellow, to manage everything for you. Give me a note now to your lawyer, while everything is fresh in our minds. Trust me. I'll get him to draw up a fair agreement, stipulating, of course, that the lady or any of her emissaries will not approach you, or, indeed, that neither you nor any of your emissaries will approach her. It will all be done without trouble or bother to you, beyond the signing of your name to the final document. Do write me that note, now my dear fellow and I will take the whole difficult business off your shoulders.'

And Dickens, with an unmistakable air of purpose, went across to the writing table beside his host, selected a sheet of paper and sharpened a quill like a devoted clerk. He then drew up a chair and wrote rapidly and fluently before replacing the pen in the inkstand, blotting the paper and passing it over to his host.

There was a long silence, a very long silence. I held my breath. Could everything be worked out as easily as this? It was not true justice, of course, but I had little desire to see the noble lord tried for murder. The important thing was to put others out of danger and Dickens' solution would also solve the problem of Lady Rosina.

Eventually Lord Edward spoke. There were two bands of hectic colour upon his cheekbones that owed nothing to the paintbox and his hand trembled as he took the pen into his hand.

'And that will be the end of the matter if I do as you say?' His voice shook.

'You have my solemn word that if you keep to the terms of this document and neither seek to see or to communicate in any way with Lady Rosina, that both I and Mr Collins will keep silent about all that happened here in this house.'

Dickens waited for the signature and then took the paper into his hand, holding it carefully near to the fire until the ink was dry.

'Come, Collins,' he said to me. 'All has now been settled. I'll give the inspector a few days to investigate, to follow up some fruitless leads, and then I'll visit him. I'm sure,' he added with one of his verbal flourishes, 'that I can convince him and Scotland Yard that some itinerant with a grudge against Lord Edward, who after all has been a magistrate for the last thirty years, managed to take a potshot at the man dressed as a marquis while he lay on the floor of the stage. Scotland Yard are good at handling this sort of thing. The matter will have almost been forgotten by the newspapers when they make the announcement. And,' said Dickens grimly, 'I'm sure that we can both trust Lord Edward to keep his side of the bargain and allow Lady Rosina the comforts due to her station in life.'

EPILOGUE

Last night I dreamed of Lady Rosina. Dressed all in white, she stood at the gate of an asylum and with slow and solemn gesture, she beckoned to me. As I came near to her, she looked deep into my eyes and pointed towards an unmarked grave in the distance.

Then I awoke. I was confused for a minute but soon came to my senses.

The Woman in White, my new novel, the book that was going to make me rich and famous throughout the English-speaking world, was a huge success. It had been published by Dickens in his magazine *All the Year Round* and then the hardback edition had hit the world. Already, barely a month after publication, it had earned me over £1,400 in royalties – an enormous sum, almost as much as Dickens had paid for his magnificent house and country estate at Gad's Hill. Last night, Dickens, himself, had thrown a party to celebrate my success. He had made a speech which had brought tears to my eyes and caused me to gulp down more champagne than was good for me.

The champagne, I thought, had brought about that bad dream.

Lady Rosina was alive and well, enjoying the generous allowance paid monthly by her husband. I had brought her a signed copy of *The Woman in White* and we had laughed together about the news that young Charley Dickens, returned from abroad, was now madly in love with the daughter of a publisher and was all set to marry his Bessie and settle down. We avoided the subject of Nelly and the sad separation of Dickens and his wife, and spoke only of *The Woman in White*, my masterpiece, Lady Rosina called it and related how she had seen, every week, huge queues standing patiently outside the printers of *All the Year Round* waiting eagerly for the next edition of *The Woman in White*. She, herself, had bought one every week for the sake of my story.

We said nothing about her husband. I could see from her affluent surroundings that he had kept his bargain. He was now Secretary of State for the Colonies in Lord Derby's Conservative administration and so did not wish to attract any more publicity about the treatment of his wife. Nor did we discuss Dickens and the huge success of his latest novel, *A Tale of Two Cities*, about a golden-haired girl who met her father for the first time when she was eighteen years old.

Lady Rosina wore white, a high-necked, long-sleeved, silken dress, draped with a soft snowy Indian cashmere shawl, and she swore she would never wear any other colour again. We discussed her latest book. She had written the title, a splendid title, *Shells from the Sands of Time*, but was seeking ideas for its content and I promised to think about it. It was the least that I could do.

The Woman in White was set to bring me fame and fortune for the rest of my life and perhaps for even hundreds of years in the future, and her appearance at Knebworth in that month of July had been the inspiration for my most successful book.

AUTHOR'S NOTE

Dear Reader,

This book is inspired by my interest, not just in Charles Dickens and his friends, but also in Ellen Ternan whose name is so connected with his.

So, who was Ellen Ternan?

A huge majority of the English-speaking population of the world would probably say that she was an actress who became Charles Dickens' mistress, but I am convinced that she was not his mistress, but his daughter.

Oddly, I originally came to this opinion from what one might call the internal evidence. I was rereading *A Tale of Two Cities* and for the first time was suddenly struck by the enormous force of the emotion in the scenes where an adult daughter and father meet for the first time. And Lucy in *A Tale of Two Cities* was physically almost the exact image of Ellen Ternan: 'A short, slight, pretty figure, a quantity of golden hair, a puzzled expression and a pair of blue eyes . . .'

Dickens, I've always felt, writes poorly about love between a man and a woman – Lucy's relationship with Charles Darnay is cardboard sentimentality – but he writes with great intensity about this relationship of a father and newly-found daughter.

Dickens, himself, states that the idea of writing *A Tale of Two Cities* came to him in 1857 which was the year when he first took over the role of protector of the Ternan family, Mrs Frances Ternan and her three girls, Fanny, Maria and Ellen.

'Young enough to be his daughter' say various reproving voices of biographers.

But could Ellen Ternan, in fact, be his daughter? Do dates make it possible, or even feasible?

Ellen was the youngest of three children. Her mother, Frances, married Thomas Ternan in 1834 but he died of syphilis in 1846. The link between Frances Ternan and Dickens was an actor called Macready. He was one of Dickens' best friends and a very good friend and patron of Frances Ternan who had acted with Macready since her earliest years playing opposite him in many Shakespearean plays – Ophelia to his Hamlet when she was younger and then Gertrude, Hamlet's mother, in the same play many years later. In May 1837 Catherine Dickens suffered a miscarriage after the tragic and sudden death of her seventeen-year-old sister, Mary Hogarth. Dickens took his wife to Broadstairs seaside to recuperate but he himself travelled up and down to London, staying overnight in order to visit the theatre and see his friend Macready. He would certainly have met Frances Ternan at that time.

The following January Dickens resolved to keep a diary. He went to Yorkshire to investigate schools and began to write *Nicholas Nickelby*, which is suffused with a sense of theatre throughout. The Crummles theatrical family, along with that memorable character 'The Infant Phenomenon' (the two elder Ternan girls had been on the stage since the age of two), has now become a household name, but it probably shows the influence that the Ternan family had upon him. Dickens writes in his diary about attending a banquet in honour of the actor Macready and it is very likely that the Ternans were there, also. The interesting thing is that three pages have been torn out of this diary in January 1838. Could it have been something about Frances Ternan, which in view of later events, he decided to get rid of?

Ellen Lawless Ternan was born in March 1839, so where was Dickens nine months earlier, in June 1838? On 6 March 1838 Catherine, Mrs Dickens, gave birth to her second child Mamie and was plunged for months into that condition of physical debility and post-natal depression which had afflicted her after the birth of her first child, Charley. This was possibly a time when Dickens, as a very vital and active young man, could potentially stray. Mrs Dickens was recuperating in the countryside in Twickenham where Dickens spent all his week-ends, but he was up and down to the city of London on an almost daily basis. There are many recorded meetings with the actor Macready during the next few months and doubtless there would have been opportunities to meet Frances Ternan, a gifted actress from early childhood and an extremely beautiful woman, married to a bad-tempered, untalented failure of a man, who was now ill with syphilis. Dickens was an obsessive theatre fan, went two or three times a week. During that winter, in Drury Lane Theatre, Mrs Ternan had played Desdemona to the famous Kean's Othello, while her husband played Iago – to extremely poor reviews. Dickens undoubtedly saw these performances and would have been sorry for Frances Ternan.

On 29 October 1839 Kate Macready Dickens was born, six months after the birth of Ellen. Portraits, I feel, show a resemblance between them, especially the ears and the nose. Kate was supposed physically and otherwise to resemble her father more than any of his other children.

In 1846 Thomas Ternan died of syphilis when Ellen was only six. He had been confined to a hospital for the insane for many years previously.

In 1857 Ellen Lawless Ternan was eighteen when she and her sister played parts, with Dickens, in the play *The Frozen Deep* which took place at the end of August 1857. At the end of the performance, Dickens gave Ellen Ternan a piece of jewellery – a brooch or bracelet. This came to Mrs Dickens' notice and there was a huge row. Kate Dickens said her father ordered his wife to see Mrs Ternan – and this is odd, because it almost appears as though Dickens wants to make recompense to Mrs Ternan as well as to care for Ellen Ternan and to take her from the life on the stage which she hated.

In May 1858 Dickens decided to separate from his wife. He was an emotional man, but his fits of fury at the imputation that he was having an affair with Ellen Ternan seem excessive – if she were really his mistress. However, if she were his daughter, this would be more understandable, would make his almost hysterical behaviour much more reasonable. In my opinion, he behaved like a man who has been much wronged.

In 1858 Dickens set Ellen Ternan up in an establishment with her mother. It is now that he began writing *A Tale of Two Cities* – a story about a father and daughter who meet for the first time when the daughter is eighteen years old. Later he took a house for Ellen and her mother, in Slough and then in

France. At the railway crash at Staplehurst, both Mrs Ternan and Ellen were present. In fact, right through the Dickens and Ellen years, Mrs Ternan appears to have been a constant presence.

In 1859 *A Tale of Two Cities* was published. It is a rather over-sentimentalized portrait of fatherly and daughterly love where the heroine bears a strong physical resemblance to Ellen Ternan.

Interestingly, it appears as if several people were in on the secret of the relationship. To one lady friend (a highly respectable Victorian lady, according to the biographer Peter Ackroyd) Dickens wrote that 'Nelly would be distressed and embarrassed if she knew that you knew the secret of her history'. (NB not her position – her *history*. I think there is a significant difference.) Another lady, Mrs Fields – an extremely strait-laced American lady – wrote rhapsodically to Dickens about how he was going to see his beloved. (She was unlikely to refer to a mistress in those terms.) She also hoped that despite 'mistakes that he had made in the past' (perhaps having an affair as a young man) that he would now be happy.

One of things that struck me, and partially led me to this conclusion, was that Peter Ackroyd, a meticulous and tireless biographer, was totally puzzled about the relationship that Dickens had with Ellen Ternan and eventually came to the conclusion that it was a non-consummated relationship – something he deemed as very odd! Interestingly enough, he didn't take that sideways step, which I have taken; less odd, I think, than the guess that a highly sexed man like Dickens would live with a pretty young girl in a 'non-consummated' relationship.

No, I think Dickens was the father, not the lover, of Ellen Ternan, and didn't want to destroy his relationship with his public (and Queen Victoria) by confessing to the affair with an actress. He also didn't want to attract shame on to Mrs Ternan, but otherwise wanted to make it up to his illegitimate daughter. It is somewhat overlooked, I feel, that in making provision for Ellen, he also cared for Mrs Ternan.

I am fairly sure that he confided the secret to his sister-in-law, Georgina and to his daughters, Kate and Mamie before he died. They summoned Ellen to his deathbed. Afterwards they were very friendly with Ellen Ternan who went on to make a good marriage with a clergyman. She had children with him, although she was then in her late thirties which makes one wonder why, if she were Dickens' mistress, she did not have children by him. Despite much research no one has ever found any evidence that there was a child.

Henry Dickens, Dickens' youngest son, had children who went to a birthday party held for Ellen's children, which, once again, makes me think that the Dickens family all knew of the relationship. All that nonsense about Kate saying that there was a child and it died is just hearsay. It was quoted ten years after Kate's death by a friend, an elderly woman (suffering from the early stages of dementia), who wrote, with the help of a journalist, a book called *Dickens and Daughter* and perhaps wanted to beef it up; probably she knew nothing as Dickens' children and sister-in-law guarded his reputation with great care. Moreover, a scandal may have injured the huge sales of his books in this Victorian era.

Of course, no one will ever know for sure, but I do think that it is feasible that Dickens was Ellen Ternan's father.

I would be so interested to know what others think of that and would love to hear from you on my website: www.coraharrison.com